INSPIRED BY TRUE EVENTS

Miserable Business

A STORY OF CHICAGO'S INFAMOUS
PROHIBITION MOB BOSSES

PJ Eiden

Print ISBN 978-1-09837-995-7

eBook ISBN 978-1-09837-996-4

CONTENTS

It was June 1930 when H.L. Macklan stepped off the steam train in a place where he didn't belong. As sparse afternoon raindrops began to spit from the sky, he put on the scorched suit coat and dark hat. Being fully aware of the truth of things, it felt good to be alive.

CHAPTER 1

Boom

The young mother lost focus on the Bible verse, stopping mid-sentence. Her attention snapped to the outline of the open window visible through the thin cotton draperies. Another tremor rippled the drape's lace fringe.

She closed the leather-bound book without marking the page.

Her daughter, tucked beneath the blankets with hands folded, reopened her eyes. "What's wrong, Mommy? Aren't you gonna read the prayers?"

The woman cupped her hand over the child's mouth while she listened to the percussive blasts echoing in the distance. *Boom, boom, boom, boom.* Water in the nightstand glass pulsed and rippled.

The child twisted her head side to side, tiny tears rolling back on her temples. The mother loosened her clutch over the girl's mouth.

Staring at the outline of the window, the woman reached and fumbled for the switch on the bedside lamp. In the darkness, she took hold of her daughter, sweeping her off the bed along with the blankets, the girl thumping on the hardwood floor.

The child began to sob. "I wish Grandpa was here!"

"Shh, Sarah!" The woman began to quiver. With each short breath, the collar of her nightgown shook with small quakes, her chest rising and falling. Even her forearms and hands moved in tremors as she busied herself tucking the blankets beneath the girl. "I'm sorry, honey, but you can't make a sound. Bad men are coming."

Outside, the thunder grew louder with each exchange. *Boom, boom, boom.* The raging mob battle was hurtling closer.

In the full-length nightgown, the woman scrambled on hands and knees over to the wall, reaching up behind the draperies, pulling the window low, to a level just high enough to still peer through.

Over-powered tires squealed around the street corner, echoing across the neighborhood calm.

The mother couldn't control her outburst, "Oh God, they're coming this way!" Her words were buried by the drone of engines rising to speed. Light flooded the room as two mob cars of the latest muscle barreled toward the home.

A dark Chrysler sedan made an aggressive swerve, banging full-on into the side of the second car. Sparks flew in the darkness followed by the distinct flash and sound of a handgun discharge. *Boom.*

The second car careened off the street, bounding through the picket fence, plowing into the front of the family's home with an earthquake of wood splinters.

The Chrysler skidded to a stop, shifted to reverse, lurching backward.

With the mob battle spilling onto her property, the woman slammed the window down, swarmed over the child, and drove her face into the bundle of blankets. The mother's grip paralyzed the girl.

Out on the street, the driver's door of the Chrysler swung open. Jack McGurn, a man quick to violence when it came to retaliation, slid off the seat with a face twisted in rage and an automatic gun equipped with two handgrips. While his gangster life of excess was beginning to show, the skin on his knuckles still bore the white scars of a street fighter.

Notorious throughout Chicago, no one doubted Jack anymore. Today, he had a reputation to uphold.

He stepped clear of his vehicle and assumed a rigid stance with the weapon held waist-high. He pulled the trigger back and the gun erupted. *Boom, boom, boom.* He clobbered the crashed car with a judgment of bullets.

The roar of the machine gun mixed with shattering sounds from every window in the home's first-level parlor pouring glass out onto the floor.

In the bedroom upstairs, the woman and child sobbed with nearly silent screams through the agonizing pounding. The mother, holding both of her hands over the child's ears, kept her own eyes closed, but couldn't stop the penetrating flashes of light in the otherwise dark room. *Boom, boom, boom.*

When the blasting finally came to an end, the two of them were buried deep beneath the bed, sobbing, shaking, and praying not to be discovered.

The mother kissed her daughter's disheveled hair then brought her mouth right next to the girl's ear to whisper. "Are you okay, honey?" The frightened child could only nod.

McGurn stepped toward the car wearing an out-of-place gray overcoat. He moved with crouched, deliberate steps like a wolf drawing in close to hiding prey. His overcoat trailed on the ground, as if in obedience, while he approached the back of the pin-cushioned vehicle. He crept along the driver's side and thrust the muzzle of the gun through a shattered car window. He used it to probe the interior.

Satisfied no life remained, he stood upright again, turned, and used the gun's barrel to notch the front of his hat up while he considered the house. The first level looked like it belonged in a war-torn village. He'd learned the hard way about doing a thorough *clean-up* before leaving execution scenes. Under his breath, he muttered, "Let's see who might be watching from in there." Jack left the mutilated car, picked his way up the intact portions of the porch steps, and crossed to the entrance. He reached around inside through a broken window to unlock the front door.

In one motion, he pushed the door open while he raised the barrel of the shouldered rifle. From the entry, the pale-yellow city lights filtered in through the shattered parlor windows. Ribbons of shredded curtains cast streaks across the ruins of furniture and peppered walls. The sofa was marred with bullet pox of escaping wool popcorn. The one-time centerpiece of the home was now but a splintered radio cabinet with a broken crystal dial. Jack stepped over the threshold into a maze of glass shards spread out across the floor. Each footstep commenced with a muted crunch.

He poked his head into the various doorways on the first floor and stopped when he reached the base of a wooden staircase leading up to the second. Jack kept his gun barrel trained on the top of the stairs where a pair of closed doors caught his attention. He thought it was odd the house would be empty at this time of night in the middle of the week. By the looks of the place, he was sure somebody was living here.

Up in the bedroom, with ears still ringing, the woman tried to suppress her sobs while she slid out from beneath the bed, stood upright, and stared at the closed door. She was in shock and trying to comprehend what had happened. Her child was scared. From beneath the bed came a soft whisper, "Mommy, don't leave me under here."

The woman got on her knees and poked her head beneath the bed frame. She tried to smile as she whispered. "Sarah, honey, Mommy's going to look around downstairs for a minute. You're safe under here. I'll be right back."

The girl ignored the response, scrambled out from under the bed, and raised her slender arms in the air. Despite the child being over half the size of her mother, the woman scooped her up. In a complete state of uneasiness, the mother made careful steps to the bedroom door and took hold of the white ceramic knob.

At the mid-level stair landing, McGurn released the gun's magazine and checked the ammunition. Satisfied, he snapped it back into place with a distinct click.

From inside the bedroom, over the sounds of her squirming child, the mother heard what she thought were almost inaudible clicks of metal coming from somewhere out in the parlor.

McGurn continued his sneak up the steps until an oak floorboard squealed like a rusty hinge.

Inside the bedroom, the woman's eyes flew open at the sound of the alarm. The color drained from her face. She released her grip on the door handle, squeezed her child, and began backing away. Someone was in her home just beyond the door.

Through the remnants of the first-floor windows, a faint but rising wail of a police car siren echoed in. McGurn stopped and turned toward the direction of the sound. He'd have to get moving immediately if he hoped to leave the neighborhood before the cops arrived. He shouldered his gun and pointed the muzzle at the doors on the upper level. McGurn drew his forefinger back from the guard to rest lightly on the gun's trigger.

As he squeezed, he swung the barrel of the gun across the second-floor wall from left to right in a single pass. *Boom, boom, boom, boom.* A line of a half-dozen bullets strafed the wall and splintered the painted wooden doors.

The wail of approaching sirens grew louder. McGurn lowered the gun, turned on the stairs, and began to retrace his footsteps to exit the home. In his haste, each step sent glass skittering across the floor like the shattering of china plates. The dark-colored Chrysler rumbled back to life and disappeared through a lingering haze of gun smoke.

CHAPTER 2

Roaring

In the shadows of the recessed entry of a two-story brown brick nestled among the buildings on Terrace Street, the single bulb of an electrified gas lamp cast a glow on a sign with faded yellow letters spelling *The Granary*. This was the place they'd been searching for. A well-dressed man around the age of twenty raised his hands in the air and thumped both his buddies on the back. "I knew we'd find it, boys!"

His friend with the shock of wild red hair turned and poked him in the chest. "What a great idea to bring the girls along!"

At a quarter past nine, a large man stood just inside the door wearing a vested suit and a black hat. Through the hatch, he surveyed the evening guests who'd accumulated outside. He munched on a handful of pretzels. The salt was having its intended effect, and he reached for the bottle of beer stashed under his stool. He listened to the group of twenty-somethings puffing on tobacco cigarettes while they discussed a new sports coupe rumored to take its sleek shape from the design of an airplane. The man had heard enough. He drew back the latch and pulled the thick door open. Light poured out from the entryway. He took a moment to survey the young people eye to eye. They stood frozen, waiting for the verdict. He broke the silence with a nod. "You kids look all right. Come on inside." Out of habit, he glanced up and down the street as he waved the three couples into the club and swung the door closed behind them. He drove the bolt back into its rightful place and took another glance through the hatch.

From back in the club's entertainment room, the unmistakable brassy sound of a saxophone player pouring his heart out made the girls smile. The large man turned toward these well-heeled patrons. The young women were wearing low-waisted dresses, bell hats, and each carried a small purse. "You ladies look like you've come here for dancing."

Grins and nods spread across the group.

"This should be a fun night as we've got a fantastic jazz band who will take the stage soon. I really like them. They've traveled all the way here from the French Quarter in New Orleans!" The man took the final swig from his beer bottle. As he swallowed, he tipped the empty bottle in the direction of the young people and shook it side to side. "Aw, I should tell you kids. Unfortunately, there's been some sort of delay with today's shipment. If we run dry, we may be forced to shut down a little early tonight."

—— • ——

In the summer of 1920, a sense of euphoria was taking hold of the country spirited by the end of the Great War in Europe, surprising new prosperity, and women now having a vote. A sweet perfume was blowing through the air saying, *Hurry, don't miss the best of times!*

All of Chicago seemed to have gone mad. Everyone was caught up in the delirious scramble to make it big and, more important, everyone believed they could. Toiling in a factory or the field from sunrise to sunset was a thing of the past. Smart young people were borrowing as much as possible to invest. Best friends whispered, "You can't lose on Wall Street." From shore to shore, America was prospering. The stock market kept climbing higher and higher and, astonishingly, had grown tenfold since the turn of the century.

Chicago, in particular, had become the envy of the nation. At the crossroads of America, this was the best place to be. In the shimmer of Lake

Michigan, the downtown skyline soared to new heights. Modern buildings were being designed and built with strong bones of iron and skins of impressive granite or even stainless steel. Chicago was taking its place among the world's commerce centers. The city was rich with Midwest resources, a bountiful workforce, and abundant opportunities. Everyone said, soon this would be the epicenter of the country.

Daily newspapers were a sensation in the city and a conversation starter for everyone who was up-to-date. Crowds swarmed corner newsstands each morning as the press circulation trucks tossed the bundles to the street. Particularly during elections, disasters, crimes, and scandals, newspapers became a valuable commodity. When news was interesting, people horded their daily print like gold coins during a calamity. They often read the paper several times throughout the day to memorize the particulars.

Radio broadcasting now provided the latest news information even to rural communities. As a new form of entertainment, people found listening to the radio was a thrill like going to the movies for the first time, but from the comfort of their home. Families gathered around their radios to listen to everything from jazz and swing music to the wit of Sam 'n' Henry. Deluxe radios were a sign of prosperity and most displayed them as the centerpiece of the family parlor.

Nighttime in the city came alive with young people. The downtown filled with the sounds of laughter and singing. Everyone wanted to look like a success with gentlemen in coats and ties and ladies wearing their best dresses with pearls. Keeping up appearances with friends was important. The most popular evening streets all had a club. They'd have music like jazz and blues with live acts, some had dancing girls, and all had plenty of spirits. Regular citizens couldn't deny the excitement created when defying the law. Drinking beer, gin, or whiskey was like gambling on horse races as storm clouds built in the afternoon sky. Place your bets now because any race could be the last. Rumors had it the government men were coming.

CHAPTER 3

The Sanctuary

On a sultry night in 1923, Hank Macklan, the leader of a liquor transport, abandoned his post counting cash stacked on a whiskey crate. Bullets began to rain down intending death on his men outside where they were about to unload a truck. Hank had to help save his men.

Overtaken by worry, he ran from the shelter of the stockroom into the street where thunder echoed. *Boom, boom, boom.*

From the sidewalk, he flung the Lincoln sedan's passenger door open, dove inside, and put the key in the ignition. The mighty V8 roared to life. Hank stomped the accelerator and erupted from the curb in a rolling cloud.

Before he'd even cleared the block, two shooters emerged from the neighboring buildings and sprinted to a dark sedan parked along the street. The chase was on.

The hitmen wasted no time and cut off from Halstead Street through a narrow alley out to Clybourn, which sliced diagonally along the river.

Hank was forcing his way north through the thick evening traffic on Kingsbury Street. At the point where Kingsbury merged with Clybourn, the shooters could see the Lincoln sedan slipping in ahead of them at the narrows.

"There he is!" The man in the passenger seat leaned the upper half of his body out the open window while aiming a rifle. Just as the hitmen's car bounded out onto Gardner behind Hank, the gunman sent a spray of bullets rippling across Hank's trunk.

Bullets pierced the car's seats, making Hank a victim. He swung the automatic out his car window, pointed the gun backward, and peeled off several rounds to deter them from pulling even. While the second car tried to evade the response, Hank swerved off onto Webster Street. The shooters tore around the same corner after him and returned volleys through his front fender and cowling.

Now Hank had the room to make his move. He used the advantage of the big engine to push the car until the speedometer reached seventy miles per hour. The city became a blur.

Block after block, the Lincoln bounced over each cross street. Sparks lit the roadway as he bottomed out in one rough intersection better suited for the clearance of a horse carriage. Hank was putting distance between the vehicles.

His mind flashed back to Halsted Street. *How many of his men were down back there?*

With the accelerator pressed to the floor, Hank focused on the rearview mirror. The headlamps behind him faded, but the searing heat in his abdomen wasn't going away. Hank slapped the gun down on the seat beside him. *How are these thugs still getting our delivery routes? We change them every week!*

Easing his grip on the gun, Hank reached across to work his shirt loose from his trousers. The pain came from his left side with blood bubbling out just above his belt line.

As the car forged ahead, the motor began to ping and clatter. Steam erupted from the sides of the engine compartment leaving an unnatural haze in the car's wake. Inside, the fetid smell of hot oil and overheated metal began to turn the air toxic. Hank coughed and choked but was even more concerned about a sudden drop in his speed. Something was wrong under the hood.

Despite the burning in his left side, Hank trained his eyes on the roadway while he kept himself propped up against the interior of the door. His hand trembled as he reached to twist the mirror in his favor. He took a corner at

Willow Street and drove the messed-up Lincoln into a dated neighborhood. He cut the motor and rolled the sedan into the shadows near a large tree. Thankfully, Chicago had never been good at street lighting. The radiator kept on steaming from an assortment of bullet holes.

The street was as still as midnight. Hank stared beyond the windshield at the pale glow coming through stained-glass windows. As he opened the car door, empty brass shell casings rolled off the running boards and scattered on the ground.

Hank limped across the sidewalk and labored up the stone steps to make his way inside the old church.

Two elderly widows dressed in black were leaving the sanctuary. They paused near the granite holy water font to wait for Hank who was leaning over it. He muttered an apology and dipped his right hand in the cool water. A crimson stain radiated out from his thick fingers. One of the widows cinched her grip on her friend's arm and pulled her friend away. Hank took a seat among the empty pews.

Father Whelan, a middle-aged Irish priest with wavy chestnut hair and graying sideburns, made his way from the confessional booth to the dark figure seated alone in the back of the church. As he approached, there was a sense of urgency in his native brogue. "I'm taking confessions tonight and I can hear yours if you like before I close up." Hank lifted his head from the seat back of the pew in front of him. The priest recognized the familiar face, but his smile soon faded. Hank rose, turned away from the holy man, and headed back toward the entrance.

Hank paused at the door, easing it open a crack. A police car passing on the street slowed alongside the wounded sedan, shining a spotlight. Brake lights came on and both doors of the police car flew open. An officer emerged from the car, a gun in hand. Parked over a puddle of brass, the Lincoln was peppered with bullet holes. He twisted the driver's door handle and pulled it open. He holstered his sidearm and reached inside. From the car's seat, he took the submachine gun by the front grip and backed out with it raised in the air like a trophy.

Inside the church, a voice came from the shadows. "You know Henry, your father used to talk to me about things when he was alive. We could talk, too, if you like."

Hank slid his hand inside his suit jacket, reaching for a holstered thirty-eight caliber pistol. Drawing the revolver, he turned toward the priest, thrusting it into his stomach.

Father Whelan winced and grabbed at the gun with both hands. "Why Henry? What have I done to you?"

Hank froze and stared at the white collar of the priest's shirt. His hand began to tremble. He eased his grip on the revolver and moaned, "I can't do it!"

Father Whelan exhaled a deep breath. His heart was pounding as he held the pistol that could have taken his life.

"My name is Hank! People now call me Hank."

A doubting look came over the holy man's face, and he shook his head. "Are you sure your name isn't *The Hammer* as in *triggerman*? I've been told it's your nickname now." Father Whelan looked down at the gun. He noticed the thick blood on his hands.

Hank groaned.

"Henry, you've been shot!" The priest took a small step back and noticed a dark stain showing inside Henry's suitcoat. "Where are you hit? Maybe, I can help."

Hank reached over and took the pistol back before he slumped against the wall.

The priest stepped to the door, locked the heavy bolt, and turned the lights off inside the church. He hugged Henry beneath his arms and helped him walk. In the dim light of the church candles, they made their way toward the priest's study off one side of the altar area. "Henry, you may not know this, but when I served as a chaplain during the war in Europe, I was also a stretcher-bearer. I patched up many gunshot wounds back in those days. I keep an old bag with medical supplies here at the church."

Hank turned his head to consider the man laboring to help him.

As they limped into the complete darkness of the study room, Father Whelan supported Henry with one arm and swept his other over the top of a wooden table, knocking various books and papers off. He helped Henry take a seat on the table's edge. "Stay here now. I'll be right back." Hank rested while the priest retrieved a burning candle and a pile of white worship cloths from the sanctuary. He stepped to a set of wall cabinets and collected a kerosene lantern along with a tattered leather postal bag. The priest set them down next to Henry. He lit the old oil lamp and moved it around next to the wound.

"Let's get you out of your coat and shirt, so I can see the damage."

Hank struggled to slip his coat off.

"The pistol holster will have to go too."

Hank stared at the priest. He wondered whether the holy man was merely attending to injuries or trying to take his weapon.

The priest used one of the linens to dab away the thickening blood around a pair of bullet wounds. White cotton cloths turned red as he worked his way into the torn flesh. The holy man strained to examine the wounds. "Based on what I can see, Henry, everything down there looks like blood. Are you packing a four-leaf clover? It doesn't look like you have serious internal damage."

The stoic look on Hank's face didn't change.

"I'm not a surgeon, but I can stitch things shut to stop the bleeding. I'll pray for healing. Within a day, you'll need some bromine to fight wound fever. The *fever* is what got most soldiers who died on the battlefields in Europe."

The priest opened a locked cabinet with bottles of dark-colored wine. Each had a special prohibition permit label for *sacramental-use-only* pasted over the corked end. He placed a full bottle on the table. "Sorry, I don't have anything stronger. Drink plenty because this is going to hurt!"

Hank watched the priest sigh as he pulled the postal bag closer. "Just get on with it. I can take it." Hank broke the sealed label on the bottle and pulled the stop loose with his teeth before taking a deep draw.

Father Whelan opened the leather case and took out a roll of gauze, a can of powder, a half-filled glass vial, needles, scissors, and some surgeon's thread. He arranged them out near the end of the table and began to sterilize a needle with a lit match. "Henry, please lie down."

Hank handed the wine bottle back to the priest and rolled on his side. The priest helped him swing his legs up on the table.

"While I work, why don't you spill it? Tell me how this happened."

Hank took his time responding. "Why? Are you trying to distract me, or stealing a confession?"

The holy man pulled a chair close to the table's edge.

"The Chicago *pouring business* isn't exclusive for that Italian, Torrio, and his underling Capone." The gangster was eager to point out the moral differences between the rival gangs. "North of the river, we play the same game, but we do it with integrity. Earning our living the old-fashioned way, we won't sell *coffin varnish* from polluted bathtub stills or flavored industrial alcohol. We only sell genuine quality products made to drink. We don't poison people as you read in the newspaper headlines."

Father Whelan nodded. The story was a good diversion for the lack of morphine.

"We respect boundaries. Torrio's hoodlums parade on the southside without interference." Hank took several deep breaths. "Father, but they've turned their streets into sewers of sin. Nothing is sacred or off limits! They even use women for a money-making business."

Hank paused to catch his breath. "They own over a hundred brothels. To them, humans aren't worth anything. No more value than a racehorse or a dog. They use them up and kidnap more immigrants coming off the boats next week. Those women are vulnerable."

Henry gasped at the pain. His instincts made him reach for the wounds.

"Hold on now." Father Whelan took Henry by the wrists and pulled his hands back. "Sorry, but you must stay out of the way. Try gripping the table's edge."

Father Whelan slid his wire-framed glasses back up through perspiration beads forming on his nose. His forehead wrinkled as he peered at the details of the damaged flesh.

Hank took in a slow deep breath. "The hatred grew with prohibition. Today, Chicago knows the crime bosses share mutual loathing.

"This is far more than bickering over neighborhoods and taverns. The venom between Johnny Torrio, the brains of the southside, and my boss, Dean O'Banion, runs deep. They go back and forth from war to peace. Like school-yard children, the two will play nice for a while and later get in a shoving match over something trivial like who gets the best seats at the ball game. Egos can be a powerful invisible force. Behind the scenes, we're always scheming on how to get rid of Torrio."

The priest almost couldn't contain himself. He wanted to lecture Henry on the sin of taking lives and the virtues of forgiveness. He hesitated, thinking it more important to keep the mobster talking.

"The southside crew operates out of pure gluttony and madness. The Torrio mob right now has more money and power than the Roman Empire, but they still want what's on everyone else's plates too! The rats have barged in up here, trying to take our Gold Coast. You know where the rich folks live. They want the whole city."

The priest's gaze was fixed on Hank's face now.

Hank continued, "They will learn. We don't tolerate trespassers. We'll send their mothers some nice flowers if you know what I mean. If we can keep a lid on it, they make nice luggage for an evening drive to the woodlands."

Father Whelan closed his eyes for a few moments. He shuddered at the thought of the hellish violence so common in Henry's business.

It was time to stretch the skin back together and stitch things shut. "Henry, this last step will be punishing pain. Hang with me, this is going to feel like I'm pouring salt in your wounds."

Hank moaned. "Shittttt! You aren't kidding! Is that needle actually a big rusty nail?" He took a few shallow breaths and propped himself up enough to drink hard from the wine bottle. Then he settled back on the table.

———— ● ————

The suturing resumed. Hank's face distorted, and he clenched his teeth together. He mumbled while trying to keep his mouth closed, "I need to tell you about my threats from John Scalise and Alberto Anselmi." Hank's words trailed off into groans.

The priest prepared another length of surgeon's thread. He took no pleasure in this punishment, even for a mobster. "Sorry, I tried to warn you this would hurt." Father Whelan paused when it hit him. "Oh, my Lord, did you say Scalise and Anselmi? Aren't they the pair of assassins they call the *Murder Twins*?"

Hank studied the figure of Christ on the wooden cross hanging on the wall. Next to it was a frame with a tattered photo of a youth rugby team. He closed his eyes for a moment and exhaled a long breath while he considered his response.

"Yes, they're the notorious murderers."

The priest set the needle down and stared into Henry's swollen eyes. "How in the world did you get tangled up with such dangerous men?"

Until now, Hank had been in denial about the threat. He was a man with a brave exterior, a solid rock for his underlings, and struggled to share with anyone the terror he felt. Hank couldn't keep it to himself anymore. He had to tell the story. "It just happened, Father. I don't deserve to be a marked man, but I am."

The priest was wary about alarming Henry, but he wanted him to understand the gravity of the situation. "Henry, you're not just marked. You're being hunted by the worst of Satan's demons!"

Hank swallowed hard.

"Hide here a few days until they forget about you."

Hank shook his head. "No. No, they will *never* forget what I did to them."

The priest shook his head and tried to understand. "Why not? What do they think you've done?"

Hank looked away.

———— • ————

A couple of long minutes passed and neither man spoke. Hank took several slow breaths. He opened his eyes and watched the flickering light patterns on the ceiling. "This started the last time I tried a legitimate gig. A friend of mine told me about the Oliver Sharpe Company on west Thirty-Fifth Street. You might know the area. They are part of the big manufacturing complex. They have almost a thousand employees working there doing printing work like bookbinding."

Hank continued, "Some months ago, thieves broke in during the night and blew the safe open in the payroll clerk's office. They made off with twenty-thousand dollars!"

Father Whelan considered his words before he began. "Henry, you know in the book of Psalms, it says, 'Surely men of low degree are vanity, and men of high degree are a lie: to be laid in the balance, they are altogether lighter than vanity. Trust not in oppression, and become not vain in robbery: if riches increase, set not your heart upon them.' Henry, did you have something to do with this robbery?"

Hank glared at Father Whelan. "Thank you, but no, it's quite the opposite."

The priest finished stitching the wounds.

"Henry, do you hear something?" The pounding on the rectory door was faint at first.

The pounding became louder and more urgent. Father Whelan wiped the last of the blood from his hands with an altar cloth and rolled his sleeves down. "I'd better go to the door."

Shielding the flame of the candle he carried, he made haste through the hallway to the residential entry. The pounding grew more intense. "Just a minute, I'm on my way!"

CHAPTER 4

The Office

Two weeks prior in an upscale neighborhood, well-polished shoes trod the sidewalks of Huron Street after 5:00 p.m. as men in tailored suits and women in sensible heels pushed their way into The Office. The gin joint was a modest midtown affair with ample tables, service over a spotless bar, a long wall of unread books parked on shelves, a display case of White Owl cigars, and a small stage for entertainment. The low chandeliers seemed to coax after-work crowds to settle the unfinished business of the day from a plush lounge chair. The watering hole had become a haven for working women to express their independence by purchasing an after-work drink.

Rachel Hilson paraded in past a throng of admiring men who ogled her with glossy eyes. She took a seat at a table in the back next to her coworker, Evelyn Smith. "Evie, why do you *always* do this?"

Evelyn smiled with satisfaction, knowing exactly what she'd been accused of. "What do you mean, dear friend? Didn't I agree to meet you here to grab a drink after work?"

Rachel grinned at her sophisticated pal. "You did. But you always slip into one of the *back* tables so you can listen to jazz."

Evelyn paused while the saxophone player on stage finished a long wavering tone. She gestured toward the performer. "You see? What could be better?

Doesn't this guy sound amazing? I get lost in the way he improvises. You never hear the same thing twice."

Rachel shook her head. "There's no problem with his music. It's quite fine. But we could be hanging out with some of those rich-looking guys standing at the bar *and* listening from over there!"

Evelyn's brow furrowed. "No, they would be a distraction, and we don't know them, do we? They might be criminals looking to kidnap us."

Rachel smirked. "Would it be so bad if a rich guy were to steal you away to his castle on a hill somewhere?"

Evelyn smiled. "Rachel, remember, we are in Chicago. There aren't many castles or even hills around here. Most of these guys are probably hourly wage workers, just like you and me."

"Oh, you know what I mean, Evie. Let's have a cocktail before we head for home."

The musician finished with his set, tidied his music case, and stepped off the stage to pack it for the door. On his way out, he passed near the table. Evelyn reached out and touched his coat sleeve. "Hello, I have to tell you how much I enjoyed your session. You have an amazing way with a brass horn."

The musician paused for a moment. "Why thank you, it's very kind of you to say."

He noticed the curious lack of drinks on their table. "I should probably tell you, I don't play as a profession or anything. I sneak up there in the afternoon sometimes before the real performers arrive."

Evelyn couldn't contain herself. "Really? You don't play as a professional? You're one of the best jazz players I've ever heard. I'm sure, you would make a fine living doing this."

He smiled. "No, I don't use sheet music or anything. I play whatever comes to me."

"Wow! When will you be back? I'd like to hear you play again sometime."

Rachel butted in, "Evelyn you're certainly being bold today."

Hank smiled and stared into Evelyn's infectious blue eyes. "I would like that."

He took a moment to think about it. "It's not a scheduled thing for me. Generally, I find it soothing to play a quiet joint when I have a lot on my mind."

Evelyn sat back in her chair. "Well, I'm glad I caught you. It was certainly a pleasure to listen to you unwind. Have a good evening."

Evelyn's feeling of triumph was obvious.

Rachel sensed she had something to say. "What is it now, Evie? Out with it!"

Evelyn beamed. "There! *That* is how you meet an interesting man."

Rachel chirped, "Oh really? Thanks for the lesson. So, I'm curious now, what's his name, Evelyn, and how would you ever see him again?"

Evelyn bristled at the challenge. "Oh, hush! You know what I mean. Even you must admit, there are better ways to meet men than to hang out with a crowd of drunkards because they look like they might have money. Anyone can shine up their shoes for a night."

CHAPTER 5

The Dance

The current nightmare wasn't over yet. Even with his side stitched, Hank was in pain and somewhat light-headed as he kept quiet while lying on the table with one hand gripping the wine bottle standing beside him. Down the hall, Father Whelan turned on the entrance lights to the rectory and unlocked the door.

Two weary-looking uniformed police officers stood on the stoop shoulder to shoulder. One held a flashlight in his hands and the other removed his hat and placed it beneath his arm. "Evening, Father. We are sorry to disturb you at this hour, but we might have a dangerous situation here in the neighborhood. We wanted to ask you if you might have seen anything suspicious tonight."

"Good evening, officers. I'm glad you're out patrolling, keeping us safe. Even with all the arrests being made lately, there are still many reports of crime in the city. I'm curious, what are your names?"

"I'm Officer Mulaney, and this is my partner Officer Richter."

The priest reached out and put his hand on Officer Mulaney's shoulder. "Your accent sounds familiar. Are you by chance from central Ireland?"

"Why, yes, I'm from Roscommon. My parents still live there. Did you grow up in Ireland too?"

The priest smiled. "Well, it's awful dark out there, would you men like to come inside for a while?"

Officer Richter spoke, "Thanks, Father, but we don't have time. We need to talk with all the neighbors along this street if possible. Can you tell me, was the church open tonight?"

Father Whelan nodded. "Yes, of course. Every week we take confessions on Wednesday evenings."

"Did you have any unusual visitors or thugs come into the church tonight?"

Father Whelan studied their faces. "Well, I spent most of my time in the confessional. But I checked the church over before I closed up and the sanctuary was completely empty. We had a small group this evening, and I knew each of the church members in attendance. There were no strangers in the crowd. Why do you ask?"

Officer Richter continued, "As we were patrolling tonight, we spotted a Lincoln V8 parked just down the street. We've never seen expensive cars in this neighborhood. Besides, this one had been through a storm of bullets. We found a submachine gun inside and empty shell casings strewn about on the ground."

"Jesus save us! The thought of armed thugs lurking outside the church is alarming," Father Whelan gasped. "Confession night is always rather quiet in the church. I didn't hear gunfire or sounds of any disturbance. We have elderly people attend on Wednesday. I wouldn't have let them leave if I thought there was a dangerous criminal loose in the neighborhood!"

Officer Mulaney raised a hand. "We don't know if the driver is still around or not. Our squad is investigating some sort of mob shootout a couple of miles from here. Most likely one of these thugs ditched his car on the street and either got picked up or headed out on foot."

The priest crossed his arms. "Well, it still doesn't give one any comfort until you arrest him. At this point, all we can do is pray for our safety and his repentance. Speaking of prayers, would you men like to bring your families to Mass this Sunday? I could do a special blessing for your safety on the job."

"Oh, thanks Father. We'll think about it. For now, we better keep moving. Please call the police station if you think of anything or notice anyone in the neighborhood who doesn't belong."

"Yes, officer, I will. Sadly, these are dangerous times. Thank you for your bravery. Good night."

Father Whelan watched the two officers walk back toward the street and turn next door to interview the neighbors. He turned the lights off and picked up the small candle once again.

Hank was sitting upright when the priest returned to the study room. "Let me help you stand. I'll find a spot for you in the rectory."

"First, who was at the door?"

Father Whelan had the upper hand now. "It was the cops who found your car. They wanted to know if I had any fugitives come into the church tonight."

"What did you tell them? Did you lie for me?"

The priest paused for a dramatic effect. "I did the dance."

Hank blinked twice in rapid succession. "What do you mean?

Father Whelan tried to conceal his smile. "I'm a priest and I try to live by the Ten Commandments. I stepped carefully around their questions with truthful answers. I also invited them to our worship service on Sunday." Father Whelan chuckled. "It made them squirm and go away."

Hank showed the first smile since he got off the operating table. "Say, if this priest thing doesn't work out, you may have a future in *the business.*"

Father Whelan shook his head. "Don't count on it, wise guy."

Hank laughed at the reference until he felt a pain surge through his sutured side.

"All right, Henry, you need some rest. This will likely be a miserable night. If you were in a hospital, they would give you morphine and put you out for a few hours. Keep the wine bottle close.

"Take a seat here in the rectory study, while I set up a folding army cot."

Hank fought his natural urge to help and took a chair next to a wall of bookshelves. He stared at the rows of volumes.

"Henry, we were interrupted by the police visit earlier. Now finish telling me *why* the Murder Twins are hunting you."

A shiver spread over Hank. "Well, I told you how I got hired."

"Oh, yes. I remember."

Hank gave the highlights. "After the break-in and theft, the Oliver Sharpe Company decided to stop keeping their payroll cash on the premises until it was needed. They found the bank and trust located two blocks away was willing to help."

Father Whelan unfolded a wool blanket and covered the cot while he listened.

"The new process for payroll day included the clerk preparing worker vouchers and envelopes for the bank to fill. In the afternoon, the clerk went to the bank to audit the count as the vouchers were filled. He carried the cash box the two blocks back to the printing office in time to hand them out at the end of the shift."

The priest set a candle and box of matches down on a small table near the cot. "Sounds like a problem solved."

"Not really. This only worked well until Sam, the payroll clerk, became crazy suspicious of people watching him. Sam believed he was being followed on the street. The company president didn't feel it was safe for the nervous little man to walk alone with tens of thousands of dollars on him." Hank took time for several deep breaths.

"OK, go on please."

"I got involved when I hired on as the payroll guard to keep the money safe until employees collected their wages. It was legitimate."

Father Whelan was waiting to hear about the pit Henry had fallen into. "What about Scalise and Anselmi?"

Hank swallowed and cleared his throat. "I didn't know them until my third week of escorting the clerk. I wish I'd never laid eyes on those barbarians!"

"Henry, be honest with me."

Hank raised his hand, signaling to stop for a moment. He took another draw from the wine bottle, swallowed, and began. "It was a cold and windy Friday afternoon in April.

"I escorted Sam to the bank and trust, and everything was normal as a morning sunrise. I waited in the lobby while he and two bank clerks did the counts in the back room." Hank snickered. "It always felt odd to me to sit in the bank with two pistols under my coat."

Father Whelan shook his head.

"About 3:00 p.m., Sam was all set with the money. As was our procedure, when he returned to the front lobby, I stepped out on the sidewalk to look things over. With a nod through the window, he joined me for the march west toward the plant. He was a nervous sort like I've never seen.

"Sam hugged the storefronts as we walked and glared at each passing car on Thirty-Fifth. We were about a fourth of the way there when I noticed a sedan at the corner of Racine Street blocking our path. I told Sam to stay alert while I reached inside my coat. I had my hand on the pistol under my left arm just in case."

Father Whelan leaned in close to Henry.

"We passed another couple of shops when two men got out of that car. One of them disappeared around the corner on Racine. The other walked straight toward us. I noticed the bulge under the left side of his overcoat, so I alerted Sam. 'Watch out! He's packing.' Sam scrambled into a leather shop while I took a position behind a metal lamp post. The shooter coming our way was Alberto Anselmi. Alberto held a pistol in his right hand and raised his arm straight out like a knight's lance. He kept marching down the middle of the walkway, cocked the gun, and fired at me.

"When his shot shattered the glass in the car parked behind me, I lost it."

The priest reached up to cover his mouth.

"I don't think he expected me to be armed. I fired back. When my shot went off, Anselmi rushed to the nearest store entryway. He had the angle on me. As I ran across the sidewalk, Alberto got off another shot, which clipped my coat sleeve. I got behind a brick pillar at the leather shop. Through the store window, I could see Sam crouched between a couple of steamer trunks with his arms wrapped around the cash box. I waved at him to stay down. The store owner watched me while he tried to save his hide by kneeling behind the sales counter.

"I heard screams down the street behind me. When I looked back, the younger robber with drooped and misaligned eyes was coming from the east. This man turned out to be John Scalise. He had a pistol in each hand. I saw a young couple drop their packages and run straight out into the moving traffic to avoid being shot.

"I was in a bad location and had to move before they boxed me in. As a last-ditch attempt, I ran straight toward Anselmi. Before he figured out what was happening, I dove into an open stairwell leading up to the second floor. It wasn't a great spot, but I wasn't out in the open." Hank's voice dropped to a whisper. "That's when it happened."

"What happened, Henry? Tell me."

Hank swallowed hard. "When Sam saw me run for cover, he decided he couldn't wait any longer. He panicked and tore out of the store. Sam was a clumsy man. In his haste, he smacked right into the door frame and knocked himself to the ground. The cash box broke open on one end. I don't think Sam saw it though, because he got up and kept running with those envelopes dropping out the box. I heard the commotion and shouted to him, but he passed right by me like he was in a state of shock. Before he got far, two different sets of shots rang out.

"I saw the profile of Scalise at one of the storefronts holding the gun out. Before he could shoot again, I fired in his direction.

"But Sam was already down. Scalise ran right through the street with his guns still in each hand. I heard car tires screeching to a halt up and down the block. Anselmi scooped up the broken box and ran toward their car still parked at Racine. I went out to Sam, but it was too late. His lifeless body was face down in a pool of blood." Hank closed his eyes again.

Father Whelan used his shirt sleeve to wipe perspiration off his forehead. He admired Henry's courage to face true evil and not cower when being attacked. "Henry, how horrible to see Sam get gunned down." The priest took a moment to collect his thoughts. "So, if the Murder Twins picked this gunfight and got the cash, why are they still trying to kill you? Is it because you were a witness?"

Hank studied the floor. "Unfortunately, there is more to this story." He took a breath. "It gets worse.

"After the shoot out, I grabbed a bag from one of those shops as it was my duty to protect the transport. I scooped up the litter of loose pay envelopes from the sidewalk and tossed them in the bag. I headed straight for the Oliver Sharpe Company to give them the bad news and the rest of their money.

"When I got to the Racine Street intersection, two police cars came up with sirens blaring. The officers in one of the cars thought I was leaving the scene with a suspicious-looking sack, so they slammed on the brakes. They were out of the car and had their guns on me before I could cross. I stood there with my hands in the air staring at the building I was trying to get to. Before I knew it, they took the money, both of my weapons, and put me in handcuffs."

"But you were the payroll guard. That should have been easy to explain. Did they turn you loose?"

"No, they wouldn't listen to me at all. I got thrown into a crowded holding cell at the jail until a judge could hear my plea. I was charged with the payroll robbery and Sam's murder."

Father Whelan protested, "That's terrible! The company should vouch for you."

Hank nodded. "There were many witnesses on the block mid-afternoon who, unfortunately, saw me running around shooting a pistol and bagging up money after Sam was killed. Based on the witness interviews, the police convinced the company president this was an inside job planned by me."

Father Whelan pushed his chair back from the table. "Did you serve time?" He asked in a distressed tone.

Hank took a seat on the cot and tried to roll on his side. "The jail time was the least of it."

The priest helped him get comfortable. "I don't understand."

"After I was locked up, the cops pinched Anselmi and Scalise with the rest of the payroll cash. The police threw them in the same holding cell I was in."

The color drained from the priest's face. "My God, what happened?"

In a somber voice, Hank mumbled, "They beat me within an inch of my life."

The priest gasped with his hand covering his mouth.

"Crooked eyes took hold of me and Scalise did the slugging. I had three broken ribs before the police stopped the torture."

The priest reached out and touched Henry's arm.

"On this night, the joint was overflowing, so they cuffed us and pushed us back into the same cell with the other criminals. Before I blacked out, Anselmi kneed me in the kidneys and gave me another to the groin."

"Did you see a doctor?"

Hank scoffed. "Why would they do that? They just blamed my condition on my bad behavior and said it served me right. I could have died from that beating."

Father Whelan was puzzled. "Why are you still a target?"

Hank took a deep breath. "My case came to court first, and I was angry. My defense didn't stop at just proving I was working for the Oliver Sharpe Company when I collected the loose pay envelopes. We also went so far as to prove the slugs collected from Sam's body matched the guns Anselmi and

Scalise had on them the day they were arrested. The ballistic evidence helped to set me free and later was used to put them in prison for a long stretch."

"You did the right thing. Those murderers deserve to rot behind bars!"

"But there's a problem."

"What are you saying, Henry?"

"They are well connected. The twins work for people who pay off prison guards and courtroom justices. In six months, they got some sort of retrial. No surprise, the witnesses each developed amnesia and the police *couldn't find* the evidence on the slugs that had been used to put them in prison. The whole thing got tossed. They went free. Now they want revenge."

The priest's face was as pale as the collar on his shirt. "Henry, these men have no fear of hell. They deliver the Devil's wrath wherever they operate!"

Turning to the patient, he added, "While these stiches will stop most of the bleeding, after you get home, you'll need to take it easy for a few days and limit your activity while the internal wounds have a chance to heal.

"A free bonus will be the scars you're left with."

"Great, your fancy needle work is all I need to turn some heads at the beach this summer."

Father Whelan had to ask, "All right, tough guy, before we call it a night, I've got one more question."

"What do you want to know?"

"Aren't you scared?"

"Do you mean am I scared of hitmen coming from the other side of town?"

"Yes, Henry. Aren't you scared you will be the next person they assassinate?"

"No, not really. Even if I'm a marked man, I don't care. If these thugs don't stick to their side of town, the undertaker will be very busy." Hank winced as he moved to get more comfortable. "You know, Father, in Psalm 68, it says, 'Let God arise, let his enemies be scattered: let them also that hate him flee before him. As smoke is driven away, so drive them away: as wax melteth before the fire, so let the wicked perish.' "

The priest took a step back and took a fresh look at the vigilante lying on his cot.

———— • ————

Hank was getting sleepy. "How well did you know my father?"

"I knew Hudson very well and your mother Mattie, too. Your uncle Edward was a friend. When I came to this parish from Ireland, they were the first members of the church I got to know. They reminded me of my family back home. I thought they were kind and generous. It took a couple of years before I figured out the family business."

"You didn't turn away from them?"

"Your father wanted absolution. We're *all* sinners. My job is about forgiveness."

Father Whelan brought Henry a glass of water.

"It took a while to get over the thought your dad and his brother were in the cruel mob business. But I realized they still had souls. They didn't take pleasure from killing and would never do their business in the presence of children or wives. I often saw them at funerals they caused. They gave me money to share anonymously with widows."

Hank's eyes were nearly closed, but Father Whelan pulled up a stool to sit next to the cot.

"Your mother was a real pearl. She tried to blend in as a regular housewife. To me, it seemed she lived in denial about the crimes that put your family in a better home." The priest shook his head. "Her death at thirty-eight was very suspicious. Your father became bitter."

"What about Uncle Eddie?"

"Your dad and uncle made a powerful team. While Hudson knew how to handle a gun, found the soldiers, and worked the streets, your uncle Edward was the real architect behind the business. He made the tough decisions. Edward set the spread for betting on races, bought the bootlegged liquor, and worried about the cops.

"As soon as we laid your dad and your brother Robbie in the ground, Edward became the next target. I was told, Torrio put a double-sized bounty on your uncle because he blamed your family for some nasty attacks on the southside. Rumors were the Torrio hitmen fought over who put the bullets in Edward. As a result, I don't think Torrio ever paid his big bounty. I doubt he cared. He just wanted your uncle gone."

Father Whelan covered his face with his hands as he considered the painful family history.

"You know, Henry, your father never wanted you in the crime business. It's why he kept you in school even while your brother worked with him. His life as a mobster was too dangerous to raise a family."

Hank pulled the blanket over himself. "But with Dad gone, George Moran, one of the right-hands for O'Banion, felt sorry for me being on my own. He put me to work. My poor father would roll in his grave if he could see me."

"Isn't George the one they call *Bugsy?*"

Hank pointed at Father Whelan. "Oh, be careful! George hates the nickname. People who think he's crazy call him Bugsy. He's not. But he might kill anyone who uses the nickname."

"I'll be sure to use *George* in the future." The priest got up and slid the stool back from the cot. "Well, Henry, you should hit the hay now. You need to rest. I'm nearly done for the night, too. I'll just tidy things up in the study room before I turn in."

"Good night, Father. Thank you for patching me up. You know I couldn't go to a regular hospital."

"I know, Henry. I was happy to help." He paused for a moment. "Think about stopping back for a confession anytime you'd like. I'm always here to listen."

Early in the morning, Hank left a fistful of cash on the cot, gathered his things, and slipped out the back door to the alley. He was on a mission.

CHAPTER 6

Moving Company

Hank caught a cab and rode through the quiet morning streets to a working-class neighborhood in Sheffield. The cab drop was four blocks from the house on the next street over. In the crime business, he couldn't be too careful. Hank kept a low profile but moved along with purpose.

As he approached on the side street, a Chevy sedan slowed just as it crossed ahead on Potter Avenue. Hank stopped short of the corner and watched it from the side of a neighbor's house.

As the car sat idling on the street, he couldn't identify the two occupants from his angle, but he could see the passenger waving at the house with a pistol in his hand. The passenger door opened a few inches. Hank drew his thirty-eight caliber.

A second car approached from the opposite end of the block. As it stopped, the headlamps flashed three times. The first vehicle shifted into gear again and resumed moving. The passenger door swung shut and they accelerated off. As the car turned the corner, the morning sunlight lit up a trail of bullet holes on the back fender.

Hank waited to be sure the street was clear before he moved toward the story-and-a-half bungalow. Vinnie saw Hank step in from the side door. "Hey, boss, where were you last night? And what's with the pistol? Is everything OK?

"No, Vinnie, things are not okay. I've been busy trying to lose those goons since last night. I eventually got away, but not before getting the new car shot up and taking a couple of slugs in the gut. Have you seen the cars out front with guys casing the place?"

Vinnie jumped up and moved to the window. He eased the curtains back and studied the street from end to end. "I don't see anyone."

"Well, they may be gone for the moment, but I'll bet they're coming back with reinforcements. We've gotta get out of here, now! You round up the guys and get them moving. Go tell Willy to load a rifle and watch the front while we leave through the alley. Let the guys know to use the back door to load up. We should all scatter. Have everyone head out in different directions, and we'll meet up at the Clay Street rental tomorrow morning."

"Hold on, boss. I've got some bad news, too."

"Vin, what is it? We don't have much time here."

"Those filthy rats were layin' for us last night. The situation was ugly, boss. Real ugly."

Hank worried about his crew like a parent frets over their children. He knew each of them would risk their lives for him, and he didn't want to lose any of them. "How are the boys?"

"We were in a spot! They tried to butcher our gang. Allen and Remi got banged up. We took 'em to the doc, and he did as much as he could. They're upstairs."

Hank took a step back. "How bad is it? Can we get them into a car?"

Vinnie scratched his head. "I think so. I'm pretty sure they're both asleep right now."

Hank, rattled by the news, tried to refocus. "Later today, Vin, you'll have to find us another car. The Lincoln V8 we got from my buddy in Detroit overheated after being shot up. I ditched it a couple of miles from the ambush, but the cops found it last night."

"Ouch, what a tough break. It was the only *fast* car we had. Our other slowpokes are still running because those hitmen left us alone and chased after you. Someone has a bounty on your head!"

Hank could have spit. "The bastards just won't leave me alone. If that Lincoln wasn't so fast, I'd be dead right now. Those goons couldn't keep up once I broke away."

Hank recalled the image of the line of bullet holes on the car he saw idling out front. "Vinnie, we have to get moving. I'll grab some things and go on ahead to open up the place on Clay Street.

"By the way, did the doc send along any bromine?"

Vinnie was caught off guard by the medical question. "Yes, I think we have the stuff." He snickered. "I'm not sure who screamed louder last night when the doc poured the first dose on Allen and Remi's wounds. Do you want to be their nurse?"

It occurred to Hank that the quiet in the house was unusual. "Where is everybody?"

"Bernie's back in the kitchen making something to eat. Carlo and Willy are downstairs using the new billiards table."

Henry was surprised. "Nine-ball at this hour?"

"No. They're down there to clean up the guns." His face became serious. "Willy got mad when we were outsmarted by the Murder Twins. He told us it will *never* happen again. He got Carlo to help him. They are using the table to tear each gun down and go through them all with oil. We had two automatic rifles jam when we were pinned down. We got by with a sawed-off and a pistol, but it can't happen again. People could have died!"

"What about Tony?"

"He's playing poker in the kitchen with a new guy named Nick."

"Hey, when you find us another car. Bring it to Clay Street, but park it in the alley behind the market. The neighbors there can't suspect anything."

Vinnie stepped to the door. "I've got it, boss. They won't see any fancy cars."

Hank stepped into the kitchen. The table was littered with playing cards, cash, and a couple of Coke bottles. Nick shouted, "Aces! Finally, I've got you dead to rights!"

Nick was a young man about nineteen with an easy smile. He didn't look anything like a gangster with his head of wild brown hair and lean build. The youngster put his hand of cards down on the table with a triumphant smile.

"Hi, Nick. I'm Hank. We spoke by phone. I'm glad to see you showed up today. Sorry to cut your game short, but we've gotta pull the tent stakes and get out of here fast. It looks like Torrio's hoodlums followed us home last night, and now they are planning to whack us. They could come back at any minute."

Both card players rose from the table.

Nick reached his hand out. "It's good to meet you face to face, sir. How can I help?"

Hank was impressed by the enthusiasm. "You're coming with me, Nick. We have to move the two wounded men upstairs over to a rental place I found on Clay Street."

Nick hesitated. "OK, but Tony tells me you have some questions before I can work with these guys?"

Hank nodded. "Yes, I do, but the interview will have to wait. We can talk later after we get these guys resettled. Everyone else is going to head out now."

Hank turned toward the parlor room. "I'm going upstairs to check on the boys and get them ready. Nick, you get a set of keys from Vinnie and pull one of those tin lizzies up near the back door. Keep your eyes open though. We may have visitors at any moment."

"Yes, sir."

— • —

Hank took hold of the handrail and made deliberate steps as he climbed. The sutures in his side pulled each time he raised his left leg. At the top of the stairs, he turned down the hall, twisted a handle, and eased the bedroom door open. The squeak from the hinges woke Remi.

Hank moved in next to his bed. "How are you doing, Rem? It looks like the doc has your shoulder and arm all wrapped up."

"Boss, we thought you were dead. Did you get away clean?"

"No, they drilled me in the car. I got stitched back together though. I should be OK." Hank pulled his shirt loose and raised it enough to show the bloody gauze patches. "Rem, man, I hate to disturb you guys, but those bastards are still after us. I just saw two cars out front casing the joint. We gotta get out of here fast."

Remi began to pull the blankets back.

"Can you move?"

Remi turned in the bed as best he could. The pain in his arm spiked like someone drove a nail into the shoulder joint. He winced.

Hank saw it.

Remi tried to smile. "Yes, I think I can. But I don't know about Allen. He's got a concussion or something."

"Rem, tell me what went down."

Remi moved to sit on the edge of the bed. "Our vehicle was the last of the pack when we turned onto Milton Avenue. It just happened another car came up the street behind us right as we slowed for the drop. Before I knew it, automatics opened up from the second-story windows and I couldn't back out. Since it was getting dark, all I could see was the fire from their gun barrels. It was coming down from both sides of the street like lightning and thunder pounding on us. I still can't make the ringing in my ears stop."

Hank moved in close to Remi. "I'll help you with your shirt."

"Allen and I were pinched, so I pulled our car up next to the liquor truck. Just, as the truck driver tried to get out his cab door, he got nailed and crumbled on the ground. The shots kept raining down on the street. We slid out between the vehicles and tried to fend for ourselves. Allen got hit in the neck and head before we even got our feet on the ground. With blood running down in his eyes, he fired back with a pistol. We were trapped like hen house chickens on slaughter day."

Remi kept talking while Hank moved over toward Allen.

"We held our own 'til I got jammed up. A pair of shells bound my gun tight. I tried everything, but I couldn't break them loose."

Hank kept his hand over the wounds in his side. He was frustrated about the attack. "What happened?"

"The shooters got pretty bold when I couldn't fire back. I could make out the shadow of one of them as he fired from an open window. When he stopped to reload, I grabbed the sawed-off from the car and gave him both barrels of buckshot. The blast buried him in broken glass."

Allen moaned when the raised voices in the room brought an end to his sleep.

Remi continued, "I couldn't reload fast enough to keep up. We were barricaded behind the vehicles. The last time I reached over the car hood to fire the shotgun, I must have leaned right into a spray of bullets. Slugs tore through my shoulder and knocked me backwards. While I lay there bleeding, I could see the truck driver in a heap with his face on the ground. I thought I was going to die just like him." He stopped for a moment and swallowed. "My prayers were answered when I heard the V8 roar in the Lincoln."

Remi put his hand on his forehead. "As I was lying there on the ground, one of those shooters ran past me and tossed a lit pack of dynamite in the back of our truck. He was on his way to their car to chase after you. I was too slow to get away. I thank God the fuse burned out on that dynamite. It never blew up.

"I can't figure out what they were trying to do. Don't you think it's strange they didn't even try to steal the booze?"

Hank considered this clue.

"Once they were gone, our guys rushed in and helped get me and Allen out of there before the cops showed up. The next thing I remember, I woke up on a table in the doc's back room."

Hank studied Allen's head wrap. "How'd he do last night?" Hank stepped in close and nudged Allen's bed with his knee to keep him awake.

"The doc said Allen was very lucky. If the gunshot in his neck was an inch either way, he would be dead right now. Though the doc did say the bones in his skull could be cracked some."

Remi was up and out of bed now. He moved towards the door. "Boss, it was bad. How'd they know we'd turn on Milton anyway? We keep changing our routes. I think they're gunning for you."

As Hank helped Allen get on his feet, Remi's comment hit him again. *I think they're gunning for you.*

——— • ———

The Clark Street rental was ill-prepared to be a nurse's station. The beds lacked linens, the bath had no towel or soap, and the kitchen was without plates or forks. Fortunately, it had adequate window curtains. Hank pulled the blinds closed to darken the bedroom. "Nick, the guys are resting now. Come join me in the kitchen for a while."

"Sure thing." Nick braced for the conversation to come. His shirt had blood streaked on the side from helping move Rem and Allen.

The stains didn't seem to bother Nick even on his first day. It was a fair sign Hank might have a keeper. He waited at the simple table like a judge presiding over a courtroom. He nodded to the empty chair on the opposite side. "Take a seat, Nick.

"The reason for this talk is to figure out who you are and what makes you tick. You can also learn a few things about what we stand for. If either of us doesn't like what we hear, we go our separate ways now and avoid a dangerous problem."

Nick nodded in agreement.

"On this crew, we trust people with our very lives. As you're aware, we got attacked last night. The guys took good care of each other and everyone is alive today. This is the type of trust we need."

"OK, Hank. I get it."

Hank pulled his chair around the table to face Nick. "I have a few questions I like to ask to get things rolling. First, where are you from originally?"

Nick smiled. "This one's easy. I grew up in St. Louis."

"OK, now tell me, what family do you have?"

"My folks emigrated from Germany in 1890. They had four kids here after they arrived. My brother and two sisters still live in Missouri." Nick thought he could handle these types of questions with ease. His stress level eased a little.

"So Nick, who do you trust?"

This was an unexpected question. He didn't know why Hank would ask it. What difference did it matter who he trusted? He took his time answering. "This may sound odd, but in Chicago, I trust myself right now. I tried working with a partner when I first moved to the city. We did some small-time pickpocketing and minor theft. The next thing I knew, I found our place cleaned out. He took everything. So, other than me, I guess, I trust my family."

Hank nodded. "What are you good at? What sort of skills do you have?"

"For specialty skills, I tried my hand at safe cracking once. For a short while, I worked with a guy who broke into business safes. Before he could train me, he got thrown in Joliet." Nick scratched his head. "I'd like to learn more about how to open safes, but I also like dealing with numbers. Maybe someday, I could keep some books or other records."

Hank made a note of it in his small brown notebook. "Thanks. Here's the next one. What are you most afraid of?"

Nick was stumped. "This is a tough question." After twisting in his seat for a minute, he got up from his chair, walked around, and stood behind it. "I guess I'm most afraid of disappointing my parents. If I got sent to prison, I think it would kill my dad."

Hank's brow furrowed. "Why do you think so?"

"My dad has been an honest man throughout his life in both good times and bad. He believes when things get tough, you just work harder. You never take another man's possessions."

"So, he doesn't approve of your life's work?"

"No, he wouldn't approve if he knew about it."

"So, how did you end up in this business?"

Nick plopped down in his chair. "Poor choices. For a while, I worked for a lumberyard on the southside. A couple of guys I knew there began doing some jobs on the side to make extra money. Before long, they didn't need to work in the hot, dusty lumberyard anymore. The last time I saw them, they wore expensive suits with neckties and hung out with pretty girls."

Hank nodded. "New question: If you worked for us, what would you do with the money?"

Nick pushed his chair back. "What I would do with my money is none of your business."

Hank noticed the fire in his young associate's face. "You're right, but I want to know how long you plan to work?"

Nick thought this was out of line. It showed on his face. "At this age, I guess I don't know. I assume it would be for a long time. This isn't the type of regular job my dad has so it's hard to say.

"How many more of these questions like this do you have?" Nick took his seat again.

"Just a few more." Hank carried on, "So, who are your enemies?"

Nick stroked his forehead. "I don't have any major enemies. The cops have been after me a few times, but I keep moving around so they won't catch up with me."

Hank studied Nick's face. He appeared to be telling the truth. "Here's the last question: How do you want to die?"

Nick bolted from the chair and it tipped over backward with a clatter. "What the hell kind of question is that?"

Hank wasn't fazed by the drama. "Everyone thinks about it in this business. So how do you want to die?"

"I don't! I'm not even thirty years old!"

Hank crossed his arms and pushed back in his chair. "This is a dangerous business, Nick. Men get killed on the Chicago streets every day now. If you join the crew, at some point, people will shoot at you. Are you going to shoot back or run off?"

"Look, I don't have a bad temper, but if someone takes a shot at me, I'm pretty sure I will return the favor." Nick stared at the creases in Hank's face. "I mean if it's the best option and all."

He continued, "Now if you ask me to walk into a room filled with armed thugs who want to kill me, I'll have second thoughts about your sanity."

"Fair enough. It would be true for any of us. How well do you handle a gun?"

At this question, Nick's face picked up some color. "While I wasn't in the army, I've shot plenty of pistols and a rifle a few times."

"I assumed you were too young to have served in Europe. I want you to practice shooting with the guys. You've got to be able to hold your own in a gun battle. I hope it doesn't come down to this, but it is better to be prepared."

Nick's smile soon faded when Hank asked the next question. "Have you ever killed a man?"

Nick expected this to be part of the interview. "I've never felt the need."

"But would the thought of taking lives bother your conscience?"

Nick stood up and stepped toward the sink. He paced back and forth a couple of times, staring out the window at the street. This was a deeper question.

He rejoined Hank at the table. "I grew up going to church on Sundays and I felt the sting of the belt on my behind, so I know the Ten Commandments."

"It appears you know right from wrong. Well, we don't hire out as killers, but we do defend our part of the city and the business we've earned over the years. We don't relish in taking lives, but it happens. If it bothers you, this isn't your line of work."

Hank wasn't finished yet. "I don't have a problem with men who have strong beliefs and may look down on this miserable business. You must be completely in on this if you work with me. Otherwise, you'll be timid in a gun battle and others will exploit it. I've seen it happen before.

"Here's an extra question, what terrible secrets do you have?"

Nick had a blank expression now. "Nothing, really. I had a girl back home I was sweet on. We were going to marry after school. Once we graduated, she picked someone else. I have a notion to go back there and make his life miserable somehow."

"You sound pretty normal to me." Hank laughed. "Why don't you take your seat again, please. I want to tell you a few things about how I operate this gang."

Nick took his place and pulled his chair in close to the table.

Hank led with the most popular topic. "First, I want everyone to share in the success of the business. For example, when we sell a load of liquor, I cut everyone in on a slice of the profit."

Nick smiled.

Hank pushed on. "Don't get too excited yet. When you're new, this won't be much, just some extra spending money. The more you contribute over time, the more your share of the pie grows."

"It seems like a fair way to operate. I'll work hard to earn my keep."

"Great, Nick. We understand each other. There are a few more things. I like each guy to have his own plan. If you stay in the business long enough, there's a fair chance you could die. So, if you join the crew, you need to put some money away for life *after* being a mobster. In other words, you need an exit plan. It works the best if there is someone you trust to give money to as you go. It has to be out of sight, waiting for you, if you need to retire on the spur of the moment."

Nick looked bewildered. "I don't know who I would trust completely. Maybe my folks, but they would ask too many questions. It might sound crazy, but I've always trusted my older sister."

Hank nodded. "Would you still trust her even if she didn't approve of how you earned the money?"

Nick scratched the back of his scalp. "Yes, she can keep secrets better than anyone I know."

Hank added some notes in his notebook. "That might work."

"We're not saints, but we won't sell women or drugs."

Nick nodded.

"OK, I don't want your answer now. I want you to think overnight about your stance on your willingness to take lives. We'll talk again tomorrow."

Nick had never had a deep conversation like this in his life, but he understood why, and he respected Hank for grilling him.

"You should head home now."

Nick felt he had at least a fair chance of making the crew. He was curious about working for Hank. "Thanks, I appreciate the brutal honesty about what I might be getting into. You're an unusual patriarch."

"Hold on now!" Hank waived a finger in the air. "We don't use those expressions around here."

Nick was confused. "Why not? Aren't you in charge of this mob crew?"

Hank nodded. "Most days, I feel like more of a circus master. But I'm just one of the guys, Nick. Yes, I make the decisions, but I'm certainly no better than any of them."

The two shared a laugh.

Nick got up and turned for the door. "All right, I'll speak with you tomorrow."

———— • ————

It was quiet at the Clark Street rental when the morning sun brightened the window blinds. Rem was sitting up in the bed talking to the recruit. "So Nick, did Hank talk to you about his *crime academy*?"

Nick nodded. "I think so. Do you mean training with each of you guys on guns, driving, and other stuff?"

"Hank is as serious as a courtroom judge about training recruits. If you don't have the skills, you won't ride with us. Better pay attention, too. When you're finished, he'll put you through the wringer on everything you learned. If he doesn't think you've got what it takes, he'll send you packing. He'd rather see you find another job than to put lives at risk."

"OK, OK, I get it. Man, he seems like a hard-nosed boss." Nick tossed his hands in the air.

"There's another side to Hank, too."

"What do you mean, Rem?"

"He's quite the musician. It may sound odd, but he looks at this gang like an orchestra. Each of us has a role to play, but he wants everyone to know how to play all the instruments in case someone has to leave the band."

Nick was curious. "Why do you call him a musician?"

Rem tried to smile through the pain. "Oh, if you're around here long enough, you'll hear him on the brass horn."

"The trumpet?"

"Oh, no. For Hank, it's the saxophone—his true love."

"Really? I never took him for the type with those thick fingers and all."

Rem smirked. "None of us did. But don't be fooled by thinking he's an amateur. The man knows his way around swing music. Sometimes, he plays in little joints around this side of town. You should hear him."

CHAPTER 7

The Academy

In an expanse of unused rural land twenty miles outside Chicago, the remnants of the overgrown drive were hard to discern from where it departed the dirt road. The broken-down fences, obscured by layers of vines, were clues leading to a farm site from the past. As Hank swung the car off the road and began to push through tall grass, underbrush scoured the sides of the car. He pointed toward the abandoned farmhouse and silo becoming visible through the trees. "We're headed to those buildings back there."

Hank turned toward Nick, smiled, and thumped his new man on the shoulder. "We've got the whole day here to work on skills. Are you ready for the crime academy?"

Nick had a concerned look on his face.

The weeds were knee-high around the house and the front door was hanging from a single top hinge. The breeze swung the door around like a lighthouse spotlight. The dull red paint on the barn appeared to be a final sunset on a pioneer's dream. The horses and livestock were long gone, but an old plow remained parked in the tall grass next to the barn. The leathers on the plow were withered away and rust consumed the metal.

This place held a long-forgotten story of a family who toiled during the hard decades before the value of crops rose enough to make farming a viable business. In the late nineteenth century, people struggled to raise enough cattle to support a family. It was honest work, but it was filled with countless unforeseen losses, livestock disease, and financial disasters. The structural remains of a wooden windmill stood adjacent to the barn and the chicken coop looked like it had been the victim of an air raid. The missing wooden roof shakes were strewn about on the ground.

Nick was puzzled. He raised his upturned hands waiting for someone to tell him this was a joke. "What do you mean this is it? There is nothing here but some crappy old farm buildings."

Hank took the challenge. "You're right, Nick. This old farm is in shambles. But the beauty of an old place, this far off the beaten path, is no one cares if we make a little noise today."

Nick was tempted to bail out of the car and walk the road back alone, but the whole crew had made the trip and he hated to disappoint them. Hank seemed so cheery about the prospect of training. "You mean to shoot guns?"

"Yes, we will shoot a few guns, Nick, and learn about the *whole business*."

Nick's apprehension soon faded away. He was curious about their plans. The other two cars pulled into the farmyard and parked in the overgrown weeds.

As the crew piled out, Hank didn't waste any time. "OK, before you guys get too far away, listen here for a minute. It's been a while since we've done this, so I want to remind you of a few things. First, remember no one ever goes inside or walks behind the old chicken coop. The coop is our shooting gallery. If you walk behind the building, you're likely to get popped. Are we clear on this?"

While everyone nodded their agreement, Nick noticed the splintered bullet holes in the walls of the chicken coop. It looked like a giant woodpecker had been at work.

"Next, I want each guy to load and fire all the guns. Willy will run through each one with you on how to pull them apart in case someday you get jammed up. You must be able to do this even with your eyes closed. I mean it. We don't leave here until everyone runs through them again."

Willy nodded his agreement.

"With Allen back on his feet, he'll open up the brewing school. Allen, there is old equipment stored in the barn, and you'll find some grain samples in there, too. Set up your stuff inside, and we'll cycle through. With your bad wing, you may need a little help with the heavy items."

Allen raised his good arm as a gesture of willingness. His other, still bound in a sling, remained at his side.

"I'm going to talk about our customers, what they want, and about planning your exit from this group someday. The exit I'm talking about means a plan for how much money to save and finding someone trustworthy to keep an eye on it.

"Bernie will cover the need to switch liquor shipment routes frequently, back-up plans when stuff happens, and using our doctor when someone gets hurt. Vinnie is going to go over knife fights, how people die of stab wounds, and how to defend yourself."

Vinnie swung his left arm behind his back, while he motioned with his right extended ahead of him as if he were in a sword fight.

"Before we begin, here's what I believe about trust. I handpicked each of you guys because I thought you had the guts and brains to be in this business and you appeared to be a fit for this group. I trust you and expect you to trust me. As you know, we all share in the profits when things go well. At the same time, we have a code of honor. If you ever abandon this team in some way or steal from us, there are no second chances."

Nick swallowed hard when he reflected on his urge to run off when they had first arrived.

Hank set the wheels in motion. "Hey, Tony, do you mind going into the house and grabbing a pile of targets from the kitchen?"

"Sure thing, boss."

"Willy and Carlo, would you guys pull the guns from the trunk and set up a table or something?" Willy went around to the trunk, and Carlo headed towards the barn.

When Hank finished speaking, Nick walked past a well pump and over to a scraggly apple tree growing next to the house. He stood on his tiptoes to pull a green and red apple loose from a low branch. On one side, the piece of fruit was marred with a couple of wormholes, so he turned it around before he took a bite from the safe side. The tart flavor made him pucker and reminded him of the apples he grew up with.

Hank came over and spoke to Nick. "Let's get you firing a few pistols."

Nick smiled as he tossed the apple core into the weeds and wiped the sticky juice from his hands on his pant legs. "I'm ready." The pair walked to a small workbench table Carlo had retrieved from the barn.

Willy balanced four of the tin plates he brought from the house on the pairs of nails protruding from the wood siding on the chicken coop. The plates were arranged over a section of wall riddled with holes like the tin lid on a pepper shaker.

Nick marveled, "If a guy misses the plates, it will be tough to tell where your shots went."

Willy joined him at the table. "We've all taken our turn at the wall. There's no shame around here. Sometimes it takes a while to get used to these short guns."

Nick ran his hand along the side of the sawed-off shotgun.

Willy reached past it and picked up a Smith & Wesson revolver. "The 12 gauge is deadly at close range, but we build up from the basics. This pistol is a thirty-eight caliber. See how you press this release right here on the side to open the cylinder? Now hold it with your left hand and spin the cylinder to load each chamber with ammo."

Nick picked a few shells out of a box and dropped them into the cylinder holes. He swung the cylinder back into the gun and held it with his right arm extended toward the target.

"To be accurate, you're going to need a good firm grip using both hands. Hold your arms out straight and sight down the barrel. Before you shoot, I want to warn you, a thirty-eight will sting a little when you fire it. But again, a tight grip is the best way to limit the pain. You can't be afraid of it. Step up here, draw the hammer back, and take your best shot."

Nick emptied the weapon in a wild pattern of firing.

"Good! Now get rid of those empties. First, turn it over with the cylinder rolled out and knock the brass loose. Do it again. This time, focus your aim on the centers of the plates."

———— • ————

The barn was all set. Dust-laden light filtered through the windows on the crock of malted barley resting on a high bench next to several blue-glass jars of hops, a small drum of dried yeast, a pail of water drawn from the hand pump, and a row of steins to drink from. On the floor, a copper tub filled with cool water held several drowning brown bottles.

Allen, not quite limber with his arm bound, offered an animated lesson on the finer points of brewing lagers. By design, the water in the copper tub liberated the labels from the brown bottles. Nick helped to open each one for the class to sample which led to a lively debate on how to influence flavor.

With their rivalry unleashed by the beer, Vinnie seized the moment for an all-hands knife fight in the middle of the yard using wooden daggers wrapped with rags bound by string. There was no debate. With skillful footwork, Willy, bearing the mustache of a swordsman, made quick work of several opponents before most of them had realized the fight was on.

———— • ————

Balanced on top of an overturned orange crate in front of the parked cars, Hank addressed his men spread around him in a half-circle. He looked a bit like an armed college professor standing there in his box-toed shoes, brown twill pants, summer hat, and suspenders draped over his white shirt with a slung holster for his thirty-eight. No one dared to look away.

The message was brief, a few statements really, connecting each man to the mission they longed to understand.

Hank studied the group. "You may have wondered from time to time, what business are we really in?

"When I was a young lad, my father was a mobster, too. I never understood why. I'm not sure he did either. It was the business he knew, and from time to time, he saw it pay pretty well. But it was a far too dangerous way to support a family.

"A family needs much more from you than money. They need safety, stability, and time with you. Eventually, both my parents and my brother died. My father had not considered this possibility, nor had he prepared for it.

"This fact changed me forever and now I run a different sort of show. Some think it's tough to get into this gang, while other gangs will hire anyone who comes along. I surround myself with crackerjack men to run a clean operation and work together to survive.

"Our mission boils down to this: We play a part in the *entertainment* business. We help the hardworking people of Chicago unwind and have fun. Our job is to run liquor and tobacco distribution for a good portion of the North Side. We deliver when promised and keep thieves away from both our supplies and our customers. Once a speakeasy owner trusts us, they often want us to arrange their bands and performers. We work with the best.

"While they are busy serving patrons, we keep the fun going. It's simple. It's also dangerous.

"In a perfect world, a fifteen-dollar case of whiskey crosses the border from Canada to be sold to one of our joints in Chicago for ninety dollars. Unfortunately, this amount of money attracts every sort of thief and hoodlum imaginable. They are all after us and the booze. You can top things off with the federal raids and state's attorneys trying to make a name for themselves, too.

"Our business is different than others. There are things we aren't willing to do. We don't run brothels and don't believe in them. None of us will sell or use drugs like opium or cocaine. We will not be hired assassins, but we do defend what's ours. And finally, we don't beat on our customers. Turns out, they aren't very loyal if you do.

"There are two hundred men in a dozen different crews working for the North Side. From time to time, we agree to partner with a few of them for larger projects. It's part of the deal we've signed on for.

"Now, within our group, we share profits when times are good. Today, times are very good!"

The men broke into cheers. One yelled, "Remember, Hank. We don't take any wooden nickels around here!"

Hank smiled. "We also take care of each other when times are bad. We each agree upfront never to cross anyone in our crew or skim from the take. If you do, there are no second chances. None.

"Besides making money, ultimately, our goal is to stay alive long enough to enjoy it. We trust each other with our very lives.

"It's simple. It's how I run things. Are there any questions?"

Hank made eye contact with each of them. He stopped at Bernie. "Bernie, you've been around here the longest. Do you have anything to add?"

"No, Hank, you know your onions."

"Well, if not, here is one for each of you. Which is more important? To get rich, or to get out alive?"

The faces in the group turned serious.

"Of course, you might say getting out when you're rich is the best answer.

"It's true, but it puts you more at risk. I want to talk to you now about planning an exit strategy for when things turn from bad to worse. Mark my words, someday, when we least expect it, they will."

Hank stepped down and moved closer to the men. "We each need to save for an early retirement, which could occur at any time."

He walked over and pointed out the bandages still wrapping Remi's head. "What if you get banged up tomorrow and have to quit? Would you be ready to be out of work awhile or move to a new town somewhere if you had to? This business is a merry-go-round. If you stay on the ride long enough, the music will stop for you one day. I know a lot of guys who thought they got rich in this business. But after a stretch in prison, they came out with nothing. Others had moved in and taken everything while they were in the slammer.

"It's amazing how easily it disappears unless you park some of it out of sight. My sister and I became destitute teens when our father was killed."

———— • ————

Hank used four brass tacks to pin a wrinkled Chicago map on the side of the barn. The guys gathered around taking seats on old crates and small drums. He drew a heavy line around the North Side boundaries on the paper. "This is the area where we do business. You need to memorize these streets. Outside this area is no man's land for us. We stay out of there.

"We run things from Howard Street up here on the northside of Roger's Park, dropping south on Kedzie and the Chicago River to make our west boundary down to Randolph Street on the south." His finger trailed the boundary as he talked. "While we own everything between the river and the lake from Roger's Park down to central Chicago, there are other crews from the North Side to help cover this. Be sure to speak to me before you work any fresh land."

Vinnie spoke up. "Hank, it's all well and good for us to stay on our side. But, what about thieves that cross a bridge?"

"That is a good question, Vinnie. Now, if some dimwitted Andy Gump from the other side of the river peddles his swill in our neighborhoods, we need to crush him right away. Once they take root, it's hard to pull the weeds from your garden. Stay on top of *maintenance work*."

Willy added, "I'd start by cracking some melons of the guys who bought the outside booze."

"Hold on a minute, Willy. I can see how you might feel that way. But unlike the garlic squads from across town, we don't shake down our speakeasy owners. If they buy someone else's booze, we hit hard against those suppliers. Otherwise, our rivals keep bouncing around trying to steal more accounts, too. It's better to attack the knuckle heads directly, typically by stealing their loads.

"If things get worse, we try to remove the leader of the gang. It's a risky move that can open a larger fight.

"I want to switch subjects now and talk about trust. Our customers trust us. What do you think they trust us for?"

The group volunteered, "Quality booze, class acts on the stage, and deliveries when promised!"

Hank called on Nick. "Nick, what else do you think they need?"

Nick felt the eyes on him. "Protection to keep the other gangs away?"

Hank nodded. "Yes, I like it.

"So how do we do this? We all know, we've been getting hammered lately while making deliveries. So, we're going to change a few things.

"First, we're going to stop acting like a military supply line. We won't use the big trucks for merchant deliveries anymore. Those mules haul a lot of booze but are too slow and make an easy target. When they get hit, we risk too much.

"No, we'll bring those loads into warehouses and like a racehorse runs, do our drops with cars rather than trucks. We'll move faster and stay light on our feet to get in and get out. We want to be hard to catch up with, so we'll need more cars and more of you to be runners to make this work."

The guys looked back and forth at each other.

"The change shouldn't hurt anything for our dry goods. The cigar lines are easy to cover by keeping some stock in each car.

"Now Bernie is going to say some things about a new game plan for routes."

Bernie stepped up to the map. "Guys, whether we like it or not, other gangs are watching us. When they see the chance to steal our loads, they will, and we could get shot at in the process. It's a miserable business.

"So here's what we've gotta do: Keep throwing them off by changing routes, days of the week, the time, the vehicle, the driver, and more. I mean everything has to change, and often. I'd even switch to running the whole route backward from time to time or arrange some drops early in the morning. Our customers know this is a dangerous business, and they will work with you."

Vinnie nodded his agreement.

Bernie continued, "Now, for a warning. If you decide to use the same route twice in a row, you might get away with it. But every time you repeat it, the risk that you are going to get hit rises.

"Am I being clear?"

All heads nodded.

CHAPTER 8

Sieben

Decades earlier, Michael Sieben built a multi-story brewing house in the German style with a handsome brick facade at 1466 North Larrabee Street. When the prohibition curtain fell in 1920, the Sieben family was put out of the beer-making business.

Dean O'Banion and Johnny Torrio were both rivals and partners. They both could profit by working together to exploit the thirst created by the Eighteenth Amendment. It was the perfect storm for mobsters, a prosperous new world begging for a drink while banning all legitimate breweries from providing it.

The street-smart Irishman and the Italian businessman couldn't have seemed more different. Yet there were mutual benefits for working together. The unlikely pair took over the brewhouse as partners with a deceitful promise to make non-alcoholic beer. It was a hand-shake agreement to peacefully divide Chicago and prevent gang wars.

Dean's Irish curiosity was killing him. "Why, did Sieben give it up?" It seemed mad a master brewer would walk away from business when there was no competition.

Torrio thought it was obvious. "We'll get our way, Dean. The horse is out of the barn now for Sieben. He can't brew anymore under the new law.

Furthermore, it took years to pass the amendment and no one knows how long it could last. So he released his men."

"I assume you know a few of them?"

"Yeah, I did." Johnny dug through paper in the brewing office file drawers and produced the former employee list. He waived the page in the air. "Right here."

O'Banion smiled. "The first step will be to get a few good guys on our payroll."

Torrio had devised a plan. "This is how we'll make it work. First, make small batches of the non-alcoholic stuff for a month or so. This is not what people really want but legitimate we must look. Maybe we could make some root beer for kids, too."

Dean agreed, "Old man Sieben and the cops will be snooping around when we first get going. We should keep some stuff around here for show."

Torrio finished explaining his plan. "Once the parade is over and things settle down, we'll brew small batches of real beer, but still packaged with the fake-beer labels. It will take some time to get the process down. Afterward, we can do what we want. I don't think we should let anyone pick up at the brewery for now. Let's truck it out to our own warehouses and relabel it there." Torrio snickered at the thought. "We can each claim to have the best beer in the city. No one needs to know it's the same stuff!"

<hr />

Dean's face was hot. His hand shook as he dialed the phone number. The phone rang several times and finally a voice crackled in from the other end, "Hello, who is this?"

"Hey Johnny, it's finally you! This is Dean. Where have you been the last month? Are you dodging my calls? I left you messages."

Torrio sighed. He might as well get this call over with. "I've been a little busy, Dean. I didn't know you needed something."

"Oh, yeah? No one told you I called? Well, I did *several* times, and I am again right now!"

"Jeez, cool it, Dean. It's not too good for your health to get so wound up."

"What's that? You could say I'm a little hot under the collar. You're right."

"What's the problem? Is the brewery running OK?"

"Yes, the brewery is still running fine now after two years. But you and I have a much different problem. It's those scums, the Genna Brothers, who you call friends. They are all over my map selling cheap liquor to my best accounts. Accounts who normally pay me a premium!"

Torrio sighed again. "Hey chum, sorry about your luck. This sort of thing happens to all of us. I have my own set of problems."

"Not so fast— This is your problem. We had an agreement. You keep your crews working on your side of the river, and we do the same. Then all should be at peace in the land." Dean wasn't done yet. "Unfortunately, this isn't happening today. Your pals are working on the wrong side and they are killing our business! You've gotta keep your dogs on a leash or somebody is going to get hurt. I mean soon!

Torrio was silent as he didn't want to upset the powerful Genna family with such a trivial matter. They ruled Little Italy and the Near West Side with an iron fist.

Are you going to take care of this, or should I?" Dean's fiery Irish temper boiled over. To him and his gangs, it was open season on Genna liquor shipments. The hijacking attacks would begin in earnest.

——— • ———

Trust was a rare commodity in the bootlegging business. Dean kept his own insurance policies. By the spring of twenty-four, he never missed the monthly appointment. Dean rolled his car in to park along the curb at Halsted Street. The officer inside the bakery shop set his newspaper down and left a steaming cup on the table. He emerged, scanned the street in both directions, then approached the idling car.

The policeman leaned down inside the open passenger window.

"Afternoon, officer. It's gonna be a warm one today." Dean reached inside his suit coat and retrieved the thickened envelope. He shifted the car back into gear but held the clutch.

The officer, still leaning in the car window, folded the envelope flap open, and ran his thumb across the bills. "I've got something."

"What's that?" Dean stared straight ahead through the windshield, reached down, and turned the car engine off.

"The Farmer's Almanac says the weather is about to get even hotter over at Sieben."

Dean turned his head to face the policeman directly. "What do you mean?"

"Your little brewing enterprise with Torrio *is on the list.*"

Dean felt his face flush. His eyes narrowed. "Get it *off the list*, now! That's our arrangement."

The policeman watched a passing freight truck lumber down the street. "Sorry, you don't have a get out of jail free card on this one. The chief is leading the charge himself. I can't stop it."

Dean fumed. "How much time?"

"You got a couple of weeks. They're coming for you on Monday, May 19."

Dean closed his eyes. The knuckles of his left hand turned white as he gripped the steering wheel. He clenched his other in a fist and pounded the wheel repeatedly. "My name is on that building lease."

The officer stood upright again. "Not my issue pal. Unless you like wearing horizontal stripes, I'd retire soon and leave town."

—— • ——

The looming raid consumed Dean's thoughts. Sieben had been their premier source for high-quality beer. Stress began to eat away at him until he couldn't think about anything else. He tried midday drives to take his mind off the police officer's prediction.

His friend Earl Weiss decided to tag along one afternoon with a trunk of beer. Their drive ended at an empty city park.

By physical stature, Weiss, was not an impressive man. Slightly below average in height with an unremarkable build, he had brown hair, bulging eyes, out-turned ears, and a sober grim face. Indeed, he might have matched the basic profile for a community dogcatcher.

But despite his looks, Hymie, as his friends called him, was a fiercely loyal man, especially in times of trouble. "Dean, you've got to find a way out of this mess with Torrio."

Dean struggled with just two hours of sleep. "Yes, Hymie. Now tell me something I don't already know. I'm on the lease. Johnny and I are both going down for this. But, more time in prison isn't an option for me."

Weiss paced around on the lawn and offered Dean a foaming bottle of beer. Dean stared at the Sieben label.

Hymie uncapped another. "I might have something."

Dean rested against the fender of the Studebaker and took a sip. "What do you got in mind? I'll listen to anything at this point."

The pair started a slow walk.

"This might sound mad but, what if you could sell your share of the brewery before the raid?"

Dean stopped walking. "Why would I ever? It would kill our business." He studied the bottle in his hand. "We need more beer, not less. I don't want to sell out!"

Weiss nodded. "I know we need the beer, but after the nineteenth of May we have to face the fact it won't matter because the brewery will be locked up. This train has already left the station."

Dean set his bottle on a park bench, walked over to the car, and kicked a white-walled tire. "You have an interesting idea, but it could be almost impossible to find a new buyer within a couple weeks."

Hymie threw his empty back into the open trunk. He liked using provocations. "Well, how might we?"

Dean rubbed his hands together. "I don't know."

"What would keep you out of prison? There must be someone who's after more beer."

Dean smirked. "Well, wait a minute. If I *was* going to sell my share, there's really only one buyer that makes sense—Johnny. But if he won't listen to me about getting the Gennas under control, why should I think he'll listen to me if I offer to sell out?"

Hymie took his time. "Because this is different. Very different."

Dean dug for more. "Why do you think so?"

"First, because you know about the coming raid, but he doesn't. Second, he will call you back about the brewery because this is high quality beer. He'll jump at owning the entire source!" Hymie tapped on the car fender. "The question I have is how can you convince Johnny you're serious about selling your share? He'll ask, *why* you'd be crazy enough to sell out of a great business when there is a shortage of supply?"

"That's a good one." Dean began to pace. "I may need a night or two to mull this over."

CHAPTER 9

Dean

On November 10, 1924, Dean O'Banion, founder of the North Side Gang, pushed aside his bootlegging business for the day. Out of respect and appreciation, he went to work in his part-owned floral shop preparing arrangements for the funeral of a mob peacekeeper named Mike Merlo.

Merlo had lost a battle with cancer. Mike's work was a precarious balance of negotiating a never-ending stream of peace treaties between rival gangs. The funeral was expected to be enormous as Merlo worked for gangs from all sides of Chicago and beyond.

Dean arrived early and worked alone in the shop's backroom. As he was busy clipping special flowers brought in for the event, he heard the ring of the brass entry bell at the front door. Dean called out, "I've got my hands full back here for the moment. Go ahead and look around if you like. I'll be with you shortly."

An instant later, when the brass bell gave a sharp ring a second time, he stopped working. In his limited view, no one was visible out in the store. He set the flowers aside. Before he finished drying his hands on his heavy canvas apron, the bell sounded yet a third time in an odd slow fashion.

Curious, Dean picked up the partial arrangement and headed for the front. When he stepped into the store's display area, three serious-looking men dressed in hats and long dark coats stood facing him from the other side of the sales counter.

A nervous chill raced through Dean. He knew the faces. These were the worst of men. The very worst.

He kept a cool appearance on the outside. "Ah fellas, I assume you're in town for Mike's funeral?" Dean set the flowers down on the counter. These men wouldn't come here to talk about floral arrangements. They were more likely here to talk about bloodshed.

Frankie Yale, a notorious mobster from Brooklyn, stepped up to the counter and extended his hand. "Yes, Dean, the funeral, of course."

When O'Banion ignored the offer of a handshake, Yale turned and motioned toward the two comrades standing behind him. "Dean, do you know John Scalise and Alberto Anselmi?"

Dean recognized the misaligned eyes of John Scalise and shifted his gaze quickly to the older man, Anselmi. Alberto was cursed with an intense stare and stoic Sicilian face. The odd couple had a peculiar appearance that made peaceful citizens decide to cross the street mid-block rather than to pass near them on a walkway.

Dean gave a slow nod to the Murder Twins. He'd seen them in action fighting for the Genna crime family on nearby Taylor Street. When it came to gun battles, they were butchers.

It slammed Dean like a runaway train. His only pistol in the shop was stowed in the back room. He was caught completely unarmed standing in front of an execution squad.

Yale extended his hand again. "We're all here for Mike and what he's done for the syndicate right?"

Dean assumed this was supposed to be some sort of peace gesture, but the story was a load of bull. These weren't the type of men who attended funerals to show their presence or extend condolences to families. These men were cold-hearted contract killers who kept to the shadows and sold more funeral flowers than Dean ever had.

Dean thought about making a run to the back room for the pistol, but the beasts in his midst would never allow it. As it was, there was no choice. Dean succumbed with great trepidation to shake Frankie Yale's hand.

Like a trap snapping shut, Yale grabbed Dean with a crushing grip. The two of them struggled, Yale dragged Dean around the end of the counter, twisted his arm, and pulled him in close. Yale's face was red with a horrid grimace. He delivered the message directly in Dean's ear, "Listen here you ungrateful cheat. I'm here for my pal Johnny Torrio. Do you remember him? He paid you a half a million bucks for your share of the brewery you knew damn well was due for a police raid. Now, Johnny's lost everything, and he's sitting in prison while you play with your flowers."

Dean tried to pull away. Yale wouldn't relent. "Mike Merlo, the peace-keeper, is gone now, so your day has finally come."

Dean struggled to get his hand back. His face was as white as a ghost. "Just wait a minute, Yale. Torrio has been selling whiskey to *my* saloons on *my* side of town. He asked for this fight!"

Frankie kept his grip on Dean's hand but pushed him back at arm's length. "I don't want to hear no lies from you. Time's up. No more talking."

Scalise and Anselmi rushed in from the sides with pistols drawn and fired point-blank. *Boom, boom.*

Dean collapsed face down on the floor. The three assassins watched him wither. Yale, with a grim smile, set about finishing things. He grabbed the pistol from Anselmi and fired one more shot. *Boom.*

—— • ——

When the word of Dean's murder arrived, George Moran, Hymie Weiss, and the reckless Sicilian Drucci were working the north end. By the time they got back to Schofield's Floral Shop, the street was choked with police cars, curious bystanders, and pressmen taking photos. Hymie was determined to see Dean at any cost. When he got through the street crowd, a pair of unnaturally large police officers guarded the front door. They grabbed Hymie by the shoulders.

One of them questioned, "Hey, buster, where do you think you're going? There's been a crime committed here and no one is allowed inside."

Just as Hymie started to turn back, the officers released their hold of him. He reversed course hard, catching them off guard, and shoved past them. Inside, he sidestepped the other men until he made it to the sales counter. He found Dean on his back. The medical examiner was going over the wounds.

Hymie saw the bullet holes in Dean's chest and neck. His head was twisted to the side in a distorted fashion. Just then, the pair of police officers caught up. One of them used his nightstick to clock Hymie from behind.

Hymie was dizzy from the blow and fell to the floor. One of the officers ran his hands around inside Hymie's coat and retrieved a handgun. He raised it in the air. "Hey, look what we have here!"

He rolled Hymie over on his back and stood with one foot planted in the middle of his chest.

Hymie moaned from beneath the officer's foothold, "Who did this to Dean? I wanna know who the shooter is."

The larger officer kicked him in the ribs. "What difference does it make to you anyway? What's your name, buster?"

Hymie gave a fake name to the policeman.

"How do you know the victim?"

Hymie blurted out without thinking. "Ah, we are..." His voice trailed off.

The cop was quick to respond. "So, you're one of the Northsiders. Should be no surprise to you this happened. Everyone knows about the dirty trick Dean played on Torrio."

Hymie was mad. "You're on their payroll, aren't you?"

The officer looked away.

Hymie tried to get his attention. "You're not going to do a thing about this, even though someone was gunned down here today in cold blood? Who exactly shot him?"

The policeman got Hymie up off the floor and pushed him toward the front door. "Why would I tell you anything about the shooter, so you can hunt him down? No, you boys better clean up your act, or we're gonna stop your little booze-running business."

CHAPTER 10

Transition

It was a raw November day in 1924. The autumn wind raked the last leaves from the trees and sent them tumbling through the Chicago streets like miniature tumbleweeds. The outdoor markets were packed up for the season, and the streets were deserted. Hank spent the day with Hymie Weiss and George Moran at a rural sportsman's club. They sat in a private lounge area. They needed to get out of the city and regroup after the murder of Dean O'Banion.

Hymie led the discussion. "For God's sake, Dean was thirty-two years old. If Torrio can get to him, I swear none of us are safe. Has the world gone mad? Can't a guy take shelter on his own premises?"

Hank knew the feeling of loss. He was doodling on a scrap of brown paper. The dark and shadowed sketch showed three men with guns hovering over a collapsed body. "I saw them you know."

Hymie barked back, "What are you talking about?"

"I saw Dean's murderers."

Hymie got up and stood over Hank. "What *exactly* do you mean?"

Hank tore his drawing in half, crumpled the scraps, and threw them into the fireplace. He looked up at Hymie. "I was too late to stop them from killing Dean."

George crossed the room and stared at Hank. "Who were they? I want names!"

"I didn't know what they had done. Dean was busy making plans for Merlo's funeral. I drove to the shop to talk to him. I thought he might need help with all of those floral arrangements. As I approached Schofield's, I passed a sedan leaving the block heading south on State Street. Frank Yale was behind the wheel with Scalise and Anselmi riding in the car. I can still see it in my mind in slow motion. Scalise turned as we passed and glared at me. He was yelling something, but I couldn't hear him.

George turned away in anger.

"I left my car in front of the floral shop and headed inside to tell Dean about the dangerous sharks cruising the street." Hank closed his eyes, reliving the tragic scene. "I found him when I ran inside. Dean was lying in a heap beside the counter. He was surrounded by blood-soaked flowers. His cutting shears were there, but I never saw any gun. I shook him for a long time, but he was gone. I got back in my car and raced down State Street trying to catch up with those three killers. I drove for miles, but I never found them. They had turned off somewhere and vanished."

Hymie spoke first. "It was just a crazy idea. Dean shouldn't have crossed Torrio. Selling the damn brewery to him the day before a police raid may have seemed like a smart move, but at what price? How do we pick up the pieces after this?"

The anger raging inside George reached the boiling point. He unloaded like a volcano spewing molten lava on everyone. "I've had enough of this intolerable scum. We're going to crush these snakes with everything we have once and for all. I'm not talking about an eye for an eye. I want each of their heads cut off and stuck on a pole on Main Street! I don't care how many men it takes. This is war!" The words echoed across the room.

His rant continued. "We can't tolerate these cowards and their rotten underhanded murder. It's one thing to try to get the best of each other. It's completely different to murder someone working in their own legitimate business with their guard down." George pitched his glass at full strength into the brick fireplace where it shattered into a thousand pieces.

A steward rushed through the door. When he saw the red rage on George Moran's face, he apologized for interrupting and backed out of the room.

CHAPTER 11
The Pain

On that horrible day, Hymie Weiss lost his best friend and inherited the leadership of the North Side Gang, a task for which he had never longed. The Italians and Sicilians would soon find out, killing Dean was the worst move they could have made. A war was underway in Chicago. They just didn't realize it yet.

Unlike his Italian counterparts, Hymie wasn't content leading from behind while directing others to do the dirty work. He detested the business of prostitution and was completely unafraid of death. Invisible to anyone who didn't know him, Hymie Weiss had become a nasty powder keg with a lit fuse. No one would get away with killing his friend.

There, in the morning shadow of the largest Catholic Cathedral in the city, the brazen gangster took over operating the North Side Gang from the same small office above Schofield's floral shop on State Street.

Hymie was the real brains behind the Sieben Brewery swindle and, for a period, was the negotiator of peace with the bloody Sicilian Genna family on nearby Taylor Street. Earl Weiss was a vicious man who once shot his own brother in a disagreement. He was an in-your-face force to be dealt with, but when a truce was possible, he could bring himself to the table with an assertive yet amicable tone.

Josephine Simard, a lanky dancing showgirl with a pretty face, but a gold digger, was his weakness and the one woman who'd tolerate him. Not exactly a match made in heaven. Earl was enamored with her primped-hair beauty, and she with his money and the excitement of being a gangster's girlfriend, despite the fact she already had a husband living back in her quiet home province of Quebec. It was a secret she never revealed to Hymie.

Unusual for a tough, fearless leader of Chicagoland bootleggers, Hymie was adept at making plans and negotiating with both rival gangs and the cops. When he wasn't crippled with incapacitating migraine headaches, Weiss was a strong leader for the North Side. While locked in prison serving an unbearable six months for bootlegging, Hymie vowed to never be taken into custody again due to his ill-health.

Upon the death of his best friend Dean O'Banion, Hymie became obsessed with killing Johnny Torrio and his rising star—Al Capone.

CHAPTER 12

Mother

In the quiet hours of a mid-winter morning, Hank tried his new key in the door lock and made his way successfully into the office above Schofield's. He flipped on the lights and surveyed the rooms. It was here somewhere. The place could have used a secretary for organization, but it wasn't a large office. He was determined to find the box with his father's possessions. George Moran confirmed he'd seen the box more than once.

Hank started by probing through the desk drawers. Then he moved on to dragging items down from the closet shelves. There was a sturdy-looking typewriter that appeared adequate to anchor a ship at sea. There were books and paper records, some picture frames, and an old lamp, but no box.

On the floor below, beside a chair with one missing arm, was a shotgun with a busted stock, a barrel-shaped basket, some old calendars, and a rolled-up map. He pulled the basket out of the closet and, on the floor beneath it, was a plain box built from wood strips.

Hank retrieved it and put the box down in the middle of a desk. He removed his coat and hat, collected the old oil lamp from the closet, and placed it on the desk. He struck a match from a box sitting next to an ashtray and lit the lamp. In ink, the name Hudson was scrawled across the box lid. The box was large enough to hold a pair of men's shoes. He was curious why George Moran and Hymie Weiss would have kept it around after all this time. Hank assumed they had lost track of it.

He pulled the cover off the box and set it aside. The contents were a hodgepodge of things his dad owned at the time of his death. There was an old brass pocket watch. Hank took it out and wound the stem. He held it next to his ear and listened to the smooth ticking of the mechanism. He picked up a well-worn Sheffield pocketknife with a folding blade. Hank pulled the blade free and smiled as he thought about his father using it more often for car repairs rather than self-defense. There were racetrack betting stubs and a photo with curled edges of his mother in her teen years riding a horse.

Hank drew a Colt forty-five revolver with wooden grips from the box. The cylinders and chamber were empty. The gun had an easy balance as he sighted down the barrel at a clock on the wall.

At the bottom of the wooden crate, Hank found it. He almost didn't notice it at first. It simply lay flat face down beneath the other odds and ends of his father's life. It was a long thin brownish-gray book with a heavy paper cover clad in canvas. The canvas material was dried and cracked at the binding, flaking apart in slivers once bound with glue. The print on the front had blue letters with the faded, but discernible words *Travel Journal*. To Hank, it didn't make much sense. His parents never traveled for leisure. He wasn't sure they knew how.

The cover popped and cracked as the stiff binding yielded to the separation of opening. Inside the first page, taped in place, were two black-and-white photos of young children playing in the sand on a beach. The note between the photos was in his mother's hand. It read, *Robert, Henry, and Gloria, South Carolina, July 1900*. Hank had no memory of the ocean.

He kept turning the tattered yellow pages. The book's meaning changed, beginning with a peculiar section containing numbered columns. Hank wondered if this is where his father began to use the book after mother had died. The dates along the left side descended like daily record keeping. Each column to the right appeared to contain records of bets. His dad must have been working the

Chicago North Side. Hank assumed he was running numbers games. The last column to the right listed amounts with dollar signs. Small at first but growing into the hundreds and a few thousand as the months went on.

Here and there were notes in his father's handwriting. He found one on the fifth page. *Check out a move into the Gold Coast.* Halfway through the book, he found another. *Get out of this business before something else happens.* The word *before* was underlined three times.

Near the back of the book, Hank noticed the ragged remains of three pages ripped from the book. The next intact page contained a handwritten scribble beginning with, *Johnny Torrio is stealing our...* The rest of the page corner was torn off. What remained didn't say what was stolen.

The final pages in the journal were wrinkled and many of the ink numbers were smeared and illegible. Hank studied the figures he could read and tried to make sense of them. The values were decreasing in size. It was clear the business was falling apart.

Between the columns, near the dates the month before his father died, was a smudged note in black ink. Hank stared at it. He couldn't quite make it out. He pulled the book close and held it there. After a few moments, he turned the book clockwise to angle it slightly. Hank looked again. He felt a surge of cold rush up his neck like a winter breeze when his eyes gained their focus on the words—*Avenge Mattie.*

Hank read the words again. He pushed the box aside and left the journal there by itself. His suspicions were confirmed. Mother had been murdered after all.

CHAPTER 13

Torrio

In gangland, all funerals were respected with a day of peace. While an odd tradition in the mobster war, bitter enemies faced each other on funeral days without violence. At the burial of Dean O'Banion, Johnny Torrio's skin crawled as Hymie Weiss glared at him with bloodshot eyes from across the casket. The message was clear.

Weiss had one goal in mind: Kill anyone rumored responsible for the death of his friend. He knew who'd ordered the hit.

The brewery swindle had put the gangs at odds, and Johnny Torrio knew enough of Weiss to be uneasy. Torrio surrounded himself with guards. The North Side Gang had already taken a swipe at Torrio's right-hand, Capone, but a car was the only casualty.

The siege was just beginning for Hymie Weiss. Johnny Torrio was blind to the fact, his unguarded apartment, at 7011 Clyde Avenue, put him at great risk.

Hymie and George sat on the place for days before it paid off. On the afternoon of Saturday, January 24, Johnny and his wife Anna were chauffeured home from a shopping trip. Before they could step from the car, the two men rushed from the street with drawn weapons.

While George Moran was merciless with his forty-five-caliber pistol, Hymie Weiss blasted Johnny with a 12-gauge loaded with slugs. *Boom, boom,*

boom. The point-blank shooting clipped the driver once and hit Johnny four times, including his jawline and neck.

Down the block, the getaway driver blew the car horn signaling it was time to go. Anna Torrio screamed in horror as she watched Johnny bleeding out in the car.

With weapons empty, the shooters were confident they had completed their mission.

Anna's mother, witnessing from above through the upstairs window of the apartment, called for an ambulance and the police as soon as the shots began.

The neighbors, horrified and confused, couldn't understand why such a gentle neighbor would be attacked like this. Johnny's alias had them fooled.

George Moran and Hymie Weiss assumed they had extinguished the leader of the Italian mob. They, however, didn't finish the job and the quick phone call made by Torrio's mother-in-law for an ambulance saved Johnny despite his grave-looking wounds.

While Johnny recovered, Capone kept the hospital protected by a small army of bodyguards. No one would get to Johnny while he was laid up.

Even at his weakest, Johnny's lips were sealed. No amount of pressure from the police could pry his mouth open. He wouldn't rat out the shooters to the cops. His outfit would be much more effective at leveling the score.

Torrio recovered physically and began to serve his sentence for his role in the Sieben brewery charge. He never returned to lead the Chicago Outfit ever again but instead handed the reigns over to his loyal friend, Al Capone. Johnny retired after prison to New York with ongoing financial benefits.

CHAPTER 14
Blame

Chicago, despite its size, could sometimes be a small world.

"Good evening, Louie. Hank and I would like a table in the back."

"Mr. Moran! Good evening and welcome again to the Green Tavern. It's always a pleasure to see you." Louie looked down at his desk. His face turned pale as he studied the reservation book. "However, we are a *little busy* tonight, Mr. Moran. Could I interest you two in a nice table in our lounge area?"

George had a smirk on his face. "Is everything OK, Louie? Come on, it's me! You always make room for me, even when it's *very busy*."

Louie was uncomfortable. "Yes, of course. But I'm afraid things are different tonight. I'm so sorry, Mr. Moran. Would you two like a seat in our lounge?"

George was puzzled. "Louie, can we wet our whistle in there?"

"Mr. Moran, our lounge offers French coffee and a variety of soda drinks."

"Come on, Louie, you know what we're looking for."

Louie wiped fine beads of perspiration from his brow. "Of course, Mr. Moran. If you'll take a seat for now, we'll get you a table in the back soon."

The two settled in the lounge and ordered sodas. Louie's cool reception bothered Hank. "George, it's been a while since I've been here, but what's up with Louie? He seemed so strange."

George poured whiskey from a small personal flask into their fizzing sodas. "I don't know. He is acting all weird over something."

"These guys still have the best steaks in town, don't they?"

"Yes, the beef comes out of Kansas. It's the best money can buy." George took a drink. "Hank, the reason I want you here tonight is to talk a piece of business I want you to take care of."

Hank put his overcoat on the empty chair sitting next to him.

"Those ruthless mongrels from the other side of town in Cicero executed O'Banion, and I'm gonna spit on Capone's grave. They have no idea the pain we're about to unleash on them." Fire lit Moran's eyes. "This is war. When we're finished, there can only be one of us left standing. We'll destroy the Capone businesses, take every one of his customers, and get rid of the king himself. His reign is over!"

Hank nodded and kept his voice low. "So, how do you plan to wipe them out?"

"I need troops to go to war with." George reached and put his hand on Hank's shoulder. "You're gonna work for me." He pointed at Hank's face. "But before you say a word, I want you to know, I won't take no for an answer. Soon, we'll own Chicago!"

Hank pushed his hat back and scratched his forehead. "What does Hymie think of this?"

"He needs some time. He's torn up with grief right now. Dean was like a brother to him. When the shock of it wears off, there's a powder keg inside him ready to explode. The rest of us have to step things up to get ready."

When Hank didn't respond, George's eyebrows furrowed. "However, Hank, if you're *not* on my side, there may not be a place left for you. Those who play a part in this war will be rewarded. Those who refuse, will become casualties."

Hank was concerned about losing control of his men. If they became part of a larger war against the Italians, he couldn't protect them the same way as when they operated as a small gang of runners.

George noticed the shift in the room's noise level. People at the tables near the entrance whispered in low tones and some pointed. He turned in his chair and thumped Hank on the arm. "What gives out there?"

Two thick-looking suits from the back secured a path towards the entrance. A blonde woman with bobbed hair and a short, beaded dress appeared behind them. She kept one hand on her necklace as she walked, and her other arm was locked with a man on her opposite side. He was wearing a pin-striped suit. As they made their way toward the door, the man turned and scanned the lounge tables. Beneath the trilby hat was a face Hank could never forget.

Hank said it first, "Capone." He reached inside his coat.

George caught Hank's arm. "Not here. Not now."

Capone placed the butt of his cigar in his mouth. He dropped the woman's arm and raised both his hands to point fingers straight at George and Hank. With his thumbs raised in the air like the hammers on a pair of pistols, he began to push the imaginary guns toward them as he slammed his thumbs down over and over pretending to fire. He pulled the cigar out of his mouth and raised the freehand figure of a gun in the air. He blew cigar smoke over the end of his pointer finger and placed his pointed finger inside his coat pocket like a holster. Quickly, the gangster and his arm candy vanished out the front door.

Hank began to rise out of his chair. George put his hand atop Hank's shoulder. "Sit down. Why chase after him? He saw us, too, and will be on high alert now. We know where he lives. Someday soon, we'll plan a *housewarming* for ol' Capone.

"You know, Capone's not a frightened cat like Torrio was. Torrio was lucky he survived our hit. He liked to keep his hands clean so when things got bloody, he gave the organization over to Capone and slithered out of town. Now, Capone isn't afraid to get into it himself. He's always raising some serious cane. Everyone knows where he lives. The thing I don't understand is how he's still alive."

"George, I can't sit here any longer. Let's get out of here and go someplace else. The back room will stink like garlic tonight." Hank was perturbed. He twisted in his chair like a thousand spiders were crawling over his skin.

George waived the host over. "Louie, I'm afraid we'll be dining elsewhere this evening."

"I understand, sir."

"But I want to thank you for recommending your fine lounge for our seating."

"Yes, Mr. Moran. It was my pleasure. I also want to thank you two gentlemen for your restraint this evening."

George nodded.

CHAPTER 15

Warehouses

The racehorse delivery plan model was working, resulting in fewer stolen loads. The Northsiders needed places to drop truckloads and stage automobiles for delivery.

Tony pulled into the alley next to an old red brick warehouse. Newspaper trash and weeds had accumulated in front of the doors. The grilled windows were thick with dust-laden cobwebs. "Nick, you sure this is it?"

"Yes, the note I made says, *2122 North Clark*. This is definitely it."

Carlo and Willy left the alley and drove their car around to the front side. "Carlo, why don't you go in the entry and check it out? We've gotta make sure nobody's around."

"OK, Willy, I got this." Carlo stepped from the car and scanned the length of the street in both directions. Vehicle traffic was light. As he entered the front door, he drew his handgun and fumbled around in the darkness for a light switch. A loud screech came from the rear of the building as Tony and Nick tried to open the truck bay doors at the alley entrance.

Carlo shouted, "You guys see signs of life back there?"

Nick shouted, "Nothing but a mouse. It's all clear, just like Hank said. We got this place to ourselves."

Carlo rubbed his forehead. "How did Hank find this old garage? What a mess. Where'd all these stacks of wood come from?"

Nick picked up a piece of hardwood and tossed it on the pile. "Looks like crate material. The kind of boards you use in the shipping business."

Tony walked toward a walled-off room with a small interior window. "I wonder if the office is open?"

He stepped into an efficient shipping office with space limited to a desk and two file cabinets. The drawers were open. Papers and files littered the desk and the floor as if someone left in a heated rush. "There's nothing in here a match couldn't fix."

A freight train lumbered past the neighborhood rattling the windows. Tony was annoyed with the earthquake of a train passing so close. "Man, I sure couldn't live down here."

Willy piped in, "Don't worry about the train. You get used to them. Let's get this place picked up, so we can get trucks in here. We got an hour 'til today's load should roll in."

Nick was anxious to help out. "Maybe we can build a fire in the back alley and burn up all this extra wood."

Willy was keeping an eye on the new kid. "Hold on, Nick, I wouldn't light that fire. Let's not draw any attention to this place. We've gotta keep things quiet in the neighborhood. Let's pile it up in stacks along the walls inside the building. Maybe we can ship the crate material out on an empty load some-time. Today, we need to make room for the truck and our cars so we can offload without the neighbors getting suspicious. Tonight, will be our first big haul out of here."

Nick agreed. "All right, Willy let's get busy."

— • —

Traveling north of the city, Hank was pleased to discover the rural highway was quiet. The remote location would be perfect to stash some reserve until they put an end to the booze going missing. He checked his pocket watch as he drove toward the barn. The truck was due any time. He stepped on the gas. The trucks were sent out two hours apart to avoid risk.

Bernie turned toward Hank. "Tell me, boss, why do you and I have to meet this load by ourselves? And why are we going to a different barn in the country? I thought you found a warehouse in the city."

Hank studied the face of his prodigy. "Bern, I haven't told anyone else this, but you and I go back a long way and I trust you." Bernie sat upright and gave his full attention. "George Moran is convinced we've got a spy somewhere in one of the crews."

Bernie could have spit. "What do you mean a *spy*? Do we gotta cop hiding among us?"

Hank shook his head. "No, it's almost worse. We may have a rat who's working for Torrio and Capone. You know we've had three shipments hijacked in the last month and a half. Somebody is flapping their gums about our loads!"

"And *you* think it's one of our guys?"

"Bernie, we really don't know who it is yet. For now, we're storing extra whiskey in secret locations. We can't miss another delivery, otherwise our speakeasies are gonna switch. Once we lose 'em, it takes a real bloodbath to get them back. Besides, we've already got two guys banged up. We can't afford anymore."

The fifteen-dollar-a-case whiskey from Canada crossed the water south of Detroit and was trucked to Chicago, where it was worth ninety dollars at a speakeasy. Hank had never seen this kind of money before in his life. The rat in their ranks threatened the whole thing. He was frustrated. *Why can't Capone's guys stick to their side of town? It's tough enough to evade the cops, let alone attacks by greedy thieves!*

A dark green truck was parked at the barn with a canvas tarp still draped over the pile of crates. The driver was busy knocking chunks of dried mud from the spoke wheels. "I took some back roads to avoid the inspection. On the last run back, I saw where the barricades were set west of Detroit."

Hank walked around the truck with the driver. "So, no one followed you?"

"No. I wasn't followed." The driver bent over to brush the dirt off the knees of his coveralls. He stood upright to challenge Hank face-to-face. "But you don't pay me enough for this work. I drove extra miles to avoid the cops this time."

Hank took a half step back and looked the driver up and down.

The driver continued, "I have an uncle who works up on the high steel constructing skyscrapers in Manhattan. He gets extra pay for his dangerous job." He reached out and thumped Hank on the shoulder with his pair of gloves. "I need more pay for hauling your cargo."

The driver resumed moving along the truck. Hank stepped in front of him and blocked his path. He pointed at the driver's chest. "Don't you worry yourself about things now. I'll talk to your boss, and we'll take care of your pay."

"Mister, I know what's in them crates and I want cash now or the next load might get lost somewhere during the all-night trip. You never know when the truck might breakdown."

Hank grabbed the young man by the shirt and pressed him against the truck. He drew his revolver and shoved it into the man's beard. "Listen, smart guy! And listen real good. You don't know who you are messing with, do you boy? We have an agreement for packing and shipping this cargo. If your boss doesn't treat you fair, take it up with him. I pay plenty. As for me, I'm not giving you an extra dime. And if you try to hold any load like this hostage, I'll come for you. And if I do, you'll need a lot more than extra pay. Now move the truck into the barn and get to work unloading it."

Bernie rolled the large red doors out of the way and the tandem axle truck pulled inside.

The driver made quick work of unloading the crates. Without another word, he disappeared down the road in a cloud of dust.

Bernie stopped Hank for a minute. "Hey, what was all the fuss about?"

"The driver thinks he controls our supply. I'll call the owner of the trucking company. The chump will need a new career before the day is over. He's lucky he has both his kneecaps right now. Other mobs would have clocked him and kept the truck."

"Do you think we left some loose ends here?"

"No, I scared him pretty good. He won't be around again.

"Now we've gotta open a crate and check the bottles."

The sides of the crates were each stamped, *Product of Canada*. Bernie pulled a crate aside and used a pry bar to pop the boards off the top. He reached around in the loose wood shavings and felt the shape of a glass bottle. He twisted it loose and pulled it from the packing material. "Maple syrup? Boss, the driver scammed us after all. These crates are full of maple syrup!"

Hank smiled at the reaction. "Bernie, calm down. There's another layer inside each crate. Scoop the sawdust out and set the pancake syrup aside. The bottom half of the crate has what we want."

Bernie set to work. Like a dog digging for a bone, the wood chips flew everywhere. After the syrup was cleared out, he pried loose the second layer of boards and found the neck of a bottle lying flat in the hidden compartment. He raised it into the light streaming down from the hayloft. The brown glass filled with whiskey sparkled in the sunlight. "This is it!"

"Just like I said. Now let's move these crates back in the stock pens over there and cover them with the tarp."

"Hank, why are we doing this?"

"We're going to bury them in straw and keep them out of sight. Just in case anyone wanders in here, we don't need to show them the stash. If one of our regular loads gets hit, I'll send you back here to collect the spares. In a pinch, this would cover us for a while."

Bernie lugged the crates over to the pens. Hank did the same until everything was tucked out of sight. The pair pulled the large barn doors closed and locked them from the inside.

"Let's go see how the other guys are doing." On the way out the small entry door, Hank grabbed a loose bottle of syrup. "Do you like pancakes?"

CHAPTER 16

The Swamp

There was more than one way to get revenge.

It was midnight, and the mosquitoes on the desolate stretch of road along the river marsh were ferocious. Vinnie hated insects. He seemed to attract the biting variety more than others. He heard the faint high-pitched whine in the darkness behind him. As the whine grew louder, it stopped with a pinprick in the back of his neck. He reached over his shoulder and slapped the bug. "Boss, how long we gotta stay out here? It's late already. This truck ain't coming tonight."

Hank brushed him off. "Our information is solid. Capone avoids the police on the main highway by sneaking his loads down this old river road. There is a shipment due tonight. You'll see."

Vinnie ran his fingers under the tight collar of the police uniform. The shirt and coat were too small for him, not that he had a lot of choice in the matter since they were stolen from a laundromat. "Boss, why did we pick this spot? We can't see 'em coming past the curve in the road. We're caught between a hill on one side and the swampy river bottoms on the other. If things turn out badly, it will be hard to get away."

Hank smiled at the nervous observation. "Like we planned, this spot makes a good trap. No one's getting away."

The freight truck was parked on the shoulder of the road with the engine hood raised to appear to have mechanical problems. Tony sat ready to move the truck out as a roadblock.

Willy paced the road with his long gun under his arm while he smoked a cigarette. He was anxious to take booze shipments from Al Capone. He walked up to Hank and Vinnie. "Vinnie, are you over here complaining again? Listen to Hank and get back to your post. We're not gonna let Capone get away with killing O'Banion. Our job here is to hit his liquor supplies. Next, Northsider's will attack his gangs. Finally, we'll erase him from the map."

Hank added, "So, we're shutting this pipeline down, right here, right now. Nothing gets through. Do you understand? You need to be ready to box in the liquor truck when they stop for the breakdown. This is happening tonight. We'll wait here until dawn if we have to."

Vinnie was getting it from all sides. He nodded his head and walked the road back to the decoy police car. He had the car backed in out of sight at the base of the hill.

— • —

At 1:30 a.m., the low rumble of a heavy engine grew in the distance. From over the rise, the skyline held a glow of light coming through the forest. Hank stepped closer to the roadblock truck and rapped on the fender. Tony nodded, started the engine, and moved the truck forward to the middle of the road without using the headlamps. He stopped using the hand brake to avoid illuminating the taillights.

The oncoming truck crested the hill on the gravel road and shook its way down the grade as rough as a washboard. Vinnie heard the rumble and saw the lights on the road in front of the car. He got the old police car running and waited in the darkness of the road bank. He felt the earth move as the truck lumbered along within fifty feet of his vehicle. *Where is Hank? Why isn't he lighting the road flare?* His hands were shaking on the steering wheel. Hank's instructions were: "Do not pull out or turn on the lights and siren until you see the road flare." The freight truck kept driving along.

Vinnie saw more lights coming down the road. *Another truck? What the heck, there's a second load?*

The next truck shook the earth as it tumbled over the road bumps. Vinnie held his breath as the big truck tires rolled past his car.

Hank lit a road flare and tossed it next to the disabled truck. Vinnie slid out of the car and jerked the tarp loose covering the nose of his car. He eased the driver's door closed and slipped it in gear. He pulled completely out on the road before he turned on the lights and then the siren. The red flashing police lights lit up the trees on the hillside. Brake lights appeared from both freight trucks. Vinnie stepped on it and drove in right behind the last truck.

He pulled the gear shift into neutral and set the hand brake. As he slipped out of the car, he drew his pistol and headed for the left side driver's door with caution. He shined the flashlight into the open side window.

The driver was ready for a cop. Vinnie saw the muzzle flash from the dark cab. *Boom.* He flinched as the shot grazed his arm. He dove in close to the side of the truck body. The driver tried to reach further around the cab side and fired again. Willy opened up from the high bank along the right side of the road. He shattered the passenger side window and showered the driver. The driver yelled and returned fire toward the muzzle flashes coming from the underbrush on the hill. Willy scrambled around to the rear of the truck.

Two men bailed out of the first booze truck. One took a position alongside the front bumper and shot at Vinnie. *Boom, boom.* Vinnie emptied his pistol and dug for more cartridges in his coat. The other driver took a knee along the shoulder of the road and fired at Willy, standing near the truck. *Boom.* The gun battle was on.

Vinnie tucked in behind the rear wheels of the truck and Willy stayed close to the right side. Still inside the cab, the driver hunkered down as the bullets whizzed along both sides of his truck.

Hank waived to Tony in the decoy truck to steer toward the ruckus. When he moved into position, Hank jumped on the running boards and yelled, "Lights!" The headlamps lit up the shooters like high noon. Before they could turn around, Hank fired two blasts of buckshot in the air.

With the opposition now on both sides and nowhere to hide, the delivery men set their weapons on the ground and raised their hands above their heads. Hank swept in with his shotgun leveled at one of the hostiles. Vinnie approached the other. They collected the enemy guns and tied the men to the bumper of the decoy truck. Willy retrieved the driver from the second booze truck and tied him up as well. His injuries were limited to the glass shards blasted into the cab.

Hank picked up the burning road flare and walked around the cargo load on the first truck. He pulled the tarp loose. The crates were labeled as *Denatured Industrial Alcohol*. Hank inspected the second load too then approached the prisoners. He held the flare in one hand and his shotgun in the other. With the end of the gun barrel pressed against the wounded driver's neck, he asked, "What's really in those crates?"

The driver tried to turn away. "Why should I help you bunch of bandits?"

Hank clicked the safety off on the shotgun. The driver's head began to shake visibly. "Because this trigger determines whether you live or die."

"OK, get the stinking gun away from me! My load is a quality gin made ready to pour." The driver wouldn't look up from his boots.

Hank kept the gun barrel against his neck. "And?"

"The second load is corn and rye whiskey. The good stuff from Canada. We rebottle it in small lots with our Old Cabin label. The joke will be on you if you try to peddle Old Cabin." The driver couldn't suppress the smirk on his face. "Everyone will know where you got it."

Hank thumped him on the side of the head with the butt of the shotgun.

The driver moaned as blood ran down from a split ear lobe. "All right, you've got your booze. Will ya let us go now?"

Hank motioned to Vinnie and Tony. "You two get these loads out of here. It will be daylight before we know it. Willy and I will take care of these goons."

Vinnie swung the driver's door open on the truck and used his police coat to brush the broken glass off the seat. The booze shipments began the two-hour trip to Chicago and the 2122 North Clark Street warehouse.

Hank set the flare down and reloaded his shotgun. He pointed it at the men tied to the bumper. "Look, here's what you're going to do if you want to live. My friend is going to untie you from the truck and lash your hands together behind your back. Afterwards, you're going to walk down into the swamp and wade way out in the muck until you're in it at least chest deep. Once you're in the mud bath, we will drive our vehicles away quietly and not shoot you.

"If you give us trouble, this buckshot will be the last thing to go through your mind. Do we understand each other?"

The men nodded.

Hank held up some lengths of rope. "Vinnie, would you do the honors?"

"Sure thing, boss."

"And here's a piece of advice for you hoodlums. If I were you, I wouldn't work for Al Capone again. Now that you've lost *two* of his liquor loads, your boss is likely to get a little emotional. As such, I expect him to put a price on your heads. The fact you're still alive walking around right now looking pretty healthy, will mean he's gonna think you *stole* his booze. No, I would keep going and find your way out west somewhere or maybe down south to get into a new line of work. You'll still have to watch over your shoulder, but you'll live a lot longer."

The pair of drivers exchanged a glance. In a moment's time they'd become the accused.

"All right, Vinnie, let's get them ready for their mud baths. Good luck, fellas. Be sure to check yourselves for leeches after you crawl out of the swamp!"

CHAPTER 17

The Escape

George pulled the car in near Union Station and turned the motor off.

Hank looked out the car's windshield in confusion, then turned toward George. "What gives George? Who are we meeting here?"

"No one."

"Then why are we here?"

George looked directly at Hank. "I've got a pair of train tickets."

"Are we going someplace?"

George didn't waste words. "No, I'm not leaving. But *you* have to."

Hank dismissed the notion. "Why would I?"

"Because the Twins are on to you and Capone is ticked off. You'll need to disappear for a while until things cool off."

Hank's face soured. "We have dodged a few bullets lately, but I can't leave the men."

"They will be fine. You have to."

"Why?"

"Hank, the newspapers say nearly five hundred gang murders occurred since the city first went dry. Good men, and tough men, too. There's a saying, *six feet of dirt makes all men equal.* After the raid you just did on Capone's liquor loads, the word on the street is you are a target to be equalized."

Hank fell silent.

George pushed, "It's only the smart ones who'll make it out alive in this business. You've got the brains to be one of them." He paused. "Just think about the survival rate of our gang. It ain't the best. I wish Dean would have gone out of town for a while, but he didn't. Your family's been a victim of the great Chicago cleansing, too."

Hank looked out across the train yard. He moaned, "You're right, George."

George took his left hand off the steering wheel, swung his arm, and thumped the side car window with the back of his knuckles. "Hank, I'm sure you know if something were to happen to me, you gotta help lead the war against Capone. He's a monster. One by one, he keeps devouring the other gangs. I've heard through an accountant friend those clowns now rake in fifty million dollars a year! We can't let him have all of Chicago."

Hank nodded. "I don't understand their endless gluttony when so many people are murdered to achieve it."

"This is another reason why I'm sending you away for a while, so I don't have to pick out your *underground furniture.* I don't think you'd look good in a pine box."

Hank took his hat off. "When would I leave?"

"The 9:00 a.m. train."

Hank couldn't believe the timing. They were making plans for the hijacked Capone liquor. "Today? But the train leaves in a few minutes and I didn't get the chance to tell my guys—"

"This can't wait," George interrupted. "In the back seat is a briefcase with cash, a pistol, and some shells for the gun. You can get what you need as you go. You'll be fine. I'll tell the boys I sent you on an errand for a while. I'll keep an eye on 'em."

"But George, there's more talk about a repeal. It could happen soon. This is no time to be gone!"

"Listen to me, Hank. You're right. Prohibition has been the greatest boon ever seen in this business. But when it's over, life will go back to normal. We've still got a dog racing track, unions to take over, loans to make, and every other kind of scam. I need men I trust. Men who can run a dependable crew. At this rate, you won't see the repeal if you're dead."

George reached behind him, retrieved the briefcase, and gave it to Hank. George reached inside his coat and pulled out two train tickets. "Now this first ticket is on The Chicago Great Western heading to St. Paul. The second ticket is for a train which goes north from there."

"Further north? Are you sending me off to a logging camp?"

"All right, wise guy. I want you to listen and listen good to this part. Whatever you do, *don't stop over in St. Paul!* I don't care what people try to tell you. Stay out of crook's haven! In St. Paul, it's not only the cops you have to worry about. If you get off the train there, within a day or two someone will surely recognize you. You'd be dead just the same as here. Capone's money has a long reach."

"OK, good advice, George. I had no idea he had men working up there, too."

"No, stay put in the train station and switch over to the Gull River Line. On the map, the train heads deep into the north woods. Go as far up there as you can on the train and find a place to hide out. Take your time. Three or four weeks wouldn't be too long. Things here need to simmer down a lot before you come back. Stay out of trouble. I loaded this briefcase from the safe. You have plenty to live on while you're up there."

— • —

Steam rolled out from beneath the base of the black locomotive. The heavy-plated nose of the engine shook as the pressure buildup neared completion.

Two short blasts from the train whistle and the ringing bell marked the slow turn of the steel wheels. Hank climbed the rungs of the passenger car steps.

The assistant conductor checked his ticket and motioned to the doorway for passenger seating. Hank walked the center train aisle and took an open seat across from a woman with two small children. The gaunt mother with a distant look, wrinkled forehead, and a mound of soiled cloth bags stacked beside her on the train seat looked down at the floor as she avoided meeting Hank's eyes. Her little boy laid his head on her lap. His dirty face and patched jeans showed the life of living with little. His sister considered Hank with clear hazel eyes showing through tangled snarly hair.

"We never rode a train before, Mister." Her young voice quivered as she spoke. "Grandma bought our tickets, cause our papa lost his job at the flour mill. We're going to live with Grandma in St. Paul while he looks for good work. Mister, are you some sort of businessman? You got a fancy suit."

Hank studied the girl's face. He never had time for children of his own. "Sure, I have a business of sorts."

"Do you have a job for my daddy? He's a real honest man."

Hank thought about the work he was in. He wasn't proud of it. "No, I'm not hiring anyone right now."

The young girl shook her head. "It's too bad, 'cause if papa found work, we wouldn't have to leave. All the men in our neighborhood lost their jobs when the factory closed."

"Girl, leave the man alone." The mother's face turned stern. "Sorry, sir, she means no real harm."

Hank smiled at the woman. "It's all right. She's not a bother at all. I like her honesty." He turned to the child once more. "Well, good luck on your trip, little lady. I hope your dad finds work real soon."

Before Hank departed the train, he opened the briefcase and retrieved some money. As the woman and her children stepped off the train, he handed the cash to the little girl with the instructions, "Give this to your mother later."

The young girl smiled. She whispered, "I will."

The St. Paul Union Depot was a busy place. There was a visible police presence with officers stationed near all the building entrances.

Hank checked in with the conductor to verify his connection. He was directed to the number two stub-end track to catch his train north. With a couple of hours to spare, Hank walked over to the diner counter in the depot. As he approached, a well-dressed man got up from a table, folded his newspaper, and came out to meet Hank. "Hello, I'm Morgan Hill. I assume you just arrived in St. Paul. I manage a hotel and restaurant walking distance from here. We have fine food and clean rooms available if you're looking for a meal or a place to hang your hat. The fare here at the depot is pretty common. We bring class to our menu."

Hank was tired and tempted by the offer to get out of the busy train depot. But the words from George came flooding back to him. *Whatever you do, don't stop over in St. Paul cause it's crook's haven!*

"Well, thanks, Mr. Hill. While it sounds like a fine offer, I think I'll stay put here at the depot until my next train comes in. You have a nice day."

Hank perched on a bench near the number two track. The Gull River train steamed its way to park alongside the platform. Several suntanned families dressed in summer clothing and some fishermen carrying sporting gear disembarked the train. Hank was puzzled no one was dressed like a lumberjack or a miner.

The train ride north was a slow scenic tour, working its way from green open farm country dotted with red barns and dairy cows into the timber of a dense forest. There were whistle stops at occasional small towns and villages. The train came to a dead-end stop at a small open-air platform on a narrow strip of land between two blue water lakes. The passengers began to gather their things and unload from the train. Hank interrupted the conductor as he assisted an elderly man with a heavy case. "Sir, can you tell me where we are?"

The conductor smiled. "This is the end of the line. The train will stay here overnight, and tomorrow we'll make the trip back to St. Paul. You'd best gather your things now. Do you have a case in the baggage car?"

Hank shook the briefcase at his side. "No, this is all I brought along."

"Well, if you need anything. The general store here is always well stocked."

Hank stepped onto the platform and stopped to study the two-story general store perched along the shore of the larger lake. The proprietors were out in front of the store along the small dirt road that disappeared into a dark forest. The sun shined through the trees with a welcoming warmth to it. He was greeted with the fresh smell of pine.

Hank crossed the road and approached a man and woman sitting on the bench out in front of their store. The man stood up and greeted the visitor. "Good afternoon. I'm Tom Swenson and this is my wife Mildred. Welcome to Hubert Landing! Can we help you with anything today?"

Hank wasn't used to this type of hospitality. He looked at a display of fishing poles and nets in the storefront window. "Well, this may be an odd question for a store owner, but would there be lodging and a hot meal nearby?"

The man looked over at his wife and smiled before he turned back to Hank. "Sure, we hear these sorts of questions from time to time when visitors arrive from the city. Yes, there is a fine resort camp a short distance across the lake to the north of here named Clark Lake Lodge."

"How might a fella get there from here?"

"Well, this road works its way around the lake to the camp with cabins, but that's a fair distance from here. I wouldn't bother with walking on a warm day like this. If you plan to stay awhile, they will come and pick you up right here."

Hank smiled. "Thanks, I'd like to arrange that."

Tom nodded. "Why don't you step inside the store and take a look around. I've got a phone in the back. I'll ring the lodge and let them know you are here."

"Thanks, you're very kind."

Hank stepped inside and took his time looking over the variety of sundries and sporting goods. The back shelves held neat stacks of clothing. A large wall displayed rifles and more fishing rods. The glass counter held large jars of candy treats, a soda-dispensing fountain, and an official-looking weigh scale.

Tom noticed Hank eyeing the scale. "Yes, besides the groceries, clothing, and sporting items, we have U.S. Postal Service, too. Tourists often send their parcels and posts from here. Our parcels go out every other day on the train. Please don't try to send anything perishable. You best eat any fish you catch while you're staying here."

Hank had never spent time at a lake. He smiled at the peculiar notion of him catching fish.

Tom crouched while he peered out the front door to look beneath the train cars. "It looks like your ride is almost here. Albert will park on the other side of the tracks. I can see him over there."

Hank looked out the window but had no idea what Mr. Swenson was talking about. All he saw was the train parked on the railroad track. "Thank you for the lodging help. You have a fine-looking store."

"Let us know if you need anything. We're always here for visitors to the area."

Hank crossed the road and made his way around the end of the parked train. There was a short sandy trail leading down to Clark Lake. The landing had a length of wooden dock where two boats were tied up. A young boy stood on top of the dock waving his arms. Hank was puzzled. He turned back toward the store to look for further instructions from Tom, the proprietor. Other than the boy, there seemed to be no one else here.

"Hey, mister. Are you going to Clark Lake Lodge?"

Hank stopped and turned toward the barefoot boy with a freckled face, wearing coveralls over a faded t-shirt. He appeared to be in his early teens. "What did you say?"

"Hi, I'm Albert. I'm here to collect travelers going to Clark Lake Lodge."

Hank was surprised. "Yes, I'm headed to the lodge."

Albert looked over Hank's three-piece suit. "Are you a preacher?"

"No, nothing like that. My name is Hank." He remained on the shore. "I've never been in a boat."

Albert smiled. "It's OK, mister. I've got a life-preserver vest along for safety if you can't swim. If you'd rather, you *can* walk to the lodge from here. It's about halfway around the lake through the woods. Though with this trusty boat, we can float right across in no time. You can relax while I do the rowing."

Hank nodded at the lake.

Albert pointed at Hank. "So, where is your luggage?"

"Only this." He shook his briefcase.

"How long will you be here?" Albert was puzzled.

"I'll stay a while, I guess. Why do you have two boats?"

"It's easy. One is for people, and I tie the other on the back for luggage and supplies. I have a few things to pick up from the store today before we head out. Are there any more passengers?"

"No, I don't think so. If it's all the same, I'll keep my briefcase with me."

The store owner, Tom, came across the road with a hand wagon. He bridged the rails at the crossing ramp and brought the load directly out on the dock. "Hi, Albert, have you been catching anything this week?"

"Yes sir, fishing is great!"

"How is your dad doing? I haven't seen him in the store for a while."

"Oh, he's doing fine. He's always looking for more people to fill the cabins."

"Of course, summer is here at last. They'll be more showing up real soon."

Albert loaded the food items into a pair of old wooden peach crates in the second boat. He covered them with a blanket.

"Well, this should be everything your mother ordered. Here's the charge slip. You take good care of Hank here and say hi to your dad for me." Tom turned the hand-wagon and began to leave the dock. He waived as he headed back to the store.

"I haven't lost a passenger yet! I'll tell Dad you said hello." Albert steadied the boat as Hank stepped into the rocking craft. "Sorry, mister, but can you move back one bench? The middle one is my rowing spot."

Hank took a firm grasp on the sides of the boat as he made a large step over the bench seat.

Once Hank settled in, Albert took his place in the boat. He pushed off the dock, leaned over the pair of oars dangling in the water, and began rowing with smooth even strokes.

"Albert, how old are you?"

"I'm thirteen and a half."

"Are you the youngest rowboat captain in Minnesota?"

Albert grinned. "I'm not sure. But maybe!"

Albert pointed. "Mr. Hank, look over there near the shoreline. Do you see the pair of loons swimming in the lake with their young baby? The little chic is sitting on top of its mama's back while she kicks around in the water looking for minnows to eat."

It took a second before Hank saw the dark fuzzball chic riding on his mother's back like a circus performer on top of an elephant in a parade. "Why isn't such a young bird without feathers still in the nest?"

"Not a half-bad question from a city guy. You see, unlike the other birds, loons build a nest right on the ground next to the shoreline. A baby loon doesn't need to fly before leaving the nest. It will grow up out on the lake where its parents can protect it and feed it. Say, Mr. Hank, if you're not a preacher, are you a banker or a businessman?"

Hank knew better than to tell the harsh truth, so he decided to do the dance Father Whelan had taught him. "Yes, I guess I am in a way. Why?"

"I've never had anyone in this boat wearing a suit before."

"Men around here don't wear suits?"

Albert paused at the oars for a moment while the floating train drifted on. "No, not unless they're getting hitched, paying their respects at a funeral, or lying inside the coffin."

Hank smiled. "Well, I wear suits every day. Most men do in the big city."

Albert scratched his abdomen through his t-shirt. "Oh, I don't think I could ever live there." He maneuvered the boat around a small shaded island. "See the spot beneath the pines?"

Hank raised his hand and shaded his eyes from the June sun. "Yes, I see it."

"It's a nice place for a picnic on a hot day. Sometimes we pack a lunch and bring families out here. There's a swimming beach off the far side with a tire swing. I always stay out here with them though. My dad says people can get pretty nervous being on an island without a boat."

Hank looked out across the lake. He thought about being in this unfamiliar place without a real plan for when he'd go back to Chicago. "I might know how it feels."

Albert dug in with the oars as the open lake breeze challenged them as they moved beyond the shelter of the island. The rustic log cabins carefully arranged along the shoreline came into view. "That is our place. Up the hill, inside the lodge, is where mom makes the meals. You can cook in your own cabin if you like, too. Each has a wood-burning stove. I stock the firewood."

"I'm not much of a cook. How many cabins do you rent?"

"We have twelve cabins plus the rooms upstairs in the lodge."

"Do you have any brothers and sisters to help with the work?"

"It's me and my sister Kate. She helps mom make the meals and do the cleaning."

Albert pulled the boat train in alongside the dock. He whisked out of the boat and began to tether the ropes to the post supports.

Hank stepped onto the shore. He paused and took in the view of massive pine trees looming over the hillside full of cabins. He offered Albert a dollar.

"How generous! But sir, it's not necessary. Our rides here are free."

Albert's mother, Harriet, stood on the lodge stoop with her hands on her hips while she watched the arrival at the dock.

Albert noticed her posture. "It looks like my mother is upset about something."

Hank made his way up the hill across the layer of fallen pine needles beneath the trees. With each step, his Oxford shoes made a dry crunch. The breeze blowing through the boughs of the trees sounded like an orchestra of soft brooms. He had never heard such a melody.

—•—

Harriet Johnson turned and walked back into the lodge to assume her post, ready to register new guests. Hank found the lodge entry and was greeted by walls of knotty wood paneling and heavy plank dining tables.

Mrs. Johnson waited behind the registration desk. Hank removed his hat. "Hello, Tom Swenson, the proprietor at the Hubert Landing store, phoned to inquire about lodging for me?"

Harriet peered at the strange-looking man through her wire-framed glasses. Her apron was still damp from washing dishes, and her hair was drawn back behind her head. "How long are you planning to stay?"

Hank sized her up. Harriet appeared to be an intense woman mired in the labors of running this camp. "I can't say for sure. Maybe a few days, maybe longer?"

She studied the pinstripes in Hank's suit coat. "We rent cabins by the week and the rooms upstairs by the day. Are you looking for meals, too?"

"I don't cook much myself. Yes, I would be interested in meals."

Harriet's response was crisp. "There's no electricity here or clever indoor plumbing like the big city has, so cabins rent for three dollars a day. Plus, a dollar and half more for breakfast, lunch, and dinner." She stared at the rich leather briefcase Hank had tucked under his right arm. "It's not as fancy as you might be used to. I make a cold lunch because most people take it along the lake."

"It sounds fine, ma'am."

Harriet couldn't discourage him. "We fry fish on Friday nights, but you have to help catch them."

"I might have to go without because I've never fished." Hank paused for a moment. "Would you happen to have two cabins available?"

Harriet's brow furrowed. Her voice grew sharp and piercing. "Why would you need more than one? Are you expecting guests?"

Hank remained calm. "I'd rather not say. Do you have two cabins available but located apart from each other?"

Harriet scrutinized Hank's face. "Yes, it's early in the season and lately some folks around here are out of a job. But don't expect any discount. Payment is required in cash, up front. We don't take bank drafts since we don't trust them much."

"No problem, I'll rent two cabins."

"What sort of business are you in any way?"

Hank took his time. "I provide *insurance and investments.*"

"Do you have anything to do with the stock market growing so high the last few years? I read about people getting rich."

It was an unexpected question coming from a resort wife running a camp in the wilderness. "No, I don't invest in the stock market."

Hank headed outside to find his cabins. He was ready for a night's sleep.

From the second-story bedroom, Harriet peered out the window into the night. The cabins were all dark except number two. It was one of the cabins

Hank had rented. The lanterns inside were burning in the middle of the night. Harriet noticed Hank's other cabin, number ten, was dark.

She turned down the lamp and crawled into bed. Warren was still awake. "We have a strange visitor with us this week. I don't like him."

Warren was exhausted, but he turned toward his wife. "Dear, what has he done?"

"Nothing exactly, but I don't trust him. It's odd. He didn't bring any luggage along and rented two cabins even though I think he's traveling alone. He didn't give me his full name when he registered and isn't here to fish."

Warren was puzzled. "He sounds unusual all right."

"But Warren, why is he here *with us*?"

Warren yawned. "It would be anyone's guess, but tomorrow Albert can show him how to catch his supper."

Harriet became quiet. After a couple of minutes of silence, Warren rolled back on his side, facing away from his wife. She leaned over him and whispered in his ear, "No, I don't want him alone with either of our children."

Warren was wide awake now. He sat up on the bedside and lit the candle on the table next to him. He waived out the match and set it down next to the candle holder base. "OK, calm down. I can take him out with Albert in the morning. It would be good to meet him."

Harriet watched the candle's flame grow to a full burn. "I would feel better if you did."

It was a fine June morning, and the birds were alive in the trees when Warren crossed the damp lawn. The lake was as calm as a mirror. He stopped at cabin number two. The low flickering light from the burning lamps was still visible through the window. He rapped on the door. "Hank, are you up? It's Warren Johnson, the owner."

He rapped on the door again. There was no answer. *Strange.*

Warren returned to the lodge and sat down at the table across from Albert. "Son, you must have a big day planned to need that mountain of pancakes."

"Mom made her blueberry syrup from the ones she canned last season."

"She's good at making syrup. Hey Albert, if we can find our new guest Hank, I'd like you to take him out on the lake. I'll tag along. When you're finished here, get a boat ready with fishing gear for the three of us and round up some bait. Your sister is packing a lunch for us."

Albert took an over-sized bite of pancake smothered with deep-blue syrup. He swallowed as he struggled out the words, "Sure, I'll get things ready."

"Let me know when you find Hank. He must have gone for a morning stroll."

Warren went outside and split some extra firewood for the evening bonfire. Albert came down the drive. "Dad, I found him. Hank will meet us at the dock."

Warren filled a water jug and grabbed three seat cushions for the boat. Halfway to the dock, he slowed and studied the silhouette of the new guest, sitting alone in the boat staring out at the smooth lake. His suit coat and hat were most peculiar for a warm day on the water. *Harriet was right. He doesn't look like he belongs here.*

Albert came across the lawn with a bucket of black dirt. "I've got some fat worms for bait. Dad, are you ready?"

"Yes, Albert, let's go."

From the dockside, Warren extended his hand and announced, "I'm Warren Johnson."

The guest reluctantly shook his hand. "Hank."

"Albert tells me you're not much of a swimmer. Do you wear a life vest? We have those, too, if a float seat cushion isn't enough."

Hank looked over each of his fishing guides. "No, this seat cushion will do."

Warren untied the ropes and took his place in the boat. He pushed the craft away from the dock. As he took hold of the pair of wooden oars, he asked, "How about pan fish?"

"Sure thing, Dad."

Hank's face was blank.

"Hank, we'll row down the shore a stretch to a place we call Sunfish Bay. This light breeze is perfect to cast along the weed lines for bluegills. Albert, would you put a float on each of those fishing poles please?"

"Yes, Dad."

Warren leaned into the oar strokes. "So Hank, have you visited the Minnesota lake country before?"

Hank smiled. "No, this is a first for me."

"Curious, how did you find us?"

A pair of geese flew past the boat, honking as they glided in to rest on the water.

"This was as far as I could get with my train ticket."

Warren nodded. "Yes, we are the last passenger stop on the Gull River Line. The railroad was first brought here to serve the timber industry. Many of the massive Minnesota white pines from this area were harvested to build homes across the country as towns sprang up. Are you from the city?"

"Why do you ask?"

Warren smiled. "We don't see many *suits* around here. You might find it warm this week. It can get humid this time of year. If you like, the general store has bush shirts and cotton pants on hand. It's just a thought."

"We'll see."

"Albert when I get the boat turned, let the anchor down and tie it off short."

Warren introduced the business of fishing. "All right, Hank, this is a cane pole. Albert has a cork float tied to the line. The sinker and hook will hang down in the water below the float. All we need to do is to reach in the worm pail and thread one of those wriggly red devils on the hook before you swing it out there next to the weed line in the lake."

Hank took the twelve-foot long pole from Warren. He watched carefully as Warren prepared his own bait and tossed the rig into the water. Hank fumbled with the fishing hook until he got a grip on it between his thumb and forefinger. He reached his free hand down into the moist black soil and got hold of a squirming earthworm. He got it threaded on the hook and swung the baited line out in the lake where it landed with a soft plunk.

"It's peaceful here."

"Yes, city folks seem to notice the sounds of nature right away. Outside of the daily train whistle, we hear the loons calling and the occasional wolf after sunset." Warren didn't waste any time landing a couple of sunfish.

Albert raised his cane pole. "I've got a good one!" He wrestled with the blue-green fish before he brought it to hand. The fish scales shimmered in the sunshine as he added it to the wire basket lashed to the side of the boat.

"All right, your turn, Hank."

Hank cast his line.

"So Hank, what makes a city guy like you take a trip alone to the north woods?" Warren quizzed.

"I guess I'm looking for peace and quiet."

Warren noticed the fish bite. "Hey Hank, your float is down!"

"What?"

"You've got a fish on the line. Lift the rod and bring it in."

Hank raised the cane pole. The fish wanted nothing to do with a trip to the boat. He raised the pole with more force. The cane bowed from the weight.

Albert yelled, "Whoa! You've got something bigger than a sunfish!"

The fish ran hard toward the right. Warren pulled his own gear out of the way and scrambled for the landing net. Hank's line rose to the surface as an angry bass shook his way out of the water and splashed back down in the lake.

Hank had never seen a battle like this. "Wow!"

The fish powered its way to the left and fought hard before Hank maneuvered it in alongside the boat. As Warren slipped the net beneath the fish, it broke the surface again and sent a spray of water into the boat.

Hank leaned forward to help Warren pull the fish in. Something caught Albert's eye. The boy looked again into Hank's gaping suit jacket and saw the handle of a holstered pistol. As Hank leaned back and took his seat again, the pistol disappeared.

Albert was silent. He felt trapped in the boat with an armed man sitting between him and his father.

Warren beamed. "Wow, what a fish Hank. Great job keeping it on the line."

Hank used a cloth to wipe the water off his face and dab his coat.

"Albert, swing the basket in here, please, and we'll add this beauty to our catch."

Albert looked down into the water. He couldn't get his mind off what he had seen. Was Hank some sort of lawman or was he a criminal? He untied the cord for the fish basket and slid the loose end along the side of the boat. Hank took it from him.

Warren spoke up. "Albert, has the cat got your tongue? Hank, I think my son might be a spoilsport for being out fished by a new guest."

As soon as the boat reached the shore, Albert jumped onto the dock and went straight to the lodge without a word. He took the main stairs and locked himself in his room. On his path through the dining area, Harriet noticed her son's pale face.

She followed and knocked softly on his door. "Albert, please open up. Are you all right?" There was no response. "If you feel ill, maybe I can bring you aspirin or a bottle of Bubble Up for your stomach."

Albert finally unlocked the door.

"Albert, what is wrong?"

He opened the door and pulled his mother inside the room. He shut the door behind her and locked the handle.

"Albert, what is it?"

Albert thought about his words. He worried it would scare her. But he knew what he saw in the boat was real. He couldn't stand it anymore. "Mother, Hank's got a gun!"

Harriet took a step back and covered her mouth with both hands. Her son never played pranks. "What are you saying?"

Before Albert could respond, she asked another question. "Where is your father now?"

Albert knew this would alarm his mother, but she had to know. "He's still down at the lake with Hank."

"Oh my gosh! Is he OK?"

Albert shrugged his shoulders. "I think so. Hank is carrying the gun under his coat."

Harriet was beside herself. "How do you know?"

"I saw it when we were fishing in the boat."

Her face turned ruby red and her lips pursed into a white knot. "Did he point it at you or your dad?"

"No, we were just fishing."

"Does your father know he's got a gun?"

"I don't think so. Dad was in a pretty good mood when we were out in the boat. He didn't seem concerned about anything."

"Go get your father right now. But if Hank's still around, don't say anything about the gun. Tell your dad, I need to see him right away." She reached out and put a hand on her son's shoulder. "Will you be OK, or are you too scared?"

Albert was afraid, but he wanted to help his mother. "I can do it."

Harriet's mind raced for options of how they might get rid of the dangerous guest.

Warren appeared moments later with Albert at his side. They went back to the kitchen area.

Harriet took Warren by the arm. "Did Albert tell you Hank had a gun out in the boat today?"

Warren froze for a moment. "No, he didn't."

Warren turned to look at his son. "I never saw any guns. Albert, is this why you got so quiet out there?"

Albert nodded.

Warren's pulse quickened. "Hank needs to leave right now!"

"I've got to confront him." Warren turned around with his hand over his mouth. He scanned the walls and corners of the kitchen for anything he could use such as an ax for splitting wood, or an oversized kitchen knife. There was nothing threatening.

"Harriet, go find Kate. You and the kids stay upstairs for a while until I've sent him away."

Harriet pleaded, "Warren just wait a minute first. Let's talk about this. Albert, go to your room for now until your father and I can decide what to do."

Albert headed toward the stairs up to the living quarters.

"Warren, what's going to happen when you confront Hank?"

"I don't know for sure, but I'll make it clear he isn't welcome anymore."

"Has he threatened you or Albert?"

Warren saw the concerned look on Harriet's face. "No, he hasn't."

"Why do you think he carries a gun? What sort of man is he?"

Warren shrugged. "Well, I don't think he's any sort of law man."

"What if this makes him mad? Could he hurt us?"

"We are a long way from the sheriff."

"Is this why he rented two cabins? I mean, is he trying to hide here?"

Warren took a moment. "Maybe."

Harriet walked around the kitchen. "This might sound crazy, but are we safer letting him stay than calling for the sheriff?"

Warren ran his hands through his gray hair. "I sure don't want any trouble."

"Warren, let's wait a minute before you stomp over there to confront him. There's nowhere he can really go tonight. Maybe we should sleep on it. If we still feel the same way in the morning, we can send him off on the train. "

— • —

Hank heard the rumble coming up the forest drive right at dusk. The black bumper and chrome grill led a cloud of dust rolling off the truck wheels. Harriet met the farm truck at the back of the lodge. She took the delivery of honey, milk, and cream. After the brief stop, Hank watched the truck head back down the driveway. The corner of a freight tarp flapped loose revealing a load of sealed wooden crates.

Harriet was busy preparing the evening snack. An unexpected male voice coming from the back entrance spoiled the calm. "If you don't mind me asking, is a local dairy farm delivering the milk?"

Startled, Harriet jumped. "Hank, I didn't hear you come in. You shouldn't be back here. I'll bring the chocolates and marshmallow treats to the campfire."

"Harriet, I have a question."

"What is it you want to know?"

He repeated, "Does a local dairy farm deliver the milk?"

Her pulse rate was still elevated. "Yes, sort of. Three Brothers Farms is located south of here, a couple hour's drive. We are on the last of their delivery stops. We've bought from them the past few seasons."

"It seems unusual they deliver this late in the evening."

"They changed to this schedule in the last year or so. I assume they switched to evenings so they can keep things cooler."

The sun was well up in the morning sky when Warren crossed the small meadow and disappeared into the faded red barn. He swung one side of the pair of large doors open and rolled out a rotary-reel lawn clipper. He placed a short chunk of log flat on its end for a makeshift workbench. Warren set the base of the mower on the stump and used wrenches and a hammer to disassemble the frame. He drew the rough grit belt back and forth over the mower's edge to restore the sharpness.

Hank hiked out of the trees when he heard the hammer near the barn. He crossed the meadow. "Warren, did you have a farm here?"

Warren turned abruptly at the sound of Hank's voice. He thought about the plan he and Harriet had settled on to not report Hank to the sheriff as the best way to keep the family safe.

"No, this property used to be a farmstead long before I bought it. I turned the old house into the lodge. This barn is the last remnant of those days. It came with the forty acres. I still use it for a fix-it shop, parking our Studebaker family car, and winter boat storage."

Albert rode his bicycle up the drive next to the barn. He made a large swing around the two men and pulled in next to his dad. "Mom needs help with the cook stove. The pipe is blocked again."

Hank knew Albert didn't like being around him, so he walked over to the lean-to shelter on the side of the barn. He lifted a tattered green tarp and asked, "What sort of wreck are you hiding back here?" The old car had flat tires and was missing a door and a front fender.

Albert was short. "We're going to repair it. Someday soon, I'll learn to drive and go wherever I want."

Hank laughed. "Does the engine in this old heap even run?" He shook his head. "Even if it does, these old cars were pretty slow."

Warren weighed in. "Speed isn't too important around here, Hank. We'll get it going for Albert. It needs a few parts. I want to teach Albert some basic things about being a mechanic."

Warren grabbed some tools and headed for the lodge. Albert jumped on his bicycle and followed along.

— • —

Warren removed screws from the stovepipe sections and began to scour the soot away with a wire brush.

"Warren, you looked like you were on a mission this morning."

"Yes, dear. I'm getting some things done around here, so I can go out fishing with Hank."

Harriet's face turned sour. "Really?"

"Hold on a minute before you worry. We'll take the canoe this time as I won't force Albert to sit in the same boat with him again. Hank and I need to get straight on some things if he's going to stay around here any longer."

"Keep your cool with him out there. We've still got to think about our safety." She wrung her hands. "Warren, at the same time, I have to admit, I like to have both cabins rented. Lord knows we can use the boost."

— • —

Warren took the back seat in the canoe, so he could steer. He made small talk while paddling out to the island. Pulling in close to the shaded shoreline, Warren eased the anchor into the water without a splash. The summer air was filled with the fresh scent from the thick grove of pines on the island. He picked up the fishing rods, then decided to set them aside for a while.

"Hank, there are a few things we need to talk about."

Hank twisted on the canoe seat and turned his head back toward Warren.

"Don't take this the wrong way, but you're scaring the family and maybe the few other guests we have coming lately, too."

Hank closed his eyes for a moment. "How? Warren, I promise I haven't done anything to them."

Warren took a deep breath. "It all began when Albert saw the gun you had with you in the boat. He saw it under your jacket when the three of us were fishing. He's been scared to death of you ever since."

Hank faced ahead again and looked at a brood of ducklings dabbling along the shoreline. He looked back over his shoulder once more. "Oh, now I understand. One minute Albert and I were getting along fine, the next I noticed he wanted nothing to do with me."

"Harriet is worried, too. She can't stand the thought of guns. She's read all the headlines in the newspapers over the last few years and is deathly afraid of them."

"Just so you know, Warren, I carry protection with me wherever I go. I'm not out to harm anyone."

"I talked it over with Harriet. Your story is a mystery here and I assume you prefer things this way. If you want to stay, some things must change. Unless you want someone to call the local sheriff, you must *blend in* with the tourists. Right now, we're afraid people won't stay here long if they're uncomfortable around you. Summers are short, and the lodge struggles to show a profit.

"I don't know who you're hiding from, but you can't carry guns around without making people panic. Trust me, this is a peaceful place. There are no threats here. We also don't want you to do business at the lodge. Otherwise, you got to move along. Are we in any danger with you here?"

Hank thought about his unplanned departure from Chicago. "No. I slipped away when I caught the train, and I chose where to stay. No one dangerous knows where I am. I've heard some men in the business have escaped to Wisconsin from time to time because they can drive up there. But your place is well off the map. Your family is safe around me. Maybe even safer."

"We don't need an armed guard. This is a peaceful place."

Hank considered Warren's requests. "I gotta think about this *blend in* stuff."

"All right, I hope I've made things pretty clear. Now let me switch subjects and ask you a different kind of question."

"What's on your mind?"

"If you don't mind my curiosity, how do you like it?"

Hank gripped the sides of the canoe and twisted around as far as he could to see Warren's face. "How do I like *what* exactly?"

"Sorry, I should have been more specific. How do you like being in the *insurance and investment business*?"

Hank was surprised by the question. "I thought you said my secrets are supposed to be safe here."

The two sat silently for a minute.

"Yes, of course, your secrets are safe here. I don't want to know any details. I'm curious how you *like* the business."

"I suppose like anything, the business has its up and downs." Hank didn't want to talk about how he felt about murder, bootlegging booze, or his hatred for Al Capone's thugs. At some level, he knew his decisions twisted him up inside.

"When I think about these cabins and the lodge that barely ekes out a living, I know there's more money to be made doing other things. There are plenty of mining and logging jobs in this state with high wages by comparison. However, that type of work is dangerous, and it rarely allows a man the time to spend with his family. I couldn't do it to Harriet or the kids. By being here every day with them, they are learning to be honest, to have faith, and develop a strong work ethic. If I were gone for days on end, they wouldn't turn out the same."

"I can understand that."

"When I married Harriet, I never promised her a castle on a hill. She was raised on a farm where everyone helped to make a living. Rolling up your sleeves was part of daily life. It's the same way around here. I wouldn't trade this for anything. At some point, I figured out wealth comes in many forms. For me, happiness comes from being healthy and raising a family."

Warren handed Hank a fishing pole. "Someday, we'll get electricity here the same as the big city has along with all the conveniences. But for now, we'll scrape by all right."

When Warren finished speaking, Hank tossed his line in the water. "I live in a different place where most men are greedy and impatient. They'll climb over a pile of bodies to steal someone else's treasure. The reward doesn't last for long because soon someone else is climbing over your dead body to take it from you. The business is a wicked, wicked way to make a living. Many men die trying to get rich. I'm trying to escape from being added to the mountain of the dead."

Warren thought about Hank's image of greed and desperation. "Is the real reason always about money? Or is there something else they want?"

"While greed seems insatiable, deep down these men act like immature boys trying to see who gets the last word in a dangerous shoving match."

"Do you ever think about another line of work?"

"Sure. But I have to admit, I've been holding a gun in my hand so long I didn't realize, at some point, it took hold of me."

— • —

By the end of the day, Hank was sitting on the front bench outside the Hubert Landing store. Tom was prepared to close for the day when he spotted the visitor. "Hi, Hank. You're cutting it close. Can I help you before I finish up?"

"I'm looking for some clothes to wear here while I'm at the lake."

"Sure, come on in here. We have a good selection for you to consider. You can try things on for size if you like. There's an inventory room in the back. Take a couple of pairs of pants and some summer shirts to try. We also have some sharp looking shoes. If you find some things that work, you can wear them right out of here."

Hank was paying for the new clothes when he saw the pile of newspapers on the floor next to the counter. "You have the St. Paul newspaper?"

"Yes, the train delivers it to us every other day. These are a day old, but you can have one if you like."

Hank stared at the headlines: *Federal Prosecutor Sent to Chicago to Put Away Gangsters, Lobbyists Push To Repeal Prohibition Amendment, Temperance Society Planning Protests!* He collected a copy on the way out the front door.

Tom shouted after him, "I appreciate your business, Hank. Have a nice evening!"

Hank walked the wooded roads back to the lodge. About halfway into the journey, the delivery truck for Three Brothers Farms roared past in a cloud of dust. Sometime later, the truck returned on the same road. Hank waived the driver down. The big truck slowed to the side of the road. The driver rolled his window down and apologized for the cloud.

Hank coughed a bit. "That's all right. I want to talk to you about business."

"OK."

"You see, I'm from Chicago and I want to know what you deliver."

"It depends on what you're buying, mister. Since I really don't know you, it would be hard to say."

"Maybe I could visit your operation some time to look things over."

"How do I know you aren't a *revenuer* or a *cop*? What do you want with an old honey and milk parlor anyway?"

"I've seen your loads when you stop by the lodge. The honey and cream business looks like a front to me. No one delivers those goods at night. There are a lot of wooden crates on your truck. I bet they're filled with brown glass bottles of *giggle water*. We pay a high premium for quality in Chicago. Is your stuff distilled twice and aged in wood barrels?"

The driver did a slow nod. "I have to be careful here. My two brothers have a say in these decisions, too. Sorry to cut this off, but I really have to keep moving. I've got a long night ahead of me."

"Before you go, what's your name?"

"Oh, I'm Walt."

"Hi, Walt. I'm Hank Macklan. One last thing I want to tell you. I take care of all the freight so you wouldn't have to drive anymore."

The driver turned and looked Hank straight in the eyes. "Are you serious?"

"Yes, but I need to come and see how you and your brothers do things. There's a lot of people making poor quality mash."

Walt took a scrap invoice and drew on it.

Hank watched him sketching. "What's that?"

Walt tossed the wrinkled sheet to Hank as he let out the clutch and pulled the truck away. He shouted out the truck's window, "Come see for yourself sometime. We make the good stuff from Minnesota 13!"

Hank watched the truck bounce out of sight over the washboard in a cloud of dust. As it disappeared over the hill, he stared into the floating brown haze and considered Walt's last comment. He pictured Minnesota 13 as a sort of secret recipe the locals knew about. With long winters, people in the north country could be pretty resourceful and might know a thing or two about making grain alcohol.

In the low evening light, Warren spotted Hank walking along the drive. "There you are! It's getting pretty dark. I thought maybe you got lost taking your hike. Can you stop by for a minute?"

Hank followed Warren into the lodge.

"Hey, it looks like you picked up some new clothes today." He thumped Hank on the shoulder with the back of his hand. "Now, you look the part."

"They certainly feel cooler than my suit."

Warren sifted through the papers on the registration desk. "Oh, here it is. Harriet showed me this curious post from the mail today. I assume it's supposed to be for you."

Hank studied the small white envelope. The addressee was listed, *To: Hank care of Clark Lake Lodge*. The return address was left blank. He studied the postmark.

Hank left without a word. He tapped the curious envelope with his hand all the way back to cabin number ten.

Hank took a seat at the table and turned up the gas lantern. He unfolded a pocketknife and slit the envelope flap loose. He drew a piece of parchment out and unfolded it to study the message written in black ink. It read: *Luke 15:24.* He stared into the flickering yellow lantern light.

Hank returned the card to the envelope, slipped it in his coat pocket, and headed back to lodge.

Warren was tipping the chairs up on the tables for the night. There was a broom perched against the counter. He stopped with a chair in his hands. "Back so soon?"

Hank realized the strange nature of the request he was about to make. "Warren, I have a question for you. Do you keep a Bible around here?"

Warren set the chair down and looked at Hank in disbelief. He wondered if Hank was overcome with regret for things he'd done. For a moment, he considered teasing him, but based on the look on his face, opted not to. "Awe, sure. Harriet keeps one up in our room. I'll get it for you."

Hank took the Bible and post back to the privacy of his cabin.

Sitting in the glow of the table lamp, Hank thumbed through the New Testament. He found the verse. "For this my son was dead, and is alive again; he was lost, and is found."

Hank studied the envelope one more time. It was time for him to return to Chicago. He couldn't get past the fact he told no one where he was staying. *How many of these posts were sent out to find me?*

———— • ————

"Hank, please take a seat over there by the windows. Do you want coffee with your breakfast?"

"Sure. Thank you for the use of your Bible last night."

Harriet smiled at the thought. Her curiosity was killing her, but she thought it best not to ask.

"Can you tell me when I can catch the train back to St. Paul?"

"Hank, the train leaves at 10:00 a.m. Are you going to be checking out?"

"Yes, I will catch the morning train then."

Hank made a point of arriving at the Hubert Landing store fairly early.

Tom welcomed him in. "Hank, how are you today? How did the new clothes work out? Do you need anything else?"

"The clothes fit fine. I will need a train ticket to get back to St. Paul."

"Sure, I can help you. Just so you know, I got a telephone call this morning. The train is running a little late. Give me a minute for the ticket."

"Tom, while you're working on the ticket, I have a question for you about local lodging. Can you tell me how many resort camps there are in this area?"

"Well, Hank, you've asked an interesting question. Today, the number is small. Including Clark Lake Lodge where you've been staying, there are four resorts near here."

Hank got the sense the mystery post may not have been such a miraculous thing after all.

Tom continued, "Things are likely to change soon. The state has announced big plans to build a superhighway from St. Paul and Minneapolis all the way up here to lake country. Right now, the roads to drive here are built through some wet marsh areas, and it takes a truck to make the slow trip even during dry weather. When the new paved highway is built and electricity arrives, there is a big city investor group planning to develop a camp over at

White Pine Cove on Gull Lake into a grand affair with a golf course and a high-class restaurant.

"We worry they might steal most of the business we get from train travelers like yourself. Warren and Harriet are in a tight spot, too. The main highway won't be close enough for us if people prefer to drive cars up here."

CHAPTER 18

Plan Of Attack

It was late June when the train steamed along out of the forest headed back across open field country toward the city. Hank thought about the vicious war he was helping wage. The Genna family hated his alliance with the North Side Gang. They had put the *Murder Twins* of Scalise and Anselmi on his trail. If he could put an end to this pair of barbarians once and for all, he could focus on the river of cheap liquor flowing through the streets of north Chicago.

Hank stared across the horizon at the distant city skyline coming into view. He wondered, *Is the whole country at war over the booze business?*

He hired a taxi at the Chicago train station to deliver him to 738 North State Street. As they got close, the cabbie asked, "Hey isn't this the place where the mobster O'Banion was taken out last year?"

It bothered Hank that their headquarters was still located above Schofield's Floral Shop. Every time he went there, he was reminded of Dean's brutal execution.

"Drop me in the alley behind the shop, would ya, pal?"

"Sure thing, mack. No trouble at all."

Hank took the back stairs up to the office. He rapped on the door and made his way inside. The shades were drawn, and the room was dark. Hank could make out the silhouettes of two men pointing pistols at him. "Stop right there!"

"Hold on a minute! George, are you here? It's Hank, put your guns down!"

One of the men stepped to the window and raised the blind. Hank was standing face-to-face with George Moran and Hymie Weiss.

"You can't be too careful around here you know." George dismissed the awkward standoff.

Hank nodded. As he flipped the light switch on, he thought about the modern convenience of electric lights compared to the oil lamps back at the lake. "I feel bad every time I come here. Someday soon, we gotta get out of this joint. There are just too many memories of Dean in the building."

George introduced Hank. "Hymie, you remember Hank. They call him *The Hammer*. He runs a small clean-up crew for us and provides security for liquor transports."

Hymie put his hand out. "Good to meet you again, Hank. I haven't seen you in a while. What's with the *ice cream duds* anyway? Were you at a picnic or something?"

Hank looked down at his clothes and smirked. "I call these my funeral prevention clothes."

He looked around the room. The door to the large safe was standing open. His gaze ran across the wide shelves loaded with fat bundles of cash strapped by rubber bands. The money was heaped in piles like it had been loaded with a coal shovel. On the table, a city map was stretched open next to a large ledger book.

George wanted to explain. "Hank here is being hunted by the Murder Twins. The Gennas sent those goons after him about a month ago, so I put Hank on a train to God's country for a couple of weeks."

Hymie's eyebrows rose. "God's country?"

"I sent Hank to northern Minnesota until things cooled off."

"Weren't you raised up there somewhere?"

George nodded. "Anyway, this might be a good time to read Hank in on our plans."

Hymie pointed across the room. "Hank, do you want bourbon or something? The crates on the desk over there are loaded with stock."

Hank took notice of the pistol holsters George and Hymie wore openly on display. There was an absence of suit coats on the hot Chicago afternoon. The ceiling fan made slow turns through the warm air. "Yes, I'll have one. It was pretty *dry* during my stay up north."

Hymie rubbed the two-day stubble on his chin. He rose from his chair and walked around the room as he spoke. "We have to pull our allies together and go after Capone's gangs in his own backyard. If we don't wage war across this city, he'll keep picking on us like sitting targets in a carnival shooting gallery. We've tried to get to him three times this year, and somehow, he's slithered away every time. We've got to cut the legs off his business instead."

Hank let the words sink in. "If you don't mind, I have a question."

Hymie studied the expression and seriousness apparent on Hank's face. "Sure, what's on your mind?"

Hank looked toward the open window. "Don't take this the wrong way, but how did we get into this mess? When I was a teenager, my father fought similar battles in this city, but no one really won. A lot of people were killed in the process, but the war never ended. It appears to me it's still going on today."

George felt the heat building on the back of his neck. He could have almost spit. "Hank, you of all people know exactly how we got into this. While I loved O'Banion like a brother, his determination to get one over on Torrio with a deceitful brewery sale tied him and all of us to a whipping post! Once the brewery was raided and Torrio went to prison, I knew there would be hell to pay."

Hymie added, "I was there for those discussions. Dean just couldn't come up with another buyer for his share of the brewery on short notice. He was willing to do anything to stay out of prison, so he turned against Torrio."

George stared at the floor and collected his thoughts. "The thing is these thugs are now out to kill us. Each one of us could die. They are barbarians, and they showed it when they murdered Dean in this very building when he was unarmed. They don't have souls. We can't let them get away with what they did here. We have to honor Dean's memory. His widow deserves justice at least."

Hank was trying to sort things out. "I know, down deep, O'Banion was a good man. My father liked him. And he wouldn't have been working all hours in his floral shop to help a grieving family if he wasn't a good man. So how do we honor Dean without putting more of our people in the ground, too?"

Hymie nodded. "We'll go after his gangs on the street. They are much more vulnerable. We've got a defector on our side now who used to be a runner for Capone. He stopped being loyal to them when Capone killed his brother. He knows the Capone liquor delivery plans and sources. We'll cut off his supply routes and take a chunk of his business. Capone will stop selling in our backyard in a heartbeat if he can't keep his regular accounts happy."

Hank looked over the street map. It was covered with small circles and some X's. A large leather-bound accountant's ledger was sprawled across the end of the table. He tapped on the binding's edge. "What's in the book?"

Weiss leaned over the green pages covered with handwritten entries in black ink. "You see this list of names?"

"Sure, I've got good eyes."

Hymie pointed at the last column on the right. "Well, Hank, those joints pour our whiskey and beer here on the North Side." He ran his finger down the sheet. "If you look at these figures, you can see how many cases we sell them each week."

Hank studied the dates and the figures entered in the book. "Yes, but why are there several of these sales getting smaller in recent months? I see some drop off completely. Is this right? Have people stopped drinking all of a sudden?"

Moran launched a gob of tobacco into the spittoon sitting on the floor next to the table. He pounded his fist on the table. "They're falling off because some mangy dogs have moved in on us!"

Hymie moved from the ledger book to leaning over the map. "This shows a clear pattern where the border customers are being stolen. Look here." He placed the gap between his forefinger and thumb over the area at the intersection of Halsted and Chicago Ave.

Hank stood up straight and looked at Weiss. "You're talking about the Genna brothers. They're the ones who were coming after me before I left town. They spend a lot of time in our area. We should clean out their rat's nest and shut down their booze running operations altogether."

Hymie took a seat away from the table. "It's true. I know Capone conspires with the Sicilians on Taylor Street. I could use a good clean-up crew in Little Italy, but it's a bloody neighborhood. It's the worst in all Chicago."

Hank took his hat off and ran his fingers around the inside lining. As he rotated the hat, he thought about some of his younger crew members and their lack of experience. Before he'd send them into this kind of neighborhood, he would need to work on their skills.

Hymie cautioned, "There are several things you need to know Hank. First, the Gennas have real itchy trigger fingers when it comes to threats. They'll shoot at the first sign of trouble. The whole Sicilian community is their eyes and ears. They set up the poor people living in their neighborhoods with home stills. So, they're all in on the action. Last, is the police. The cops get weekly payments from the Gennas. If you start a gun battle over there, the police are likely to *join in* against you. Don't ever let them arrest you. They won't bother with handcuffs because they'll deliver your sentence right on the spot." He paused to let the information sink in. "Can your guys handle this kind of battle?"

Hank was not a typical mob leader. Most of his family had died in this miserable business. Those painful memories left him with permanent scars. His first thoughts obsessed over the risks and preparation of his men. Half were young and had been with him only a year or two.

"Some of my guys are too new. They're not ready for this yet, but I have two who are experienced at *detail work*. They both have new Tommy guns. We'll be better at hitting smaller specific targets rather than a large battlefield." Hank didn't know if his new boss wanted honesty, but he wasn't about to run his crew into a meat grinder they weren't prepared for.

George chimed in, "It's time we deliver some lead poison to those cannoli pigeons!"

Hank didn't know what other resources Hymie might have to chase these clowns down. "Let's face it. This will be more than a single battle. I've been told the Genna brothers avoid being in public together. Even if we get Angelo Genna with a surprise assault, we'll have to be snipers after that to pick away at the rest of them. This will take some time, but we'll get them."

George's voice grew louder. "We also need to hijack the booze coming out of their industrial plant. This will draw them out as they can't lie low for very long without it."

Hymie filled his glass. "You mention *Bloody Angelo*. I've been told he is daring enough to hang his hat each night in our Lakeview neighborhood."

"What do you mean?" Hank was baffled.

"One of our guys swears he saw him coming out of a rental flat at the Hotel Belmont," Hymie said.

George plunked his empty glass down on the table. "Why would a paranoid rival mobster take such a risk?"

Hank was beside himself. "He's staying right here in our backyard?"

George's fuse was lit. His face turned as red as a garden beet. "He's stealing our booze business and living the high life right in the middle of the North Side! He's mocking us. I'm telling you, he needs to feel the wrath!"

Hank looked at Hymie. "I'll post a couple of our boys down there. We need to know what time he punches the clock and the kind of car he drives."

Hymie smiled and picked up his suit coat. "I like the way you think, Hank. Let's give this a couple of days before we hit him."

George looked over at his boss. "Say, are you going somewhere?"

Hymie slipped his jacket on and collected his hat on the way to the door. He paused with his hand on the knob. "Yes, there's a guy up in Evanston who invited me to stop and look at some cars and guns he brought in from out east. He sells interesting things to Capone and generally has a good idea of what plans are before the Italian goons make a move. He wants to get our business, too. I'll let you know what I find out." Hymie swung the door closed as he headed for the back stairs to the alley.

George shook his head. "I'll never know how he meets these guys. I don't trust anyone who works with Capone."

Hank shook his head in amazement. "Say, George, do we have any other maps around?"

George walked over to the closet. "We might have some back here somewhere." He looked at some rolled documents. "What sort of map do you need? Things might have changed a lot the last few years in the outlying areas."

Hank stared at the map on the table. "I could use another one like this or even larger. The older parts of town should be pretty much the same."

"What are you looking for on the map?"

It was a fair question. Hank stared at the ledger book one more time and back at the map. "I'd like to make another map like this, but showing where Capone's important customers are located. We could add their breweries, distilleries, truck routes, and all their other saloons. Maybe we should include the same spots for the Genna Brothers, too. I'd like to study where they are most vulnerable to attack and make plans to pinch them somewhere along the line."

George smiled. This wasn't anything like how they'd ever done business before. After all, what did they have to lose? As it was, customers were leaving them each day.

He stepped back from the table. "Hank, it was good for Hymie to get to know you better today. I'm also glad you and I have some time to talk." George dragged a heavy wooden chair up near the table and took a seat as if he had been planning this conversation. "Hank, I've been thinking about things while you were away. Since you're here again, I must admit, I've underestimated you."

Hank found the remark intriguing. He stepped to the table and stared at George Moran with his signature slicked-back hair and suspenders draped over his shirt. He considered George most often a man of action who lived in the moment. At times, however, George would surprise him and almost come off as an intellectual. Hank was curious where this was leading.

"Have a seat here and take a load off." George grabbed a chair and dragged it into place. Hank took advantage of it.

George didn't wait. "Your father was a good man, and it turns out you are, too. Hank, I see you as capable of many things. You're different from your dad though. You're more careful. I hear you talking about things in advance and making plans. Hudson was a good soldier. He marched where he was told to go and fixed many problems for us." George turned his chair to the side to face Hank and collected a cigar from the box on the table. He struck a wood match. George inhaled three or four times in rapid succession drawing the flame into the tobacco until a bright ember glowed at the end of the roll of brown leaves. He waved the match out in the air and tossed it on the table. "As you know, Chicago is at war over who is going to be the future king of the booze and gambling business. There's a lot of hands in the pie for now, but hands will be slapped soon as a leader emerges who wants everything. There is too much at stake here."

Hank tried to read the expression on George's face. His youthful look often concealed the fierceness Hank witnessed whenever George got angry. "First, I appreciate all you've done for me these past years to bring me under your wing. But, my goal is *not* to become the ruler of Chicago's mob business. I'm better at being the number two man."

George blinked several times, set his cigar aside in an ash tray, and began to pull on his bottom lip where chewing tobacco would normally park. "Hank, I know I can be a hothead when someone pushes my buttons. My kind of anger can get me into trouble if I make a rash decision. But are you saying if something happened and you were the last man standing, you'd walk away from everything we've built?"

Hank could hear disappointment in the response. "Well, let's say, leading from the shadows may be more powerful than being under constant pressure from all sides. Not to mention, avoiding being the obvious target can prolong one's life."

"In this business, how can anyone lead from the shadows? You gotta act quickly when you get attacked, or it's all over."

"It is true, at times, but behind many well-run organizations are masterminds, who with a cooler head, as they say, can look for opportunities, read situations, and choose the best direction without all the pressure. It might mean someone else acts as a front man."

"Hmm. I've never looked at things the way you do, Hank. Are you saying Al Capone might be a front man? You know, the guy who does public appearances and knows everyone in government, judges, and police officials, but someone else, like Torrio, is quietly making the calls?"

CHAPTER 19

The Cleansing

A dark horse was rushing toward the Genna dynasty. They'd crossed the river to steal more business but underestimated the enemy who defended it.

Hymie, George, and Hank waited for Angelo on the street outside the Belmont. They sat in the car until midmorning. "Either he's not an early bird or he stayed somewhere else last night," George speculated.

Hymie thought it still felt likely. "Let's sit tight for a while. He's probably in the restaurant right now having his last cup of coffee."

Hank leaned over from the backseat. "You want me to go in there and get him?"

Hymie pushed back. "Boys, we'll let him finish. This needs to happen out here to avoid the bystanders and witnesses. Shooting up a busy hotel can land you in Joliet for decades."

Hymie spotted a blue Chevy Roadster leaving the outdoor parking area. He pointed as the vehicle headed toward the corner. "There's the cheat! Let's catch him! Angelo is oblivious to the hell racing toward him." He turned south on Sheridan Avenue and shifted the car into second gear. At twenty miles per hour, the Chevy Superior Roadster was purring along past the neighborhood merchants.

George drove the dark sedan up along the driver's side of Angelo's Chevrolet. Angelo saw the front bumper and grill of the intrusive car and turned to see what the commotion was about. The oncoming cars blew their horns as the pair monopolized the roadway.

Angelo saw a gun barrel poking out the passenger window of the Ford. He floored the accelerator and torqued his head around. He recognized Hymie Weiss. "Shit!" At fifty miles per hour, Angelo hit third gear and put both hands on the steering wheel. He bounced through the uneven intersection at Diversey Parkway.

The bigger Ford was built for speed. The executioners took their position alongside the slower coupe. The car bouncing over the rough brick roadway disturbed the first burst of gunshots. *Boom, boom, boom.* They missed the mark. Weiss was angry. "Hold her steady, George, and get me in there again!"

As Hymie aimed the rifle at the Chevy's driver door, Angelo dropped the gear shift into second and punched the car into a daring swerve around the corner on to Deming.

The bullets from the second volley screamed past the car and shattered windows in the distance. *Boom, boom, boom.* The Ford sedan overshot the corner, and George stomped on the brakes. Tire smoke clouded the street as he backed up to Deming. The Ford roared ahead again. Hank handed a full clip over the seat to Hymie who reloaded the pistol.

Angelo adjusted his rearview mirror and took a sharp left onto Clark Street. The Ford was coming up strong. A pair of streetcars offered a brief wedge to keep the guns quiet while Angelo swung in close to the moving trains. He reached for the pistol under his coat. In a blink, the sedan was muscling its way back to pass the coupe. The big car bore down on the Chevy and moved into position.

Just past Fullerton, George took a swipe at the Chevrolet. Angelo avoided the smack but was forced up close to the curb and a busy street-side market. A woman with a stroller dove to the sidewalk with her baby to avoid being hit by the racing cars. Two street patrol policemen hollered and waved their arms to warn the shopping crowds. One officer blew his whistle as the cars raced within an arm's length of the innocents. A man tossed his newspapers in the air as the cars sped past.

The fear of death swept over Angelo. His world moved in slow motion. He had the accelerator pressed to the floor, but it wasn't enough.

At Webster Avenue, a freight truck swung out onto Clark Street in a wide turn. Both cars slammed on the brakes to avoid a collision. While lost for a moment in the drifting haze, Angelo heard the gunfire. *Boom, boom, boom.*

Angelo feels the bullets rip through him in multiple places and his body erupted in a sea of burning wounds. Shock numbed his mind. From instinct, he put the car into gear once more and swung around next to the curb. At Ogden Avenue, he turned right and accelerated, weaving out of control along to the corner of Hudson. As he passed out, he drove the car into a streetlamp post. He was unconscious when the dark Ford pulled in alongside.

George wasn't content. He yelled, "Finish him, Hammer!"

Hank slid out of the car and pointed the nose of his automatic rifle through the open window directly at the slumped body of Angelo Genna. Hank closed his eyes and pulled the trigger. *Boom.* The gun rocked in his hands.

—— • ——

The air was thick, and the overcast summer sky had the look of a storm brewing. Vinnie had the local scoop. "I'm telling you, George, this is the place. All the remaining Genna brothers, Mike the Devil, along with Sam and Peter, all live right here on Taylor Street in this three-story."

"Well, how convenient for them. James Genna has the coffee shop three blocks from here next to their liquor warehouse and distillery. I understand their gang headquarters is down at Sam's Billiards about a mile away. They sure don't try to hide very well," George said.

Hank chimed in, "How can they have a distillery in the middle of Little Italy? George, wouldn't the cops or the Feds shut them down?"

George responded, "No, the Gennas have a license for making *industrial* alcohol. You know the denatured poisonous stuff they use for solvents and fuel. As you'd suspect, this same operation also makes the booze people want to drink. They pay off local police to get advance notifications when the Feds are coming in."

"Vinnie, let's keep the car parked back here out of sight and watch the brick palace for a while. If Mike's not around, we can go check their headquarters next." Hank was a patient man.

He swatted at a pair of flies buzzing around the inside of the windshield. "Why do these guys think they can just buy their way in with law enforcement, steal the business from other mobsters, and all the while live in plain sight without a care? They've got to know sooner or later, the grim reaper will come."

A dark sedan turned in along the Halstead cross street and came to a stop next to the house. George glared at the black Buick. "Hey, what's this?"

Hank put his newspaper aside and studied the car parked around the corner. "Who is it? There are two goons in the front seat, but it's hard to tell if anyone is in back."

The Buick driver gave two quick blasts with the car horn. Hank's patience was about to pay off. "Sounds like they're picking someone up."

A few moments later, the side house door opened. Mike Genna, the Devil himself, emerged, scanning the street as he walked toward the car. A man stepped from the back of the car and made room for him.

"Hey, the guy in the back is John Scalise. He's one of the beasts who drilled me when they attacked our liquor load." Hank reached for the rifle laying on the floor in the back.

"Hold on there, a second!" George ordered. "We're too far off to do this here. Let's get ahead of them by racing around the block. We'll whack this crew at the next intersection."

"Vinnie, you're the wheelman for a reason. Now get us up Morgan Street quick before they cross at Polk."

The car roared ahead. Hank chambered a shell in his rifle and snapped the action closed. "How you wanna do this, George?" Hank confirmed the magazine clip was full. "I say, if we can beat them to the intersection, cut them off with the car and bail out like bank robbers. They won't expect it. I'll focus on the front seat, and you tear into the back. Let's keep them pinned in the car and go straight at them!"

George confirmed, "Hank, you ready?"

"Yes, I am. I want them all gone including Scalise. The whole crew is rotten." Hank took a firm grip on his rifle. His jaw was set firm.

Vinnie rounded onto Morgan and buried the accelerator. The former race car driver smiled as the car responded to his demands.

"Vinnie, if, for some reason, we're late to the party at Polk Street, you'll have to cool it down and sneak in behind them to follow. But not too close," George said.

"Get your guns ready because we won't be late!" Vinnie never took his eyes off the street.

Scavenging pigeons flushed from the street, brushing just past the car's windshield. Vinnie never flinched.

As they neared the intersection, Vinnie could see a black sedan approaching from the right. He recognized the car Mike Genna was riding in. "Here they come, boys."

Vinnie had the advantage. As the Buick slowed for the intersection, Vinnie pulled the car right in to block their path. The doors flew open. George Moran bailed out on the left. The Hammer took the right. The windows were down on the Buick for the warm day. As Hank swung the rifle around his car door to shoot, a pair of drawn pistols emerged from the side window of the Buick and started to fire. *Boom, boom.*

Hank felt a piercing sting in his right leg as a shot hit home. As he dropped to the ground, he kept the trigger pulled on the automatic. He peeled off a round of shots.

On the other side of the Ford, George was hit, too. The Buick bounced up on the curb and forced its way past the assassins. Vinnie emptied his pistol and turned to help the two men in the back. He was worried about the Buick circling the block and coming back to attack them. He guessed they had one minute before all hell would break loose again.

Hank saw the bloody shirt sleeve from the corner of his eye. "George, how bad is it?"

"They got me in the arm. I'll live."

"How about you? You were down."

"They hit me in the leg." Hank pressed his hand over the wound. "It's bleeding a fair amount. I'll need to patch this up."

Vinnie interrupted, "We've gotta go, now! You want me to head straight to the office, or do you need the doctor?"

"Vinnie, take us to the doc," George said. "Hank, how many do you think we got?"

Hank was eyeing the street behind them. How could his worst enemies pass within a stone's throw, and still be alive? "I don't know, George. This wasn't the way we planned it. As I went down, my shots were out of control. I fell behind the car door and couldn't do much. By the time I got back to my knees, they tore out of there. It was over in seconds."

As Vinnie piloted the car out of Little Italy, George used his left hand to twist the cap off a small whiskey bottle he had placed between his knees. He dropped the cap and chugged down some booze. "I blasted into the open car windows a few times before they took out my shooting arm. I had to hit something!" Shaking the bottle in front of Hank. "Here, you want some?"

Hank took the whiskey and tried to reduce his pain.

As he listened to the two men, Vinnie lit a cigarette but didn't say more. He didn't want to admit, in all the excitement, his pistol shots only tore up the car's cowling.

——— • ———

Hank hobbled around the desk when Hymie brought in the evening edition newspapers. "Have you cripples seen this yet?" He held both papers in the air. "Apparently, we weren't the only ones after Mike Genna. The Devil is dead!"

Hank stopped and stood upright. "Really? Let me see one of those." He took a copy of the *Daily Tribune* and read the headline, "'Cop's Bullets Silence The Devil of Little Italy.'" It took a minute to sink in. He read on. "'A second Genna crime family leader is killed within three weeks during a violent gun battle that claimed the lives of two brave Chicago police officers.' How could this be?"

George poured over the *Chicago Daily News*. He was skeptical. "Wait a minute! You want me to believe the police happened to kill Mike Genna on the same day we shot him up? Either he was real unlucky, or the cops are trying to take credit for our hit! I bet Scalise and his scum buddy, Anselmi, shot it out with the cops and left Mike Genna's dead body at the scene. It left the cops with someone else to blame. To frost this cake, Anselmi and Scalise got themselves arrested on a streetcar afterward.

"Either way, there's one less Genna in our neighborhood now and the murder twins are behind bars for a while. These first two Gennas were the tough ones. The others might be easier to take care of," Hymie said.

——— • ———

George was nursing a tall drink. "I think Tony Genna might be *another devil* in disguise."

Hank didn't understand the statement. "You know Tony believes he's part of the upper class and doesn't like to get his hands dirty. How would we tease him into a gunfight?"

Hymie studied his partners in crime. George appeared a bit inebriated. Hymie was pleased with the addition of Hank to the team. In the short time they'd worked together, despite living a small life, Hank demonstrated an ability to see through emotion and make sound leadership decisions.

Hymie knew a different tactic was in order. "You won't tease Tony Genna into a gunfight like other mobsters. This hit must be arranged by somebody Tony already trusts. I know a guy in his inner circle named Nerome. Tony likes him, but the feeling isn't mutual. I think Nerome can be bought."

Hank looked down at his thick pant leg where the bandages were wrapped and shook his head. "Why would he do it, Hymie? If he's been part of the Genna Gang a long time, why would he turn on the new boss?"

Hymie nodded at the interesting question. Hank was trying to understand the traitor's motivations. "Nerome feels underappreciated for all the things he's done for the Gennas over the years. I've been trying to persuade him to work for us instead. He's angry with Tony, but he hasn't quite been ready to take matters into his own hands. Nerome's initiation to join the Northsiders could be to let us take down the man he despises. We can frost his cake a bit more with some financial persuasion, too. I'll bet he'll help us with a place and time to find Tony."

Hymie peered out the second-story window at State Street below. "I'll keep working this angle while you birds heal up." He turned and pointed at his partners. "You better get ready. Before we're finished, we're going to own this town."

George raised his glass. "Finally, we'll get the respect from Chicago we deserve!"

— • —

"Hi, Tony, it's Giuseppe Nerome. I know you can't talk about private matters on the telephone like this, so you can just listen to me if you like. I will do the talking. OK?"

"Sì." Tony was living understandably in a state of paranoia since the murders of his two brothers. He was anxious to hear what his trusted friend wanted to tell him.

"OK, first, I am so angry and saddened about the deaths of your brothers Angelo and Mike. The Northsiders are violent cruel men who will stop at nothing to destroy the Genna dynasty! We are all scared of their attacks. Are you afraid of these ruthless monsters, too?"

Tony's hand shook as he held on to the telephone earpiece. He nodded his head. "Sì."

"I have been thinking about this *guerra* with the Northsiders. I could help you plan an escape while we deal with them. Maybe you would like to go back to Sicily for a few weeks to spend time with the family."

For a moment, Tony's mind escaped to his homeland and the cousins he saw at his brothers' recent funerals. "Sì."

"OK, let's meet tomorrow to make plans. Do you know Cutilla's Wholesale Grocery at 1057 Grand Avenue? I am a friend of the owner, Charles. I'll meet you there in the morning at 10:30. Have a good night and try to get some sleep. Tomorrow things will look different."

— • —

In the morning, Tony Genna drove north on Aberdeen Street and parked his car near the Grand Avenue intersection. He sat for a moment and watched the street corner. It was quiet in the neighborhood. He checked his pocket watch. It was 10:28 a.m. He stepped from the car and followed the sidewalk to the grocery. As he rounded the corner, he saw Giuseppe approaching from the east. The two men walked toward each other.

Giuseppe extended his hand. "Tony, you found the market. I promise today will change your life forever." He gave Tony a firm handshake and pulled him in close. Not letting go of Tony's hand, Giuseppe spoke into the gangster's ear, "You ungrateful monster! You've never rewarded me once for all the blood work I've done for you. Where's my piece of the pie? Do you remember what they did to Dean O'Banion?"

Tony turned his head to stare directly into Giuseppe's eyes. He heard the sound of men approaching from behind, but Giuseppe wouldn't allow him to turn. He heard the unmistakable clicks of two gun safeties.

George and Hank drove their gun barrels direct into the back of Tony's suit coat as Giuseppe stepped off to the side. Hank closed his eyes as he pulled the trigger. The gun rocked in his hand. *Boom.* George kept firing as Tony's body slumped to the ground.

Giuseppe's face was pale. His eyes were wide as he stood facing the two shooters. Hank grabbed Giuseppe by the shoulder and pulled him away from the third Genna executed in less than a month. The three of them headed for the getaway car parked in the alleyway.

CHAPTER 20
Dogs

Rachel Hilson folded the section of the newspaper twice to get it to a size needed for the file folder lying on her desk. She tucked it away inside while she stared at the clock. Precisely at 11:30 a.m., the bell rang. She jumped to her feet, placed the folder under her right arm, and dashed for the stairs leading to the typing pool on the second floor.

The employees among the sea of desks were busy complying with the new rule. All customer documents were to be cleared away before leaving the work area. Evelyn Smith was stacking insurance forms and slipping them back into the green metal cabinets flanking the sides of her desk.

Rachel skidded to a stop next to Evelyn's chair. Her face was flushed. The cord from her telephone-operator headphones was dangling from the base of her neck like a pendulum on a grandfather clock. "You're still here, Evie."

Evelyn reached over and stopped the swinging pendulum. "Of course, Rachel, you know it takes a little longer now to clear things off before lunch. You look like you're in an awful hurry today. Do you still have time to eat with me?"

"Well sure, but first I want to show you something amazing I've spotted!" Rachel planted the vanilla folder down on top of the desk papers and flipped it open. "Will you look at this?" She pointed to an advertisement in the *Chicago Tribune* and read aloud from it. "The new Fairview Kennel Club track out in

Schiller Park has added electric lights and is now open for dog racing *six nights* a week!"

Evelyn smiled. She was tempted to tell her brash young friend this was another of her crazy excuses to get out and socialize with random men. But she could see in her eyes this was a serious invitation. "Rachel, as long as we've been hanging out together, you've never once mentioned *dog racing*. Isn't racing a man's sport?"

"Oh no, not at all! Not anymore. If men can do it, women can do it just the same. They are now calling dog racing the Sport of Queens. The gals on the first floor are bragging about how much fun this is. There's even a ladies' night on Wednesday when admission is free, and they have special contests with prizes for women. We've gotta go. It will be more fun than buying a new pair of dancing shoes. Come on. After all, isn't Wednesday a special someone's *birthday?*"

Evelyn stood up and placed her hands on her hips. She saw the devilish smirk in Rachel's eyes. "Oh no. I was hoping this year maybe you wouldn't cause a big sensation for my annual milestone."

"What, and miss out on all the fun? No way."

Evelyn didn't have another invitation to go out for her birthday, and it sounded interesting enough. "Tell me, *who exactly* has gone to see these dogs?"

Rachel was floating on air now. "First, can you get away on your birthday?"

Evelyn nodded with a mix of excitement and concern.

"Let's go find Claire and Millie in the cafeteria. They went last week and want to go again. They'll take us along. Besides, it's meant to be since your birthday falls on ladies' night. And guess what else is going on at the track?" Rachel barely took a breath. "They are giving away a real string of pearls. Not those imitation beads we've been wearing. Maybe we can score the prize."

It would be two excruciatingly long days before Rachel's wish came true. She spoiled a night's sleep tossing and turning while thinking about the adventure with the girls.

By morning, Rachel had it all figured out. During the work break, the women sat together in the cafeteria. "Ladies, to make the most of our evening tomorrow night, we should leave directly from work. Make arrangements and pack your glad rags along to the office in the morning, and we'll change right after our shift. We can catch the Maywood bus out to the Fairview Kennel Club. The flier says buses run all evening until the track closes up."

Claire was a self-appointed fashion queen. "OK, girls. This place is a blast. What are you thinking of wearing for our big night? We're young, and let's face it, we're pretty. We should cause a sensation!"

—— • ——

The snub-nosed bus rounded the corner leaving a swirl of blue haze along the street. Millie pointed at the rolling coach coming their way. "This must be it. This is our chariot to the track!"

The brakes on the green and white bus announced the stop with an ear-splitting screech. Evelyn covered her ears. "Is this thing even safe to ride in?"

"Hurry up, fussbudget." Rachel took Evelyn by the arm and scampered after Claire who was busy finding seats for them. Millie was in a party mood. She clutched a bag with a few secret gifts for the birthday girl.

For each traffic stop, the bus brakes made their noisy plea for maintenance and the girls laughed. The roads to Maywood were crowded with a mix of people heading out to the track and the local folks returning home from the day's work.

The bus delivered the race spectators directly to the ticket gateway.

Millie sipped a beer sample she snatched from the welcome booth on the way in the building. A tiny foam mustache covered her top lip. As she wiped the froth from her face, she raised her arm in the air for a second sample to rally the troops. "Come on, girls, they have a dart tournament going on in the refreshments area. Follow me. Who wants to try this beer?"

Evelyn stopped and looked the place over. Several young men in gray trousers and blue shirts led leashed dogs around a grassy paddock area near a row of kennels. To Evelyn, the dogs looked as thin as a gazelle she'd once seen in a moving picture show about Africa. Crisp red flags flipped back and forth in the breeze from atop the tall wooden poles encircling the track. The fences, grandstands, and outbuildings were gleaming white with a fresh coat of paint. The place had the feel of a new attraction. The alluring smells of popped corn and roasting peanuts drifted through the entrance.

Rachel broke the spell. "Come along, birthday girl. Let's try our hand at throwing darts. It's how we can win the string of pearls."

For a moment, Evelyn looked puzzled. "Do we have time for darts? Aren't we here to watch the dogs run?"

Rachel smirked. "You silly goose. You didn't read the newspaper I gave you? We have a couple of hours of free time first. We don't head up to the grandstands for the first race until 8:00 p.m."

Evelyn shrugged her shoulders and stood with her hands turned up. "Really? My bedtime is usually around 9:30."

Rachel stepped a bit closer to see if her friend was kidding.

Millie turned around and put an end to the nonsense. "Not tonight it isn't! You work too hard. It's time to let it all out! Besides, you can sleep on the bus ride home if you like."

The women found their way to the refreshments room.

Evelyn had the look of someone who'd been asked to jump in a cold lake. "I'm not a saloon girl. I've never played darts. Maybe I should just watch tonight."

Millie was undeterred. Handing Evelyn a wooden pencil, she took the first step. "Here, birthday girl, put your name on a contestant list tacked to the wall. You'll have plenty of time for some practice. Claire can show you how to throw them. I'm going to get some real drinks for us. OK, ladies, who wants whiskey?"

Claire observed the women warming up. "As far as I can see, none of these gals has ever thrown darts before."

Evelyn's face brightened. "Say, you're right. That pearl necklace is going home with one of these amateurs. Why not one of us? Let's get on the list. I see every table in here has practice darts anyone can use."

Rachel held her left arm out straight stiff in front of her and pointed at the round bright-colored board on the wall. She studied it for a couple of seconds then bent her elbow back with her hand pulled in next to her cheek. With great dispatch, she launched her arm forward and sent a dart hurtling toward its target. The brass-tipped dart peened off the wall bricks about six inches below the board. "Darn it! I can't seem to hit anything with these silly little darts, let alone be accurate enough to score points."

Clair collected the projectiles piled on the floor near the wall. She straightened the tip on one of the wounded darts. "Have you thought about closing your eyes when you throw?"

Rachel was shocked. "Wouldn't it be dangerous?"

"Well, maybe if we first spun you around in a circle with your eyes closed. But I don't think it would be any more dangerous than you already are."

Rachel was flabbergasted. With a red face, she fired back, "Why do we have to stand so far away from the board?"

Millie stepped in. "Do you wear glasses?" Long pause. "Never mind. Have you tried drinking?"

Rachel dropped the dart she held in her hand. "Does it help? I'll try anything."

Millie smirked. "That's the spirit. I often feel the room gets a little smaller after a couple of drinks. I have a glass of whiskey for you waiting on our table."

Rachel wanted to have some fun tonight. "Can I mix it?"

Millie frowned. "Of course, you can. But I thought you were a *tough* girl."

The sun had begun to settle in the western sky creating a reddish-orange amphitheater through the clouds. The evening air dampened. One by one, the big yellow floodlights hanging from the wooden flag poles flickered on over the track and seating area. The crowd, building in numbers, cheered like they'd just been given the gift of sight.

—— • ——

The girls missed the first dog race heat as the dart tournament ran long. Evelyn was still competing. While they watched, the girls enjoyed the cooler evening air. Claire stepped up next to Evelyn. "I know we're new friends, but I've already heard about you. I feel like I know you in some ways."

Evelyn squinted at Claire with a discerning look. Evelyn was a conscientious woman, and people's perceptions of her were important. "I find this a little odd. What exactly have you heard?"

Claire was a country girl at heart. She thumped Evelyn on the shoulder with the back of her hand. "Oh, don't get a bee in your bonnet or anything! It's your reputation at work. I've heard you're a good girl who sticks to the rules."

Evelyn smiled. "Well, I'm not always so careful. I'm here at the track with the seedy likes of you, aren't I? One could get a reputation hanging out in this crowd."

They laughed.

Claire twisted her fingers around the loose ends of her hair. "Yes, but I haven't seen you bet anything."

Evelyn was embarrassed by the comment. She didn't gamble and felt awkward about betting. "Well, I'm studying the racing dogs. They all look too skinny to me. How do you pick one?"

Claire smirked before she spoke. "Well, first before we settle on the dogs, I'm curious: Is there a fella in your life?"

Evelyn smiled at the unexpected change of subject. "Well, sort of. He's a neighbor, and I know he's sweet on me."

"What's his name?"

Evelyn looked down at her tan leather shoes. One of her toes was already scuffed. "It's Sid. His name is Sidney."

"Oh, Sidney sounds safe all right. Well, how did you pick *him*?"

Evelyn stopped and stared into Claire's intelligent eyes. "Do you want me to look for a dog who makes me laugh, smells good, and doesn't bite?"

Claire had finally met her match. "When it comes to the races, I don't think you'll get that close to them. How about choosing one by how they look, or if they have a swell name?"

"Claire, are you talking about men or dogs?"

Millie barged in. "Hey, did you get a look at those two gents over at the payout window?"

Rachel stopped halfway into sipping her whiskey. Her jaw dropped. She spun around, winked at Evelyn, and nodded her head twice in the direction of the men. "Which one do you fancy?"

Evelyn ignored the school-girl gestures.

Rachel wouldn't let it go. "Look at those two wealthy heartbreakers! Seems to me they need a couple of ladies to help them spend some of those winnings they are piling up. Evie, what do you say you and I pop over there and introduce ourselves?"

Without looking up, Evelyn responded with a cool demeanor. "You think we should introduce ourselves to those two slick pinstripers? I think not."

"Why do you call them pinstripers? They're not wearing suits and besides, it's your birthday. Don't you want to have some fun?"

"If you had a choice for a birthday present, would you introduce yourself to a pest?" Evelyn asked.

Rachel looked puzzled.

"The reason I think they're pinstripers is, first take a look at their shoes. They are wearing Italian leather shoes to a dog racing track. They both have slick-backed hair, pocket watches, and expensive trousers. These guys are either investors in the stock market or attorneys who keep the mob out of prison. Either way, I don't believe either of them has ever done an honest day's work."

Rachel was stunned. "How exactly did you get so much information on them while playing darts. You never even turned around to look at them."

"Oh, I noticed them milling around out front when we arrived. I sized them up while you were getting our race programs."

Rachel was stumped. She had never bothered to make such assumptions about people *before* she met them. It simply ruined the fun of it.

Evelyn kept on throwing darts.

Rachel started to snicker.

"What's come over you?

She thumped Evelyn on the shoulder. "Don't look now, but they're headed this way."

Evelyn rolled her eyes. "Great, I'm overjoyed."

The man with deep-set eyes and a dimple in his chin stepped close and introduced himself. "Hi, ladies. I'm Robert." Pointing to his partner, he said, "My friend here is Thomas. May I ask, what brings such fine-looking dames to a sinful place like this?"

Evelyn wasn't taking the bait. She shook her head as she spoke. "Dames? Is this how you try to impress women?"

Robert didn't expect a cool reception. "Whoa, pretty lady! No insult was intended. I'm more of an admirer."

Evelyn walked around the pair and looked them over. "Well, we've seen you two stacking up cash over there like a couple of bank robbers. I'm guessing you've been to this *sinful place* more than a time or two?"

Thomas looked at Robert and smiled. "Yes, you've caught us. We even got here early today to spend time watching the dogs do their warm-ups."

"So that is how you knew which dogs would be the fastest?" Millie asked.

Thomas smiled again. "Well, sort of. But you birds wouldn't understand the mathematics of odds, dog breeding, and betting stuff. You'd be best left to pretty dresses and fancy hats."

Evelyn could feel the heat rising from her neck. "All right, we didn't invite you to our party. You wandered over here because you are off your leash or something. Why don't you take your cash and fancy shoes and shuffle off somewhere? I recommend you try the dog kennels. It's clear you need a muzzle."

— • —

Evelyn planted three darts in a tight circle very near the center of the target. She rose to her tiptoes and clapped her hands.

"I can't believe it. What a luck you are! Obviously, you've got more experience than the average gal who showed up here tonight," her opponent, a red-haired tart named Rosie scoffed. "Well, I'm headed upstairs to watch the races now. Congratulations, you deserve it."

Between race heats, the public address system crackled to life. A male voice echoed out across the track. "Ladies and gentlemen, may I have your attention please for a special announcement? First, thank you all for coming to our inaugural ladies' night. By all measures, it's been a great success. We hope you're having fun. At this time, I'm pleased to announce the winner of the Maywood Kennel Club ladies-only dart tournament." He covered the microphone with his hand. "Step up here closer and take this chair, please." Rachel pushed Evelyn in near the announcer. He returned to broadcasting. "So, tell everyone dear, what's your name?"

Evelyn leaned down near the wide chrome microphone. "I'm Evelyn Smith, sir."

The announcer smiled. "So, Evelyn, I understand you beat out the other women in the tournament tonight even with amazing participation of over fifty competitors. Great job!"

"Wow, I didn't realize there were that many."

The announcer chuckled. "Now, I'm told your dart-throwing accuracy is remarkable. Can you share your secret to success and tell us how long you've been throwing darts? It appears you've been practicing a lot."

Evelyn hesitated and cleared her throat. "Sure, I guess I can answer your questions. Tonight was actually the first time I ever tried throwing darts. It turns out, it's quite easy."

The announcer laughed. "No kidding, so you're a natural at this? Would you share your secret for how you scored so high?"

Evelyn turned back and looked at Rachel who was watching from the rear of the announcer's booth. When Evelyn was ready, she leaned in close to the microphone again. "Well, I thought about someone I *dislike* and imagined their face on the dartboard each time I threw."

The announcer and people in the crowd broke into snickers. Rachel leaned back against the wall and covered her eyes. She couldn't help but marvel at her friend's unfiltered mouth.

The announcer continued, "This is precious! So, Evelyn, may I ask exactly *who* you imagined on your dartboard tonight?"

Evelyn hesitated. "Well, I'd rather not say."

People in the crowd fell out of the bleachers laughing.

After a few moments, the announcer regained his composure. "So, can you give us a hint? Is it maybe someone you work with or an acquaintance?"

Evelyn's face turned as red as a beet. The announcer slid the microphone right up to the table's edge. She finally blurted, "This *always* happens to me on my *birthday*! We go out for some fun and it turns into a public spectacle!"

Now, Rachel was blushing.

The announcer prodded, "How interesting. So, go on, tell us more."

"I could imagine my close friend Rachel on those dart boards tonight. You see, she often drags me out to meet people when I'd rather not. But no, tonight it wasn't her. It was a fella named Robert who strolled up to me and made me mad by bragging about how much he was winning on these races."

Evelyn reached down and took hold of the long flat jewelry box on the announcer's table. She raised it in the air with her right hand. "But now, I've shown him. Thanks to the Kennel Club, I've got a string of real pearls."

Applause and cheers swept across the grandstands. The announcer took back the mic. "Oh my, this is rich. There's even a bit of revenge in there. Folks, before we kick off the second heat tonight, how about we all stand and sing happy birthday to Evelyn."

As the crowd of over two thousand rose to their feet, turned toward the announcer's booth, and joined in the chorus, Evelyn shot up from the chair and swiveled to chase Rachel from the booth. On the way out the door, she reached up, took hold of a long strand of Rachel's brown hair, and gave it a sharp tug. Rachel spun around with her hand covering her mouth. Tears of laughter were rolling down both of her cheeks. As she snickered, she mumbled, "I deserve it! But, it's sooo worth it to take you out on your birthday."

"You've really done it this time, Rach."

As the women made their way back to rejoin their friends, some people wished Evelyn a happy birthday. A few asked to see the string of pearls. She was embarrassed about everyone knowing her name now. Near the refreshments area, the crowd was thick. She stepped around a group of people who were busy talking and without warning came face-to-face with Robert, the pinstriper. Once their eyes met, they both tried to look away.

Evelyn didn't know what to say after the tale she shared with everyone. As she tried to brush past him, the crowd pressed in, and she was pushed right into him. He jumped back a little. "So, now its public knowledge, you *really* don't like me?"

Evelyn took a deep breath. "Wasn't it clear when we first met?"

"Oh, quite clear. You seem to be a woman who knows how to speak her mind all right."

"Well, you sir, are *not* a gentleman, but a pompous fool."

"I prefer to think I know my place. Despite everything, I'm still willing to teach you a thing or two about betting if you like."

Evelyn leaned in and looked him straight in the eyes. "No, thank you. But I could offer to show *you* how to throw darts."

"How kind. You are quite clever."

Evelyn stared at the stubble emerging on his chin. "I would gladly take a position behind you."

"Why, because you know your place?"

"No, so I could use the back of your pants for a live target."

"Say, you're a sassy one."

They both smirked a little.

"The likes of which you'll *never* get to know."

"OK, I can see you're capable of holding your own in a debate. I haven't found this trait in many women."

The crowd was breaking up a bit now. "Our fun is over. I'm going to rejoin my friends. Good luck with your get-rich schemes."

He shook his head. "You are *always* a comic. Well, happy birthday. I do hope you enjoy your pearls."

———— • ————

Rachel stood up from the table and offered her friend a glass. "Evelyn, where have you been? I was worried the crowd mobbed you for your jewelry"

Evelyn placed the necklace box down on the table in front of the women and opened the cover. "Oh, while I avoided being robbed, I was forced to spend more time swapping insults with Robert, the famous pinstriper. He and I got tangled up together in the crowd. We had a good verbal dance."

"Did you come out with your dignity intact?" Rachel was having fun at her friend's expense. "Did anyone push your face in close to a microphone?"

Evelyn chuckled. "No, our debate came to a draw, but the people near us got a few good laughs once they realized we were the famous at-odds couple."

Millie patted a chair's seat. "Come, take a load off. We have some gifts to share with you."

Evelyn smiled at her friends. "Hey, you ladies didn't need to get me anything. Taking me along tonight was a gift. You know, I have to admit I never go out on the town unless I get dragged along."

Rachel set the presents on the table. Each was wrapped in brown store paper. "Don't worry about it. These are a few little things we thought you might like."

Evelyn tore the package open from Rachel first. It contained a tiny perfume bottle imported from France. "Oh, how thoughtful!" She loosened the cap and smelled the fragrance. "It's flowery and fantastic! Here, see for yourselves." She passed the bottle around so everyone could smell it.

Next, she opened a package with a pair of gloves and the other was a scarf.

Claire spoke up. "Those are from Millie and me. I know it's summer right now, but soon enough, the scarf will come in handy."

"Thank you both. These are nice." Evelyn was beaming. "Gosh, everyone, even with me embarrassing myself over the address system, I've had a great time tonight. Thank you all so much!"

Millie had to chime in. "Hold on now, we're not leaving quite yet. Finish your drinks because we have some dogs to cheer for!"

—— • ——

The line for placing bets on the race was a flurry of activity with people each scouring over the printed betting programs before stepping to the bookies' window. It didn't allow much time to sort through the hounds.

Evelyn liked the sound of the name Spooky. "What kind of dog ends up with a name like Spooky? I'm guessing he's skittish and runs like the wind. I'll take a chance on him."

Rachel settled on Tornado. Millie chose Salt Shaker. Claire placed her bet on Light Foot.

The public address system crackled back to life with an all too familiar male voice. "OK, ladies and gentlemen, we'll get things set up for the seventh. Place your bets now because the action is fast, and this night will wind down soon. We run nine races an evening and this is number seven. OK, the dogs are being loaded in the traps now. We'll cut off bets in about two minutes. Again, the bookies will be closing up shop for the seventh in about two minutes."

The girls scrambled into the stands to find a place to watch the excitement. Rachel pointed toward the track. "Let's take those seats down in front."

"Ladies and gentlemen, please take your seats. Keep your eyes peeled everyone; you don't want to miss the launch of the new *automatic rabbit*.

"All right, we've got ourselves a six-dog set up for you here in the seventh. In the number one spot, we have Quick Sand. This dog's a multi-race winner and always a favorite here at Fairview. In the number two trap is Tornado, who hails from a kennel in Oklahoma. They know how to train 'em in the Sooner state. Number three is Spooky, a blue-gray with long legs. Watch this blur of speed when in the mood for a hare snack.

"Number four is Bolt. This pup was named after lightning struck her kennel. She's been running fast ever since. At number five is Salt Shaker. He's a white heartbreaker from Utah. Ladies, keep an eye out for a strong finish late in the race. In the sixth and final position is Light Foot. She's worthy of her name due to her smaller size, but don't be fooled. She's won her weight in gold coins over the last two seasons."

The line judge circled the box and prepared the gate. He stepped off the track, raised his arm, and waived a green ribbon. The mechanical rabbit dropped on the rail, caught the drive, and lurched into high speed. As the rabbit zipped passed the dog traps, the gate flipped open and released the hounds. The announcer called, "Away they go folks with Light Foot taking an early lead."

The women jumped to their feet. Rachel fanned herself rapidly with a race program even though the evening was quite comfortable. Evelyn bumped her shoulder with her own. "You OK, dear?"

"Yes, I'm just excited. Wow, these dogs are crazy fast."

"As they sail through the first bend, the front pack is skinny with three hounds vying for number one. The rabbit's got no rest as Salt Shaker is hot on his heels, yes it's Salt Shaker with a two pooch lead," called the announcer.

Evelyn leaned over to Rachel. "You're right, these hounds are bred to fly."

"Now in the back straight, nipping at Salt Shaker's tail, are Bolt and Spooky. They are inching closer to a three-dog tie. Look at the speed! What's this? Like a shot, Light Foot slips around and takes to the outside. What's gotten into her? She's stretching out for all she's worth. Now, she's lapped them in grand fashion to take away the prize. This one's anybody's guess folks. What a race we've got!

"Oops, there's unrest in the second pack as Tornado and Quick Sand pull apart. Tornado is making a move right into the middle of the lead group. As they go into the final turn, the long legs are taking over. Yes, Tornado blasts the front pack like a bowling ball steaming through a set of pins. He's got the nerve to do it and the timing in the home stretch. In hot pursuit is Quick Sand. No one's leaving this dog behind. The money is on the line now, folks.

"Tornado and Light Foot are neck and neck now with the finish in sight. Tornado forges ahead as Light Foot tires. That's it. Wow, what a race finish! You've seen a good one!

"Here are the official results. The first dog in is Tornado. Second finisher is Light Foot. The third payout goes to Quick Sand. Congratulations to all our winners!"

Rachel jumped up and down clapping. She hugged Claire, who was also jumping up and down. "Yeah, I won!" She stopped for a moment, then started jumping again. "I mean, I can't believe we both won!"

Millie smiled at the beginner's luck. "All right, ladies. Let's go collect your winnings. The good news is, we're not done yet. There are two more races to go. We've got about twenty minutes to pick the next round of winners and have a quick drink."

CHAPTER 21

The Lake

Albert brought the pair of boats to Hubert Landing. He got them positioned along the dock for loading passengers and tied them off. The store was busy, too. He headed over to collect provisions needed for the lodge.

Tom saw him come in. "Hi, Albert. Sorry I couldn't meet you over at the dock. Go ahead and take the wagon to haul your things. I can collect it later. Good news! You have a few boat passengers today. It looks like summer has finally arrived."

Albert loaded the food and supplies into the wooden crates in the second boat. As he placed the empty wagon next to the landing, a young family with two small children walked down to the shore. The father asked, "Are you the one who brings people to the lodge?"

"Yes, my name is Albert. If you folks want to take a seat in the front boat, I'll add your bags to the other one before we head out. Please save me the middle bench for rowing." Albert set to work loading everything in place.

As he turned to untie the boat, a man loomed over him, startling the teenager. The sound of his deep voice took the boy's breath away. "Are you Albert?"

The blood drained from his face. Albert stood in the shadow of a dark-haired stranger wearing an expensive-looking suit, fancy shoes, and an out-of-place hat. After a considerable pause, Albert composed himself. He took a couple of steps forward, swallowed hard, and reached in the boat for a life vest.

"Here, put this on. There's room in the freight boat. My dad will want a word with you when we arrive at the lodge."

The stranger smiled at the young man who appeared to be all business. "I would expect him to, young man."

Perspiration soaked his shirt as Albert strained to row the loaded boat train across the lake. At the dock, he called for his father, then nodded toward the freight boat passenger.

Warren cringed at his son's rude treatment of a guest. Extending his hand, he said, "You must be Pastor Colbert. Welcome to Clark Lake Lodge. I'm Warren Johnson. It's a pleasure to meet you, sir. If I recall correctly, you are here for your niece's wedding on Saturday?" Warren turned and made a secret scowl at Albert.

The minister smiled. "Yes, you're correct, Warren. She asked me to perform the ceremony."

"Well, we are pleased to have you stay with us. This should be a fine week to spend in the shade along the lake."

CHAPTER 22

The Second Barn

It was January in Minnesota. As Hank departed the train, the bitter cold penetrated his Chicago overcoat. He began to doubt he'd chosen heavy enough clothes for the trip.

At the general store, despite Tom Swenson's prodding, Hank refused to cut across the ice of the frozen lake on foot. He imagined falling through into frigid dark water. For safety, he trudged the plowed roads to Clark Lake Lodge. To his surprise, the vigorous walk warmed him.

Hank's mission began by borrowing the family's Studebaker from Warren. He had the car's fuel topped off at the filling station in town before heading southward. The afternoon sky was overcast with a heavy winter gray. A brisk wind picked up loose snow from the ground and sent swirls of it across the roadway like small white tornados. Fifty miles into the eighty-mile trip, the weather changed. As he rounded a bend in the road, Hank noticed a haze in the air ahead. Driving toward it, fine white ice crystals began to bounce off the windshield with a sound like windblown sand. When the frozen mix turned to soft flakes like baby powder, it began to cling to the glass.

Before Hank knew it, the snow became so relentless it was hard to imagine the world beneath it. The windshield wipers were of no use. Hank leaned forward over the steering wheel to watch the roadway through the last of the windshield kept clear by the car's heater. The heavy automobile stayed faithfully straight in remnants of tire tracks still visible in the new snow ahead of him. Hank kept the handwritten map close by his side on the seat.

When he turned off the highway and headed west on County Road Seventeen, there were no more tracks to follow. Hank was alone on the rural road. He crept along for three or four miles while the wind created brief white-outs. In a small valley, he crossed an open bridge over an ice-covered stream and began watching for the grove of trees noted on his map. He stopped the car at a metal sign nailed to a tree. It was covered with a layer of ice and snow. He was unable to read it. He stepped from the car and walked to the tree to brush the sign off. In the early evening light, crude black painted letters announced the location of *Three Brothers Farm*. Directly beneath the name were the words, *Private Property—Keep Out!*

Hank returned to the car and took the driveway leading back into the rolling hills. As he crested a wooded rise, the outline of a red dairy barn came into sight to the right of the driveway. It was surrounded by a wooden fence corralling several black-and-white cows standing with powdery snow on their backs. He could see the yellow glint through the farmhouse windows coming into view on the left. He pulled the car in next to a tractor and grabbed his hat.

Hank knocked four times on the peeling paint of a farmhouse door. Through the white background of wind, he thought he heard some rustling noises coming from inside the house, but no one came to answer the door. Hank pulled his coat collar up and began to knock again. He heard the distinct click of a gun's hammer pulled back somewhere behind him.

A male voice boomed through the winter wind, "What's your business here, mister?"

Hank knew the man had the draw on him. There was no reason to reach for the holstered pistol under his coat. He raised his hands in the air and turned slowly toward the voice. A well-built man in coveralls and an unbuttoned red-and-black wool coat stared at Hank while holding a shouldered rifle.

"Whoa there, friend! I mean you no harm."

The armed man held his posture. "You're no friend of mine. Are you one of those *revenuers* from the government?"

Hank processed the question. "No, sir. I am not a Fed. I'm just a man who wants to talk business with you."

"You have no business here. We don't know you. You'll leave right now, or I'll be the new owner of the big car you brought here, and you'll be buried under a pile of cow manure."

Hank still had his hands raised in the air. "Would you wait a minute? I know your brother Walt. He's the one who invited me here."

The farmer lowered his rifle part way. "Walt? What's he got to do with this?"

"Well, if we could step inside out of the weather for a minute, I could tell you about my business. I'm looking to buy some quality whiskey."

The farmer raised the rifle again. "First, tell me how you know Walt."

Hank cleared his throat. "I ran into Walt this summer while he was delivering products up north in the lake country. I was staying in a cabin up there. I spoke to him one day when he was delivering to Clark Lake Lodge."

The man shook the rifle in front of Hank. "Mister, you are lying! We don't sell whiskey to Clark Lake Lodge."

"No, you don't, but I saw the wooden crates on the back of the truck when Walt was dropping off milk and cream. The tarp came loose as he was driving away."

"What a dumb kid! He's not careful, and now he's dragged a stranger here. Nobody comes here. I don't want any rumors going around about this farm. So, I'm going to prove you've got things wrong. You drove a long way here in the snow for nothing!"

The farmer grabbed Hank by the coat collar and poked the rifle into his ribs. "Come with me, I will show you our operation."

He marched Hank to the dairy barn and walked through the milking parlor to a room at the end of the building. While he held the rifle to Hank's chest, he pulled the lid off the tank. He shoved Hank's face over the tank opening. "What do you see in there? Does this look like whiskey to you?"

Hank was immersed in the sights and smells of a tank of whole milk with a cream layer floating on top. He took a half-step back from the tank. "No, sir. It sure doesn't."

He dragged Hank to a smaller white farm building located adjacent to the cattle yard. When he opened the door, chickens scattered from their roosts and clucked at the late-day disturbance. "Does this look like a *still* to you?"

Hank gave the same response. "No, sir. It sure doesn't."

"All right, mister. You've seen enough. Now get off this property before I put a bullet in the back of your head!"

Hank kept his hands raised in the air as the rifleman nudged him towards the car. Midway across the yard, the wind gusted and swept out of a spruce tree grove behind the hill, and a whiteout filled the air. With a nose as cold as an ice cube, Hank still detected a slight whiff of corn mash blowing on the wind.

Hank stopped moving. The gun's muzzle pushed hard against his back. He turned and faced the wind pouring out of the dark spruce trees. He directed a head nod toward the trees and shouted to his captor, "It's over there."

"What did you say to me?"

Hank spoke even louder. "The still. It's over there!"

The farmer stammered, "What are you talking about?

"I know a good corn mash when I smell one."

"Mister, you got a whiff of farm smell. We spread manure on those fields last week after we cleaned out the barn. You must be from the city or something."

Hank turned and walked toward the tree grove.

The man began yelling at him. "Get back here right now, or I will shoot you!"

Hank kept going with his hands in the air. "No, you won't! After all, I'm a *customer* who wants to know the quality you're selling."

Behind the house, Hank saw it—a packed path as wide as a man's shoulders and hard as ice in a winter storm. As he entered the grove with the armed guard on his tail, he saw the yellow glow of a swinging lantern coming at them.

The rifleman yelled into the wind, "Get back to the barn and lock the door!" Before he finished yelling into the darkness, his right foot slipped off the icy trail into the deep snow. He spun halfway around and fell to the ground. The rifle flew off into the virgin white powder.

The voice from behind the lantern light echoed, "What did you say?"

When Hank was within a stone's throw from the oncoming light, he spoke. "Walt, is that you?"

The lantern stopped swinging and raised in the air. "Yes, who's there?"

Hank kept moving to close the gap. "Hi, Walt. It's been a while. It's Hank Macklan. We spoke last summer at the Clark Lake Lodge a couple of times. You invited me to come here to see your whiskey operation."

There was a short pause. Walt shook the snow off his coat, buying time while he tried to recall an invitation. "Yes, Hank. I remember now. You sure picked a heck of an evening to come out here to the farm. Yeah, sure, come with me. The still is back over here in the second barn. On the other side of the trees used to be an old farm site. The place goes back many years, and when the farmhouse caved in, we kept the barn for distilling. It's out of sight in case the government men come knocking. Say, have you met my brother Frank yet?"

"Oh, I'm pretty sure he's on his way here now. It seems he doesn't trust me quite yet." Hank kept close to Walt whose lantern lit the path. "So, Walt, how long have you boys been making this stuff?"

Walt stomped his boots to knock the loose snow off. "Well, it all started when this new corn variety was developed for the north country. As you likely know, our long winters don't leave much of a growing season this far north in Minnesota. So, the university kept on trying to develop different varieties of corn until they hit one perfect for us. Some are calling this whiskey *Minnesota 13*. It's distilled twice before we age it in oak barrels."

Before long, Frank came marching through the snow. He was carrying the rifle again, but his hat was missing. "Walt, don't show this goon our still!"

"Frank, you stubborn mule. Please listen a minute. You don't know who Hank is yet. He's from Chicago. He sells a lot of beer and booze to the taverns down there, and he's got trucks available to haul the loads. If you don't shoot him first, Hank might become a customer for a bunch of our whiskey."

Frank stood still and blankly stared.

Hank smiled. "Have you got any inventory on hand? I'd like to taste it if I could."

"Yes, we do. Let's step through the doorway over there." Walt was proud of their product.

Once inside, Walt pointed toward the wall beyond the distillery room. A pair of metal rails on the floor disappeared under the base of a sliding door. Walt drew the door back and carried the lantern into the storage and bottling room. The yellow light revealed the other half of the barn, which had heavy timber storage racks twice the height of a man.

When Hank's eyes adjusted to the dim light, he counted barrels stored on their sides four high in the racks. "How do you move them around?"

"That's easy. After we fill them, we plug them tight and lay them on their sides to roll them on the rails into the storage room. From the original hay mound, we use an old pulley on a trolley with a large rope to sling them up into the racks," Walt said.

Hank gazed up toward the ceiling. "Amazing! You have more inventory than I've seen anywhere else."

"Our priest says it's not immoral to make whiskey. We've built a large inventory by putting all of our acres into corn and working some neighbor's farm ground, too."

Hank smiled at the comment about getting the priest's approval. "But is it any good?"

Walt grabbed a two-foot long piece of hollow vine stem from a shelf and turned down an aisle. "Let me show you. First, we start with water from a natural spring here on the property. It runs ice cold year round." He held the lantern close to the racks to look at marks on the barrel lids and kept moving along. At the third rack section, he stopped and tapped the vine on the end of a barrel. "Ah, here we are. This batch should be about ready." He waved his brother Frank closer. "Let's give old Hank here a sample, shall we?"

Walt and Frank worked a loaded barrel out from the low rack and rolled it around on its side before parking it. Walt pulled the stop loose on the barrel and inserted the hollow length of vine stem down into the liquid before he covered the top end of the vine with his thumb. He drew it out carefully and drained it into a pewter cup Frank had retrieved from a hook on the rack.

Frank offered the mug to Hank. "You'll be the first to taste this batch. We haven't sampled it yet."

Walt brought the lantern in close to show the product.

Hank swirled it around for inspection.

"We would, of course, filter it some before bottling," Frank added.

"This already looks great, even before it's purified." Hank brought the cup to his nose and inhaled the fragrance of the deep amber distillate. The fiery-sweet fragrance was almost intoxicating even before drinking it. Hank tipped the cup back and let the bourbon roll over his tongue before he swallowed it. The flavor was rich and smooth like some of the best top-shelf products he'd had.

Walt was as anxious as a new father. "So what do you think? Do you like it?"

Hank didn't want to tell them it was the best bourbon he'd ever tasted. He tried to keep his cool until they had a business deal in place. "It reminds me of some products coming down from Canada."

"But, would you like to buy some?" Frank was interested now, too.

"Yes, I'm interested in talking about it." Hank kept his voice neutral to avoid giving himself away.

Frank had his hands in his pockets and was kicking at the straw strewn around the barn floor. "How much could you take?"

"It depends on how much you have. If the price is right, I'd take everything you have in this barn." Hank stared into the darkness at the empty end of the barn. "Can you plant more acres next spring?"

Frank looked over at Walt and smiled. "Why don't we all head back to the house where it's warm and sit for a spell. Art, our older brother, will be back from town soon. He has a say in this, too. He'll need to meet you before we go further."

CHAPTER 23

Fish in a Barrel

A new storm was brewing in Chicago. Vincent Drucci challenged his comrade. "Why Hymie? Why now, after all this time and bloodshed? It's been almost two years."

Hymie rubbed his temples where another round of migraines was beginning to throb. "We want to attack them again because Torrio survived our hit, and we've *never* gotten justice for them killing Dean that way. Now they won't be expecting a hit anymore. Yes, we *almost* got Torrio." He glanced at George Moran. "And even though we shot him up bad, it wasn't enough. The slippery fox crawled away to eventually recover. Now, I hear he's living in New York. Some say he still steers the ship for Chicago operations with Capone as a front man."

Moran threw his cards down on the table. "We got a lot of skilled fellas. What do you have in mind?"

Hymie got up off the couch and made a slow lap around the room with his hands folded on top of his head. "I say we charge right into the bee's nest. Capone is a creature of habit. Everyone knows he runs the show from the Hawthorne Hotel. How can we catch him out in the open?"

Drucci shrugged his shoulders. "Capone's a hard guy to get to. You know he keeps an army of bodyguards with him at all times."

"It would have to be a surprise attack," Moran said. "Something he's not expecting at all. We'll get one chance. We need eyes on Capone to confirm he's there before we make a move."

———— ● ————

Across the river in the suburb of Cicero in a restaurant on the first level of the Hawthorne Hotel, Al Capone read the daily headlines in the Chicago Tribune. A lunch plate loaded with spaghetti and meatballs was placed in front of him.

He took one look at the plate. Unimpressed, he folded his newspaper closed one fold at a time, set it aside, and pushed the plate away.

The waiter stood near the table with a towel draped over his arm.

Capone turned with his hands hovering over the plate and glared at the waiter. "What's this junk supposed to be?"

Unsure of what to say, the waiter hesitated and then ventured, "It is our featured lunch today, sir. Is it not to your satisfaction?"

Al studied the waiter's face and read his name tag. "No, *Jimmy*, it is not to my satisfaction! Do you know who I am? I don't care about the daily lunch feature. I've based my business out of here the last two years. You could say I *own* the place. So, why would this happen to me *all of a sudden*? Is it because you're new and you don't know what your job is?"

The waiter did not speak.

"Like my family, I enjoy spaghetti today the same way they prepare it back in Italy. How many times do I need to tell the chef, he makes mine tossed with a walnut sauce and some cheese?"

Frank Rio, a trusted Capone bodyguard, sitting with his colleague Jack McGurn at the next table, rose to his feet. The waiter turned pale as cow's milk.

The mob boss raised his right hand off the table for a moment. Frank took his seat again.

Capone continued, "Do you understand what I'm saying? The chef makes a traditional walnut sauce for me because *I don't like tomatoes or meatballs on my pasta*!"

The haggard waiter removed the plate from the table and took a step back. He bowed slightly as he spoke. "Of course, sir. This is completely my mistake. I will take care of it right away."

Capone sneered. "OK, now get back there in the kitchen, and I don't want to see you again until my order is done right!"

The waiter didn't need to be told twice. The door slammed behind his hasty retreat.

Capone unfolded his newspaper once more and looked over at Rio and McGurn. "Jeez, where do we get these guys anyway?" He nodded in the direction of the kitchen. "When we're done here, send them both packing."

—— • ——

The eight dark Lincolns rumbled through the west side streets and the Little Village. They did not yield to other traffic. Vincent Drucci drove the lead car, accompanied by George Moran in the front seat and Hymie Weiss in the back. The cars were a rolling arsenal.

George swung his arm over the seat and turned to face Hymie. "It's like old times with Dean, eh?"

Hymie smiled. "Your boy confirms he's there right now?"

Moran nodded. "Yes, he's there having lunch."

"Curious, how did your boy get in to see him and get out without bullet holes in his back?" Hymie asked.

"It's the damnedest thing. Even though Capone's crews swarm the place every day, the restaurant is still open to outside diners. Maybe it's some sort of cover for them. So, we sent one of Hank's young guys in unarmed three days in a row to pick up some lunch orders. Today, he saw Capone seated in the back section along the right side. He's got guards with him," George said.

Vincent Drucci nodded. "Easy as shooting fish in a barrel?"

George raised his hands in the air. "Sure, lets clean them out!"

Hymie leaned forward over the driver's seat. "You clear on the plan, Vincent?"

"Yes, we're the decoy car. We'll roll up first, and you two light up the area with gunfire to clear off any thugs on the street and make them panic. The rest of our cars will hold back a block at Cicero Avenue. Once we tear out of there, our guys will be waiting for Capone and his thugs to come running out," Vincent said.

George added, "There's no way Capone is going to sit idle or hide inside when they get hit at headquarters."

Hymie agreed. "This should work."

———— • ————

The office was a hostile place. Hymie was fuming. "What the hell happened, Vincent? How did we miss Capone?"

Vincent closed his eyes. "The lead driver for the second group didn't wait long enough. The Outfit wasn't outside yet when our cars rolled up and started shooting."

George kicked an empty liquor crate sending it crashing into the wall. "Capone and his goons hit the floor or slid out the back during the bombardment. Our guys knocked out the windows and plastered the place with machine-gun fire, but they were spraying bullets around, not *aiming* at anyone in particular. It was as if they never used a full automatic before. They put a couple of people in the hospital. One didn't even work for the Outfit."

Hymie stood next to the table still as a statue. He shook his head at the newspaper displayed in front of him. "Not only are we the laughingstock of today's headlines, now we've poked a sleeping bear!"

———— • ————

Over in Cicero, Al Capone leaned on his desk with both hands. He looked at Frank and Jack seated across from him. "I don't get it. Someone, please tell me why these guys are still in business? We've cut the head off the organization, and it grew right back. What's keeping them going anyway? Now, they're even more dangerous and getting bold in broad daylight."

Frank Rio was a trusted advisor. "The ghost of Dean O'Banion seems to still be alive. I'm told, Weiss, was a close friend. He acts like his own brother died."

"They almost buried Torrio. He's lucky to be alive. Now they took a close swipe at me?" Capone slammed his fist into the hard wood. "Frank, if you hadn't shoved me down on the floor when you did, I'd have eaten lead for lunch! We have to tear down their organization. It starts at the top."

Capone's face turned sour. He tapped the city map on the table. "Weiss is dumb enough to use the same office as O'Banion did. Get whoever you need, set a trap for him, and make no mistake, Weiss is gone. Take care of it, boys."

CHAPTER 24

Checkmate

Making powerful friends was a key to survival in the Chicago bootlegging business. So, risky as it was, in October 1926, Earl Hymie Weiss, his attorney, the attorney's investigator, and two bodyguards settled in a courtroom to watch a jury selection. Weiss was determined to help his new ally Joe Saltis beat a murder charge. Hymie provided the money for Joe's defense, collected the juror's names and those of the witnesses. Hymie could create leverage to keep a new friend out of prison. Such was often the practice of the day. That afternoon, as the hearings came to an end, the men headed to the North Side's office above Schofield's floral shop to make their plans before the trial.

In typical Hymie fashion, he parked his Lincoln across the street from the office near Holy Name Cathedral. Fresh out of the court room, his mind was preoccupied with how they would sanitize the witness testimony and sway the jury members. Everyone had a price. He would work out those details once the attorney and his investigator were on their way. The other men parked along Superior Street and headed across State Street toward the office. As was typical, Hymie was fearlessly in the lead.

As they neared Schofield's Floral Shop, the creak of a second-floor window being raised in the rooming house next door might have been the only warning. It would be odd, on a cool October day, for residents to open a window. At that moment, Hymie faced the business end of Jack McGurn's submachine gun as it trained on him from no more than fifty feet away. McGurn was Capone's right-hand for delivering retribution. It was far too late to even draw a pistol or try to run back across the street. In an instant, forty-five caliber bullets rained down on Hymie. *Boom, boom, boom.* He slumped on the sidewalk in the afternoon shadows of the same floral shop where his friend Dean O'Banion was slain.

—— • ——

With Vincent Drucci taken down at the hands of police during the struggle to re-elect William Thompson as mayor, George Moran was next in line to lead the North Side Gang. Under Mayor Thompson, Chicago reopened for mob businesses like gambling and racketeering with the police caught between free-wheeling mobs and city officials who were paid to look the other way.

Capone now had a lopsided share of the booze business. He was raking in millions and strutting around in public like Chicago's unofficial king.

It infuriated Moran.

CHAPTER 25

How Much?

George met Hank at Clay Street. It was Christmas week 1926. Hank greeted him at the door. "Morning, George. The boys told me you were here. What's the occasion?" Hank glanced around to see if the boys left things in fair order. "Do you want some coffee or bourbon to start the day?"

George surveyed the room. There was a tattered map on the wall, a heap of gambling tickets stacked on a small table, and two rifles leaning in a corner. "No, I'm all right. So, what's going on with you today?"

Hank sensed there was a specific purpose for the visit.

"Nothing big. We've got a run coming in from Detroit, but the boys have it under control. We are working on a shot-up car over at the warehouse, and I was going to see a guy about a new gambling option. It turns out people like to bet on baseball and team sports."

"OK, I want to go someplace quiet where we can talk. Hank, can I tear you away for a while?"

Hank could clear his schedule with ease. "Yes, sure. You wanna step into my office? It's pretty quiet back there."

George had a different type of conversation in mind. "No, I'd rather get out and stretch our legs. Let's head downtown."

"All right by me. I'll grab my coat."

George lingered near the door. "I'm parked out front, so jump in and you can ride along. Have you ever been to the Tribune Tower?"

Hank thought for a moment. "You want us to go talk to the newspapers?"

"No, you've got this all wrong. I have an idea and want a quiet place to discuss things with you."

"OK, boss, whatever you say."

Hank whistled as they parked the car on Michigan Avenue. The skyscraper towered over them. "She's a real beauty."

George agreed. "Around here, this is the tallest mountain we can climb."

The elevator chimed its way to the observation level on the twenty-fifth floor. "You ever been up here, Hank?"

"No, I can't say I have." Hank made his way through the glass door out to the deck. He stood there admiring the castle-like stonework encircling the building. He rested his elbows on the concrete perimeter railing. "This is quite a place. You have a view of the whole world from up here."

Hank paused a moment. "Say, you aren't thinking of throwing me off the building or anything are ya?"

"No, is there some reason I should?"

"As you know in our business, we don't invite people to the top of tall skyscrapers unless there's a purpose."

George smirked at the statement. "It's just a fine day to take a look around from up here."

The men gazed at the city sprawled out beyond the concrete railing.

"The streets below us are pretty tiny from up here and the river looks a little different," Hank said. "I mean, the way it snakes through the city. Look at all those freight boats. I had no idea so many companies were moving their crates on the water. I guess it beats the street traffic. Do you think it could help us sneak liquor in?"

"There's more than streets and rivers I'm looking at. Let's grab a chair for a minute." George walked to a couple of chairs set against the building and took a seat.

Hank followed and propped his foot against the side of a copper pipe.

George wasn't one to mince words. "Hank, how is *life in the shadows* for you?"

Hank's brow furrowed at the question. He thought about his role of directing the small crew of booze runners.

George slid his hat off his head and perched it on his knee. He ran his hands through the sides of his hair and interlaced his fingers together at the back of his head. He leaned his chair back on two legs and looked at Hank. "I mean, it's clear to me you are a natural leader. You do a better job of this than any crew boss I've worked with. As a result, your men are loyal. They do what you ask. And you all trust each other."

"Yes." Hank tapped his chest through his open coat. "I like things this way."

George believed he was about to state the obvious. "Do you realize it's unheard of in this business?"

Hank was a calm port in any storm. When things got tough, he remained objective and tried never to let his emotions take over. He believed everyone made mistakes from time to time. Everyone. But he also believed what a person did next determined the level of respect the men had for you.

"Yes, but don't tell anyone. I don't want people to think I'm soft or something."

George shook his head and chuckled.

"Serious question. Let's talk about what *you* want." George rose from his chair, donned his hat again, and Hank followed him to the railing.

George pointed toward the horizon. "Look out there. This is a big city now, and it's getting bigger every day. I read in the papers this week we have three million people living here now."

Hank nodded. "Sure, even since I've been around, the suburbs have grown and grown."

George wanted clarity from his rising star. "While we've got a nice chunk of business to the north, west following Lake Street out toward Union Park belonged to the Genna boys. Being the good neighbors like we are, you know what's left of them has been scattered to the wind now."

Like a black-and-white photo, Hank could still see Tony Genna's body crumpled on the sidewalk the day they took him out. Tony's fancy coat and cordovan leather shoes were spattered with blood.

"Moving a bit to the south, the Druggan Gang has a chunk." George made a slow swing with his arm toward the left. "Terry Druggan and Frankie Lake are a mix of Irish and German. They work out of the back of the Little Bohemia Café. They have direct connections and substantial ownership in beer breweries. Rumor has it, they make so much beer they are selling barrels to other gangs."

Hank stared out over the suburbs in the distance. The number of criminal-owned businesses never ceased to amaze him.

"Everything from there to the southwest out toward Bridgeport and Brighton Park along with a slice along the lake, Torrio has now handed off to Capone," George continued.

Hank's eyes widened.

"Hank, we can never take our eyes off him. That scum had O'Banion and Weiss executed, and you know he has his sights set on me, too. None of us can be too careful." George's forehead showed the wrinkles of a man who lived with limited sleep.

Hank closed his eyes and made no reply. In his mind, he could still see the swarms of people dressed in black at the graveyard for Weiss's burial service.

George was close to finishing his view of the gangland. "The Southside O'Donnells have a solid 40% share of Chicago. But they are at war down there now, especially beyond the Union stockyards. They've had many loads of beer stolen. What's worse is they force saloon keepers to buy from them exclusively. If they won't buy, they'll bust up the joint along with the owner himself. They inflict excessive harshness, but if you want to run a saloon on the southside, you do business with the O'Donnells, period. Now, when their beer gets hijacked, those saloons are between a rock and a hard place, but they wouldn't dare think of bringing in other stock."

Hank smiled politely but wondered if George was becoming greedy or was pushing to get Hank out of his hair.

"There are a half dozen other gangs spread around the city, too, but they're smaller. At some point, the big guys will get tired of letting them have a share," George continued.

Hank looked at the gray afternoon sky. The sun was hiding from the winter snows decorating the edges of streets and sidewalks.

"I don't mean to push you into a corner on this. But, Hank, how much do you want?"

A cool breeze raced up the face of the building. It was a bit unnerving for Hank as this conversation signaled a change in George. The deaths of the North Side leaders weighed on George. It was understandable. He was, however, the last survivor.

"Excuse me, George. What did you say?"

George repeated his question. "I want to know, Hank. How much of this city do *you* want? Should you and I divide this kingdom up?" He said it with a twist of generosity. "Are you tired of working for someone else yet?"

Hank bristled at the thought. Countless men had already died defending the small corner of the world they claimed now. The notion the Northsiders would go to war to take over the whole city seemed absurd.

George leaned in closer and half-whispered in Hank's ear, "What do you consider winning?"

Hank believed he and George held vastly different views. "What is *winning*, George? Is it a pile of money, owning lots of businesses, or some other riches? How about running a big area like the whole west side?" Hank withdrew and turned from the spanning city beneath them. He stood staring at the ornamental masonry that crowned the building. "My question is, *how much is enough*? Every man has to ask himself the question at some point. We live in a world of plenty right now, but this won't last. Look at O'Banion and Weiss. What good did it do them? The same can be said about my father and my brother. Some say my mother was a victim, too. And who's next? To me, *survival* is winning!"

He looked out over the city once more. "I know, I could build a huge crew, and we could take on the Druggan Gang, Capone, and a bunch of others. It would take many men and an ocean of bloodshed at my hand. How many would be killed on both sides in the process? To grab a big stake in this city, hundreds of men would die. Maybe more. I won't be a monster. The thought of it torments me. I couldn't live with myself."

Hank thought about Allen and Rem who had survived the ambush gun battle. "No, I don't think my guys are expendable. I handpick each one of them and work to teach them the business, including how to protect themselves. I make sure they have the skills to survive and get their fair share."

George had not found the same success. "So you treat them like family members?"

"How else would I treat them? My father made a real mark on me before he died. In some ways, I'm a reflection of him. To be in my gang, you must be somewhat like me. Respect and trust are things you earn."

"I generally don't get that close to most of our men. I don't think about these things the way you do, but I can see why you do it."

Hank rose and put his hands in his coat pockets. "I could be bitter about the life I was dealt." He began to pace the deck area. "Let's face it, my family was murdered. But I won't let anger or vengeance define me. I step back, try to learn from it, and channel the energy to become smarter. I believe there has to be a better way, or my father taught me nothing. This hellish goldmine is temporary. Either you die trying to play the game carelessly, or if you last long enough, the government men step in and shut things down. The only way to win is to get out alive. All those flowers you see at the gangster funerals are a sad reminder of the fact you can't take it with you when you're dead."

Hank tore into the heart of the matter. "George, I know I have the stuff to be a mob boss. I believe I could be a great boss and probably a very rich one. But I like the *number two* spot. At least the way you run the business I like it.

"You give me freedom and a say in how we run things. We won't do contract killing. We won't exploit women. I don't understand men who do. We don't sell poisoned liquor. So, if I'm proud of what we sell and how we sell it, why would I ever leave all this to go out on my own?"

George found Hank to be more complex and intentional than O'Banion and Weiss had been. Hank calculated his moves and considered risks. George liked his methods a lot. He had to admit, he didn't do as well himself.

— • —

For a few moments, the winter sun pierced the veil of gray clouds shrouding the sky. The slivers of light streamed down on the men. Hank realized the value of his situation for the Northsiders. "So, I teach each guy to have the best chance of survival. This is my mission. No, I don't mind being number two. I think it's the smartest place for me to be. No, I don't want my own slice of Chicago. I'm happy keeping the heat off your back, keeping the business running, and leading these guys. The attorneys we pay can help keep you on the right side of the prison bars."

"I can see why your men like you." George kicked at the base of the masonry wall. "Hank, you are an interesting guy. You're a combination of part parent, part teacher, and at the same time, one of the most lethal mobsters I've ever seen. I'm glad you are on my side. I don't know exactly how I'd fare if the two of us ever got turned against each other. We could have been great partners, but I'm all right if you just keep running your crew for me."

The gray winter sky obscured the sun once more, and the wind spirited around the observation deck, leaving a funnel of light snow taking refuge in the corners. "George, let's step inside for a minute."

George followed Hank through the framed glass door and into the building. Warm air pouring from the cast iron radiators greeted them with welcome comfort. "Yes, it's much better in here."

Hank removed his hat. "George, I have the same questions for you."

"Oh, what is it you want to know?"

Hank circled around two chairs set near a large, framed oil painting hanging on the wall. George settled in and studied the battlefield portrait of Ulysses S. Grant depicted on horseback during the Civil War.

"You've been at this a while and seen many good men fall in the booze battle."

George nodded.

"So, you've asked me what I want, and I'd like to hear your response to the same question. So, how much is enough for George Moran?"

George shook his head side to side. "Hank, I don't think like you. You've gotta understand some things. I grew up hundreds of miles from here with a father I didn't agree with or like much at all. He was a real hard nose. He didn't understand me or my way of thinking. My mother, on the other hand, was always quiet and spent her time in church praying for my father and me to stop fighting. Maybe her prayers were answered when I became a teenager because I got out on my own and got free from my dad.

"Once I made it to Chicago, I learned about crime as a *business*. I got my education from the school of hard knocks. Sometimes, I spent more time behind bars than on the outside of jail, but I learned. Today, I keep friends on the payroll in the courtroom, police department, and city hall. I see it as business insurance.

"As far as how much is enough for me?" His mouth pursed together like he was about to spit. The anger began to show on his forehead in the form of bulges and valleys. "Dean and Hymie were *my closest friends.* Capone deserves to die for them! He deserves to die, period. I won't rest until I inflict all kinds of bad on Capone. If I can't get him, I will take his business, I will get the men important to him, and I will ruin his reputation bit by bit. He struts around Chicago like the sole rooster in a chicken coop. He needs to learn he doesn't own this town!"

Even though the plan was soaked with danger, Hank knew better than to question the sanity of George Moran for getting even with Capone. To Hank, George was mired in pride, envy, and handing down judgment on a dangerous enemy. "George, what's your life worth?"

The other man studied Hank's face. "Blood doesn't scare me anymore. I got over it a long time ago. People don't recognize this as a war, because many of them die before they get the chance. As far as I'm concerned, hell's gates opened on January 1, 1920. Some people rushed in to be the first ones. Others, like me, stood back and watched for a while. Now is a much better time to clean up."

George paced back and forth. "I won't be a poor man. No, I will get my share and then some. We've never seen anything like this before. The mayor and the cops are willing to look the other way for few bucks while we do this business in broad daylight. The profit on booze is turning some regular men into Rockefellers.

"If we can't make a fortune now, when will we? Hank, I'm determined to make a pile of money before this is over. They talk about repealing the amendment in a few years. Not because gangsters are getting rich, but because the government is missing out on taxes from the whole liquor industry. But they're no better than us! They want their greedy hands in the booze business. What does liquor have to do with running a country?"

———— • ————

Later that afternoon, Hank walked the narrow alley and kicked aside a couple of empty glass bottles. He admired the new electric power lines webbing back and forth between the buildings like a giant spider was at work. At the second building, he stopped at a gray windowless metal door and knocked three times. He stood in silence and checked his pocket watch. He was sure they were here and rapped on the door again with more intensity. After a long pause, the bolt mechanism behind the door clicked back. Without fanfare, the door opened enough for a dark-haired bartender sporting a waxed mustache to poke his head out. "Sorry, we don't take deliveries until 4:00 p.m. You'll have to come back later."

As the door was swinging shut, Hank hurried his response. "Hey, wait a minute, Sully! It's me."

The door reopened, and a surprised J.T. O'Sullivan emerged. "Hank, I didn't recognize you. Sorry about that."

"No problem, Sully. It's been a long time. I'm glad to see you, old pal. Would you mind if I practice a while this afternoon?"

Sully smiled, causing the ends of his mustache to curl up on both sides. "Sure, Hank, of course. We're cleaning up now and doing some bookkeeping in the office. The place is yours."

The two men stepped inside. Sully secured the door and turned to his guest. "So Hank, when are you going to play for our patrons again? You know people love to hear your smooth turns and rhythms. You can show off solo or appear with the band we have lined up."

Hank rubbed his chin. "Yeah, I might think about performing again. Right now, my nights are a little busy. But sometime soon. I promise." He made his way to the familiar stage.

Hank eased the saxophone case open. He removed the instrument and buffed it with a cloth. He inserted a new reed and adjusted the strap. After lowering the case cover, he snapped the brass buckles down and put it aside. Hank took his place on the wooden stool set near the front of the stage.

He wrapped his lips around the mouthpiece, closed his eyes, and blew a long, slow, wavering tone. With the place empty of customers, the sound reverberated off the walls like an echo in a canyon. His mind kept mulling over the question George had posed. "How much do *you* want?" He took in another long deep breath and began to blow through the instrument while his fingers toggled the bell keys. His head twisted side to side as he lost himself in another world.

The bartender nudged the waitress, who was busy cleaning glasses for the expected evening crowd. He nodded toward the solo performer on the stage. "I've missed his sound. He's one of the best!"

She looked up from her work. "Yes, but I think it sounds sort of sad. What do you suppose he's thinking about?"

Sully stopped to watch Hank. "Sometimes he plays like someone who lost people dear to him. "

The barmaid nodded. "Haven't we all? This guy doesn't play music. It sounds like he's pouring out his emotions."

"Some people can't get enough of him. They come for his smooth music but find themselves swept away in their feelings."

The woman's face changed when she recognized him. Her mouth fell open slightly. "Hey, isn't he one of the notorious ones from our side of town?"

The bar owner turned and faced her straight away. "Yes. It's the reason he's reluctant to ever sign on for a regular gig."

CHAPTER 26

Matches

"Hello, George."

"Who is this?"

"You don't know me yet and for now I'd prefer to keep it that way. I'm a friend of Hank."

"Ok, what do you want?"

"Hank asked me to call you about the growing concern you have on the west side of town with Capone's dog track."

George mumbled, "Yes, that place drives me mad."

"I can help with that sort of thing. Think of me as a spook who can slip in and get things done quietly."

George took a moment to collect his thoughts. "I don't like this arrangement, but if you know Hank, I may be interested."

"I owe Hank a favor or two, so I did some digging. I found out your wished-he-was-dead enemy, Capone, has a nasty fight going on over in Kane County with that stickler state attorney, Mr. Carbury. It turns out Carbury is a real pickle. Did you know, he fooled the public and got elected even though he never actually went to law school?"

"Oh, really? So, the state attorney is a crook."

"Maybe. First thing when he got in office, he began raiding speakeasies in the city of Elgin and across the county. He says he ran for state attorney to reform and clean up the garbage. Now, he's arrested hundreds of owners and patrons."

George shook his head while talking on the phone. "If he's a crook, chances are he can be bought."

"No, that's the weird thing. He's made it clear he can't be bought. He refused a meeting with Capone last week and fired the sheriff's deputy who proposed it. Now, he has lawmen hanging all over the Elgin dog track that Capone runs. No one can bet a thing on the greyhounds."

George gasped. "I'm glad our track is in Cook County! We haven't seen anything like that. I'm surprised Mr. Carbury hasn't had an unfortunate accident or something. He must keep himself surrounded by police guards at all times."

"You guessed it. It's *killing* Capone's business right now."

George wanted to put this race track out of business. "Maybe we can join forces with Carbury because, more than once, Capone has brought this race-track back from things like this. I want to be sure they stay closed this time. This is a perfect opportunity to *light a fuse* if you know what I mean."

There was a pause on the line with only the crackle of static.

"Friend, are you still there?"

"Yes George, my advice would be to be careful with that. I don't think you should blow up the place. While it would be quick and easy, in the end, it would look like an attack. That could come back on you."

George tapped his fingers on the phone box. "Can you make it look like Capone is trying to do an insurance swindle with *a fire of convenience*?"

"If you could pull that off, it would destroy the track and put the fire marshal on his heels. He'll wriggle around the claim eventually because half of the local governments are on his payroll. George laughed. "But it will tie him up a while and cost him some dough."

"I like this idea better. I've got a couple of guys who are good at using matches and covering their own tracks."

George gave the approval, "Go ahead. Let's turn up the heat."

—— • ——

Just after 1:00 a.m. on the otherwise quiet night, the oval racetrack and grand-stands stood in hibernation. The greyhounds were secured in the kennel while patrons and staff were home for the evening. The clouds parted, showing the thin sliver of the moon over two men, each carrying a burlap bag and an oil can. With no resistance from the sleeping night watchman, they picked their way around to the staff entrance. With a simple separation of the door latch, they made their way inside Capone's 102 Ranch. Like the wind, they swirled through the belly of the great building's structure setting their incriminating arson time bombs, each with a fuse long enough to allow safe exit. When the stage was set, they made a final pass through the building with a box of matches.

They had safely cleared the perimeter fence before the first flames burst into the night sky. The watchman, stirred from his slumber by the crack of fire and sudden light, raced to the kennel building, screaming to wake the dog own-ers and release their stables of prized hounds.

—— • ——

Over in Cicero at the Capone headquarters, the phone rang. "Hello, this is Jack McGurn. Who's calling?"

Jack nodded in agreement to what was said on the line. "Yes, Al is certain they are responsible for what happened at Elgin. Our job is to take an eye for an eye. If we lost our dog track, so should they!"

"No, we can't take the train tonight, there could be witnesses." Jack paced with the phone receiver like a dog tied on a leash. "No, I don't want to take a cab either. You know, I've heard the latest rage is mobsters tossing lit dynamite into your cab when you get stopped in traffic. What a nasty trick!"

"No, we need a car. Besides, it will take several cans of gasoline to do this right." Jack twisted the end of the cigar in his upper coat pocket. "Moran's dogs don't run races after 9:00 p.m. If we go out around midnight, we'll have the place to ourselves. I'll stop by to pick you and the others up about 11:30." Click.

———— • ————

As if in anticipation of what was about to occur, the Fairview Kennel Club stood silent on that April night. Gone were the money-wielding patrons, bookies, jazz bands, liquor, and greyhounds. Gone also was the excitement, the thrill, and the speed of the chase.

Four men, uninvited and armed with fuel and flame, moved with a hush through the property, drenching the bones of the wood buildings before incinerating the dreams of the future.

CHAPTER 27

The Trap

Father Whelan just finished Wednesday evening confession. As he locked up the doors for the night and turned off the sanctuary lights, he noticed the light coming from the clergy study room. He couldn't remember leaving the light on.

He worked his way through the church and eased the door open to the room. Hank sat at the desk working with a pencil and paper. The priest's heart pounded. He exhaled at the sight of the familiar face. "Henry, it's you. It's been a while. I've been worried about you with all the violence going on in the city."

Hank nodded.

"Are you here for confession?"

He stopped scribbling on the page and turned and gave Father Whelan a stare of disbelief. "No, I didn't come to use the confessional."

"OK, maybe we could talk for a while." The priest turned a chair around and slid it in alongside the desk. "Let's see what you are drawing today. That looks like a cemetery with people mourning at a gravesite. Are you thinking about your father or possibly Hymie Weiss?"

Hank placed the pencil down on the table.

"Henry, your sketch intrigues me, but before we discuss it, have you heard the increasing talk they might repeal prohibition?"

"Sure, Father. They've been yapping about this the whole time. Like an old dog who can't get off the porch anymore, they keep barking." Hank lifted a hand in the air. "No, I'll believe it when I see it. The government has lost control. Bootleggers are making piles of cash. It would take a war with the Feds to make them stop now because most cops around here are lining their pockets, too."

Father Whelan didn't agree, but he respected Henry's strong opinions.

Hank twisted in his chair and tidied the wrinkles in the tablecloth until he felt the courage to speak. "Father, the reason I came here today is I believe I'm seeing ghosts."

The holy man removed his smudge-laden glasses and used a corner of the tablecloth to buff the lenses. He squinted at his guest. With a serious tone, he probed, "Do you mean the *spiritual kind*, like angels or maybe those who have died before us?"

"No, I mean I think I might be imagining things that don't happen at all. It's like every crime I witness or am a part of, I see those demon twins showing up to murder people. Yet, I can never catch them. They seem to vanish! Am I going crazy?"

Father Whelan closed his eyes and raked his fingers back through his wavy hair. "Henry, are you the single witness to these crimes?"

Hank considered his plight. After thinking, he shook his head. "No, I guess there have been a few times when I wasn't the only one who saw them. Like after the Mike Genna murder, the Murder Twins were even arrested, so I know they were real."

Father Whelan poured two glasses of wine. He handed one to Henry. "Are these monsters trying to beat you at the same games or still trying to get revenge for you helping to send them to jail?"

Hank began to speak and then stopped abruptly. He took a moment to think. "Uh, both, I guess."

——— • ———

Once a commercial hub for barge shipments, the massive gray warehouse complex stood abandoned on the industrial grounds along the river. Weeds had reclaimed the land, and the building lacked several windows lost in storms past. Pigeons had become the rightful owners, roosting freely among the open rafters.

There were rumors freight trucks were once again using the long-dormant buildings. Capone's crew began to watch the place. Suspicions were right that the Northsiders had made it an impromptu transfer hub for liquor.

Hank, a nervous hawk, insisted a man be posted at each end of the building when convoys were offloaded for the runners.

He pulled his sedan inside the west end and parked next to a stack of wooden crates. He opened the trunk of his car and retrieved two fat oatmeal-colored bags of cash for the payment. He and Nick met the two truck drivers to verify their loads parked inside the building.

Gunshots rang out at the east end of the warehouse. "Oh, crap! That's Willy." Hank swung the cash bags back into the trunk and slammed the lid. In the field beyond the warehouse, three distant shots rang out. The drivers looked panicked. Keeping his voice low, Hank started giving orders. "Someone is trying to poison our well. Throw the tarps back over the loads and move these trucks out the west end right now. There's no time to unload. We've gotta move while we still can."

Carlo ran in from the west door. While he hunched over with his hands on his knees puffing, he began to spill it. "Boss, vehicles are coming in from both sides now." He took in a few more breaths. "The west end is no good. There are men parked on the high ground in the field with rifles."

Two members from the Capone gang soaked rags with gasoline from a mason jar and lit the material with a match. They got to a pile of wood timbers and set a fire to flush out the Northsiders.

When he saw the flames rising, Hank warned his men. "Keep low to the ground and crawl to the nearest door or window for an escape. This place is going to burn to the ground!"

Within minutes, the fire spread to the two freight trucks they were about to unload. Thick black smoke began to pour off the burning truck tires. As the gun battle waged on, parts of the building's center roof gave way, falling in a series of collapses. The flames fanned by fresh air seemed to reach for the sky. During the distraction, Hank dashed toward a freight truck left stranded near one end of the warehouse. He needed cover with a better angle on the shooters.

In the shelter behind the truck, Hank reloaded the Tommy gun and crawled underneath the vehicle to position himself behind some crates. He peered over the stack to see men moving along the south wall. He leaned on the pile and shouldered the submachine gun. He took the safety off and squeezed the trigger, sending a hail of bullets through the inferno. The front of the gun rose hard, but Hank took a firm grip and kept the rounds coming at waist height as he sprayed across the wall. He heard a voice hollering from behind him. "Hank!"

Through the smoke, Hank spotted a young man's figure crawling toward him on hands and knees.

"Nick? What the hell are you doing out here? You need to get out of this place now!"

Disregarding the advice, the young apprentice crawled up alongside Hank. He grabbed him by the coat sleeve and pulled him down to floor level. "They're here!"

"Who is here?"

"We saw them as we were scrambling to leave. The Murder Twins ran into the building carrying rifles. I'm sure they've come to kill you. These other men were keeping you pinned down in this burning coffin until the Twins got here to nail the lid shut."

Hank felt panic. "Nick, this isn't good. In fact, it's terrible. Let's get moving." He took the opportunity to light up the east wall with a hail of bullets until the gun ran dry. He couldn't see if his attack was successful, but it was only meant to keep the mobsters at bay while they scrambled back to a safer position.

A shot careened off the bed of the freight truck a few inches above his head. He barked at Nick, "Get down! They're on to us!"

"Man, the shots are getting close!"

Hank flattened himself to the ground and slithered between a pair of collapsed steel beams. He paused to look back as the smoke swirled out of the way. He got a glimpse of John Scalise's round face and curly hair. The assassin carried a long gun. Hank wished he had a regular rifle instead of the Thompson. This warehouse maze called for precision shooting. Thankfully, Scalise hadn't seen him.

Another portion of the roof structure rained down on the growing inferno. The collapse created an obstacle in the middle between the gangs. Hank turned to Nick and said, "You better get out of here, kid, while you can. This is not your day to die."

Nick took a last look at Hank and hustled for the door. As he dashed through the opening, several shots tore up the door frame.

As the flames grew, smoke billowed throughout the building. Hank crouched behind a new debris pile in a position short of the wall of flames. While he loaded the gun, he strained to see the east side where Scalise was hiding. He saw a flash of metal through the smoke. Hank shouldered the weapon. He pounded the area with two bursts of rounds. John Scalise was hit in the fray and screamed out.

Several gunmen opened up on the debris pile. The bullets shredded the ruins. Hank retreated off the heap and moved away. He circled around to the other side to get a safer vantage point.

Crawling over the shards of twisted steel, he cut his left hand. He took a handkerchief from his coat and wrapped the wound. With a makeshift knot, he stopped the bleeding enough to grip the machine gun. It would be difficult to hold down the barrel of the Thompson when firing. He waited as long as he could in the searing heat. The open air from a missing section of the roof above gave an occasional respite from the choking smoke. Hank covered his mouth with a side of his open coat.

He lay in the pile of whiskey barrels and loose staves strewn among the wasteland of metal. The big gun was pulled up close to his side. He heard metal screech behind him and turned in time to see the shadows of two men in the haze picking their way through the twisted steel. The light coming through the west windows made it hard to see anything more than the men's silhouettes.

Hank's heart was pounding. He couldn't tell which gang they were from, but he didn't dare breathe a word. He froze as they drew in closer to the barrels. As they passed behind a vertical pile of roof beams, Hank rolled himself over onto his back and pulled a pistol loose from beneath his coat. He held the gun low near the side of his leg and eased the safety off. At the opportune time, he could raise his right arm to fire once he knew his target. He held the machine gun across his chest with his bloody left hand.

From the other side of the mound, Hank heard the unmistakable tumble of wood like bowling pins toppling over one at a time. Someone was climbing the pile from the opposite side. He was in no position to see this intruder and was now pinned down between the unknown men. The fire intensified, and thick smoke filled the air.

Hank kept the pistol gripped in his hand while he pinched the coat fabric and pulled it over his mouth for a breathing filter. His eyes burned from the smoke as he strained to see the gunmen closing in. The racket of shifting barrels grew louder as the man crawled over the pile within feet of Hank.

A breeze blew through the side windows for a moment and pushed the smoke back. There were the two gunmen sneaking toward Hank. The Capone thugs saw Hank barricaded on the pile. One of them had a pistol and the other a rifle. As they swung on him, Hank released the coat over his mouth and raised the pistol. There was an unexpected blast from behind Hank. One of the gunmen slumped and the other fired back at the unidentified assailant.

Hank took a bead and fired. The pistol kicked back in his hand. The other Capone gunman fell backward. The first pistol-wielding thug regained his posture somewhat and fired his gun. Hank emptied the thirty-eight on him until he wasn't a threat anymore.

There was the moan of a familiar voice on the pile behind him. It was Tony. Hank scrambled up to him. He was sitting with one hand over his heart. His shirt and coat were crimson. Hank saw the ominous hemorrhaging and spoke before it was too late. "Tony, we got them both. You saved me!"

Tony tried to smile but choked when he tried to speak. Hank reached out to him and gripped his hands. "I know my friend. We go back a long way."

The color faded from Tony's face, and his eyes grew still. Hank tried to shake him one last time, but his friend was gone. Flames began to rage through the barrels. Hank wiped tears from his swollen eyes and scrambled off. Beyond the popping and snapping, Hank could hear the fireworks of gun exchanges on the west end of the warehouse. He staggered out into the smokey field and headed down toward the river. His right hand was burned, and the left still dripped with blood. All he wanted was to place them in the cool flowing water. He headed over to the bank and knelt on the shoreline.

The fire brigade bell startled Hank. He sat back and listened to the sound as the main steel structure of the building folded with an eerie groan. In the brushy river thicket beyond him, a branch snapped.

He was not alone. Hank drew his revolver. In the panic to exit, he hadn't bothered to reload the weapon. Another branch snapped. He pointed the empty gun at the sound coming from the bushes anyway. He could make out a dark figure of a man picking his way toward him.

Father Whelan emerged with his hands raised in the air. "Don't shoot, Henry!"

Hank rubbed the soot from his eyes. "Father, what are you doing here? If I had any bullets, I could have killed you!"

The priest's face was pale. "I guess the Lord's angels are protecting me."

"How did you find me down here?"

"It's divine intervention! It happened when I was driving across the river bridge. I saw the thick smoke rising in the sky. I pulled off the road in time to see you staggering across the field. You looked like you needed help."

"I'll be all right, Father, but Tony didn't make it. He got shot trying to protect me."

The priest made the sign of the cross over his chest. "Does this war include the Murder Twins again?"

Hank shrugged his shoulders. "Yes, they were here today. I wounded Scalise in a spray of gunfire. I don't know how badly he was hit."

"Henry, do you trust me?"

Hank was puzzled by the question. His body was weak from breathing in the smoke. "Yes, I trust you. Why do you ask?"

"Don't ask me any questions. You must come with me right now. My car is parked over near the bridge."

The two men picked their way along the river shoreline brush and climbed the bank to a side street where the car was parked.

"Henry, get in the back of the car and keep your head down. We don't want any more gunfire."

Hank didn't question the instructions. He laid on his side and closed his stinging eyes. The priest drove the old model T to the rectory and pulled the car inside a garage.

"Let's get you inside and get some water. You've got to wash the soot out of your eyes and from your windpipe. We can treat those wounded hands and bandage them up. The burn looks like it's going to be a bad one."

"Father, I can fend for myself." While Father Whelan collected the first aid supplies, Hank took the damp cloth from the basin of water. He closed one eye at a time and washed his eyelids and dug soot from the corners of each. The water in the basin turned gray and opaque. "The bodies will need a holy blessing. Tony is in there, but I'm not sure you'll recognize him if the flames reached him."

"We need to pray for the salvation of his soul." The priest looked over Henry's hands. He reached into the old postal bag and dug out tannic acid. "Let's soak your hands in water with this acid for a minute, before we wrap them."

The priest stood up with a start. "Hey, while you soak, I want to show you a couple things left here after your father died."

Hank didn't know what to think or expect. Father Whelan walked to a closet and fumbled through some old crates. After a moment, he reached into a box and retrieved a small cloth bag. He placed the bag down in front of Hank and opened the drawstrings. Taking the bag by the bottom and lifting it off the table, several pieces of jewelry tumbled out on the desk.

Father Whelan picked through the pile and selected a gold ring and a pair of cuff links. "I forgot I still had these." He showed Henry the items.

Hank studied the gold band.

Father Whelan pointed out the inside. "See right there. It's Hudson's initials."

Henry marveled at the long-lost ring and matching cuff links. "How is this possible?"

"I understand your mother gave these cuff links to your dad as a wedding gift. These were supposed to be buried with your father, but the mortician missed the request. It wasn't discovered until after the burial. These belong to you and your sister Gloria now."

Hank looked closely at the ring. "That would never fit me, and the cuff links are a bit too flashy for my line of work. Will you do me a favor, Father? Keep them for now. Maybe someday, Gloria would like them."

Hank's mind wandered to his youth. It seemed like an eternity since Hank had last spoken to his sister.

"OK, let's get your hands wrapped. You will have to take it easy for a while until these burns heal. Keep them wrapped for your train ride."

Hank stared at the priest. "How did you know?"

"The grim look on your face shows you're out of options. And I know it's certainly not safe for you here anymore." Father Whelan began winding cloth around Hank's hands. "After I drop you at the train station, I'll go back and see if the warehouse is safe enough for a holy tour."

— • —

Father Whelan parked his old relic next to the police cars and fire brigade trucks. He grabbed the Bible, a couple of vials of liquid, and a small pouch from the front seat of the car then stood next to the vehicle. The firemen were picking through the last of the smoldering piles. The police were helping search for victims. An officer made a beeline toward the priest. "Father, I'm glad you're here. We found one who is barely alive. He's burned all over, but he's still breathing. Would you like to give him last rights?"

"Yes, my son, I would."

The policeman led the priest through the piles of ashes and charred metal back to the remnants of an office. There, between an old safe and a brick wall, lay a man on his side with his clothing seared to his legs and arms. A rifle with a burnt stock was lying on the ground near him. The officer kicked the rifle out of the way and cleared out a few loose bricks.

Father Whelan knelt down next to the man and whispered to him, "Can you hear me?"

The man gave a slight nod with his head. Father Whelan continued, "Are you Catholic?"

Father Whelan looked at the man's melted ears and watched his mouth. The only sound was the slow wheezing of the man's breath. His eyelids fluttered.

The priest took the leather pouch on his lap and retrieved a Rosary and the small bottle of holy water.

The priest paused for a moment and held on to the Rosary beads. "Do you confess all your sins including possibly killing, stealing property, and taking the Lord's name in vain?" He watched the man's face. Again, there was movement in his eyelids. "For your penitence, I will say for you an Our Father and a Hail Mary." He made the sign of the cross with the holy water on the man's forehead, chest, and across his shoulders.

Father Whelan reached in the pouch and collected a vial of wine and a communion wafer. He blessed the bread and the wine with prayer. "This is the Lamb of God who takes away the sins of the world." The priest folded a communion wafer in half and broke it. He folded it in half again to make a small sliver. He tore it through. He presented the crumb of the body of Christ moistened with a drop of wine and placed it in the man's mouth.

"This is the body of Christ. May the Lord protect you and lead you to eternal life." Afterward, he anointed the dying man with oil and prayed for him.

Father Whelan made his way back out of the debris. A young police officer came over and grabbed him by the arm.

"Officer Mulaney, I haven't seen you since you came to the church searching for villains. How are you holding up?"

"Hi, Father. It is good to see you again. I'm doing all right. I've been keeping my head down lately as we have so many mobster shootouts."

"Did you ever catch your man?"

"Well, to be honest, I'm not exactly sure. We've arrested scores of gangsters, but they never seem to stay in jail very long."

CHAPTER 28
Nightmare

It was June 1930 when Hank once again stepped off the steam train in this place where he didn't belong. As the sparse afternoon raindrops began to spit on him, he slipped on his scorched suit coat and a dark hat with the narrow brim. Being fully aware of the truth of things this time, he felt lucky to be alive.

Harriet watched Albert lash the ropes around the dock posts. As soon as the boats were secure, he raced up the hill toward the lodge. She recognized the profile of the man standing on the dock holding his hat and coat. She shouted at Warren, "My God, he's back! I thought we'd never see him again. Why is he here?"

"Harriet, what are you so upset about? Who's back?"

"It's the nightmare man who carried guns in the boat. You remember. He paid cash for two cabins. It's Hank!"

Warren stopped for a moment and thought about their options. "All right, calm down, Harriet. Remember, you know he also stayed here once last winter when you were away taking care of your mother. He caused us no harm. I'll go talk to him and see what his plans are."

With her arms crossed, Harriet watched Warren walk down the hill. Her lack of patience got the best of her. When he was about halfway there, she couldn't wait any longer. She crossed the porch and followed him. By the time she got to the shoreline, the two men stood close together on the lawn and spoke in low voices. Harriet watched their gestures. Warren pointed across the lake and then back at the lodge.

Harriet pretended to study the produce items in the boat crate while she loaded them into a wagon on the dock. Though she took her time, she couldn't hear the men's conversation very well. At one point, she thought she heard Hank say the word *money*. She was nervous about Hank, but she finally retreated back to the lodge.

When they were finished, Warren joined Harriet in the kitchen. He tried to lighten her mood. With a smile on his face, he said, "Do you know, you're not a clever detective?"

Through the window, she watched Hank perch on a lawn chair. "What do you mean?"

"It's pretty obvious you were trying to hear the conversation with Hank."

Harriet turned to face Warren. "Well, I want to know what he's doing here. Even with the new resort stealing our business, I won't take blood money to feed this family! I would go to work anywhere in town before I'd give in to him."

The screen door thumped. Harriet turned toward the sound of squeaking floorboards. Hank stood in the dining room. Harriet's face flushed, and she blurted out, "What do you want? Are you looking for a Bible again?"

Warren reached over and took hold of Harriet's arm.

"No ma'am, I'm not looking for the good book. I'm searching for a new life," Hank said.

The statement surprised Harriet. She came a step closer and took a broom by the handle to point at him. "You won't find one you like around here. You keep away from our family!"

Warren intervened. "Harriet, stop it now!"

She set the broom down and dried her moist hands on her apron. "Are you trying to steal our money? Well, we don't have any to give away. You can tell things aren't very flush these days. Some investors from the big city moved in over at White Pine Cove and turned a few cabins like ours into a giant affair."

Hank could see the fear in Harriet's face grow as she spoke. He took a step back and turned away.

Harriet continued her tirade directing it at Hank's back as he lingered near the door. "I guess they don't need the train to bring their customers in. The superhighway comes up from Minneapolis and slices right through next to Gull Lake making it easy for people to visit them. They have all the advantages, like electric lights and indoor plumbing, in every cabin! I heard a rumor this week they are going to build one of those fancy golf courses over there. Can you believe how much timber they'll destroy?"

Warren tried to appeal to his wife. "Harriet, settle down. We are making the best of things here. We're thankful to have a few electric lights in the lodge now, aren't we?"

Hank wandered back outside.

Warren got an idea from Harriet's rants. "Why don't we go over to Gull Lake today and look around to see what people like so much about the new place?"

"Why would a person ever do such a thing? No, I won't set foot on their property."

"Well, before we lose more customers, I thought you might want to see if there are any changes we could make to appeal to the people who want a quiet place to stay, away from large crowds. You seemed curious. Wouldn't you like to snoop around?"

Harriet was undecided. "It might feel like trespassing."

"Gull is a larger lake. I've heard the fishing over there is quite fine." Warren wasn't making things any better.

Harriet looked out the window toward the shoreline and the boats tied to the dock. "I don't suppose there is much we can do about that."

She stared at the floor. "Maybe."

Warren couldn't believe his ears. "What did you say?"

"Maybe I do want to spy on them."

Warren scratched his head. "I don't think we would be breaking any laws to go and visit a fellow business in our area. I'll let the kids know we'll be gone for an hour or so. They have plenty of chores to do this afternoon."

— • —

Harriet joined Warren in the Studebaker sedan for the drive to the Village of Lake Shore. Harriet insisted on wearing a clean dress and her church hat. She'd felt threatened by the rumors it was a first-class resort. She was certain the new retreat with all the modern advantages was ruining her family's business.

The smooth, paved highway curled its way through the afternoon shade from the dark pines. Towering at the edge of the road, a large billboard promoted fine family vacations at White Pine Cove on Gull Lake. Harriet winced when she spotted the sign. "It seems awful gaudy to me. They have such poor taste."

"I can see why people don't think about us much anymore. It seems this new place has quite a presence now," Warren said.

Harriet raised her nose in the air somewhat. "They are spoiling the landscape. A modest sign would surely have had the same effect and still give other businesses a chance, too."

As they left the main highway for the driving tour around the north side of Gull Lake, a flatbed truck loaded with inflated rubber tire tubes passed them on the sandy driveway. The young man in the cab waved a tanned arm out the open driver's window as he drove on toward the water. Several teenagers rode red-and-white bicycles along the drive. Their unofficial race to be in the lead carried on in uproarious fashion. One of them carried a soda fountain drink in one hand.

A man was waxing an overturned canoe with a wooden hull on a rack next to a lake cabin. Harriet was silent.

At a large tree-covered hill, the drive curved along the water and led to a three-story timber lodge. Women and men lounged in wicker rocking chairs on the shaded porch that wrapped around the building. Three children played in the sand. Two tossed a beach ball, while the other searched for clamshells.

The large pier extending out into the lake buzzed with activity. Some fishermen had come in with their catch, and two families were loading gear into boats getting ready for afternoon trips out on the water. Warren stopped the car when he noticed the sheen of a silver Evinrude outboard hanging from the back of each fishing boat. He watched a guest pull a starting cord. Smoke puffed out from the rear of the outboard. Moments later, the fisherman twisted the handle on the motor. The craft powered away from the dock out into the lake and splashed through the waves. Warren shook his head in amazement.

Harriet watched a young family picnicking under a tree near the shoreline. People were smiling, laughing, and appeared to be quite happy. She was perplexed. *How could this be? Don't they know about the stock market collapse and the great depression forcing families out of their homes into lives of begging?* It all seemed so unfair. "Take me home, Warren. I don't want to see any more of this."

He leaned in close to his wife's ear. "Harriet, you know this hasn't hit everyone the same way. Even though many folks are suffering, these people still deserve to be happy."

Harriet was silent on the car ride home.

— • —

When they arrived back at Clark Lake Lodge, Harriet was visibly agitated as she left the car. She noticed Hank outside searching for a chair to use on the porch. She glared at Warren, before she went off on a rage-filled rant.

She marched toward Hank, screaming, "My husband may be afraid to tell you this, but you are not welcome here! You stay away from this family and get the hell off our property right now! I don't want to ever see you here again!"

Hank was on his feet and avoided more confrontation by leaving from the far end of the porch.

Harriet's face burned red and tears rolled off her cheeks as she disappeared into the lodge. The screen door slammed behind her.

Warren intercepted Hank out on the lawn and grabbed him by the arm. "Hold on a minute. No excuse, but Harriet is upset by what she saw over at Gull Lake. She knows this place is doomed to compete against the new larger business and I'm sorry she lashed out at you."

Hank stood silent as Warren continued, "Besides, there isn't a train leaving here until tomorrow. Let me give you a ride to find a place for the night."

Hank nodded. "It's probably best."

The two men returned to the car. Warren said, "You know, my wife would kill me if she heard me say this, but White Pine Cove looks like a nice place to stay."

Hank looked at Warren, surprised by the frank comment.

After delivering Hank to Gull Lake, Warren returned and pulled the car back into the barn. He rolled the large doors shut. He took care not to make too much noise when he climbed the staircase to their room. The bedroom door was closed. Harriet was still in her dress. Her hat and shoes were strewn about on the floor. Warren picked up the hat and set it on the dresser. He took a seat next to Harriet, who was face down in the pillows.

He reached for her and brushed the side of her shoulder. She bristled at his unexpected touch and pulled away. Warren stayed close. "It's time we talk about this," he began as he stood next to the bed. "You can't treat people this way. You know the *tour* really upset you, not Hank."

Harriet raised her head from the pillow and spoke without looking at him. "That man is a monster, and I don't want him around here. You know I hate criminals. I don't want his business. I'd rather starve than take his money. We should have dealt with him properly the first time he showed up in Albert's boat." She put her head back down on the bedding.

"He's gone now. Let's go outside, get some fresh air, and talk things over."

Harriet rose from the bed and changed into her regular clothes. Warren waited for her in the dining room. He guided her toward a shaded picnic table across the yard.

As they walked side by side, Harriet raised her arms out with her hands facing up. "I don't understand. What exactly does Hank want with us?"

They stopped walking. Warren turned to her and said, "He wants to start over, and he needs money."

Harriet's eyes widened, and her mouth fell open in disbelief. "What do you mean Hank needs money? We have nothing to give him. We have mouths to feed. Furthermore, he's a monster. Why would we ever help him?"

Warren took a deep breath. He looked directly into Harriet's eyes. "Harriet, there's something I've been meaning to tell you for a long time."

Harriet crossed her arms and stood as rigid as a statue. Her eyes narrowed and her lips drew into a white knot.

Warren had never seen his wife with this much anger on her face. He pointed toward the empty table. "Let's take a seat."

With a piercing tone, Harriet said, "Can't you see, I don't feel like sitting down right now."

Before this impasse got much worse, Warren moved in and swung an arm around Harriet. He tried to guide her toward the table.

Harriet wouldn't be corralled. She twisted away from her husband to face him. "Warren Johnson, what have you done?"

Warren regained his position next to her and pressed on. "Come with me."

Harriet was reluctant. She followed Warren to the table but stood with her arms crossed. She knew she wasn't going to like what he was about to say.

The breeze sweeping through the pines muted out the rest of the world. As Warren began, he patted the bench next to him. "Take a seat. I have a long story to tell you."

Harriet remained rigid with her arms locked as she took a seat *across* from him. She stared at Warren's chest and neck but wouldn't make eye contact.

"Harriet, you know when we first met, I told you I had roots in Minnesota but worked in Chicago for several years. I also told you I bought this place as a way to make a living outside the big city, right?"

Harriet held her stare firm. She didn't acknowledge his statements.

This was going to be a tense conversation for both of them. Warren knew he had to tell her everything if there was any hope they could move on together. He didn't want to lose his wife, but it was a real possibility if he wasn't careful with his message.

"I told you before we met, I worked as a manager at a beverage company. Well, it's true, but there's more to the story. What I didn't tell you was I worked for my older brother Hudson, and we brewed beer for clubs in Chicago."

Harriet glared at Warren's face. Both the corners of her mouth curled down with distaste like she'd swallowed bitter poison. "You mean illegal beer, don't you?"

Despite the summer heat, Warren felt a chill come over him. He stared at the cracked planks of the table's top. "When my father Martin emigrated from Europe, he arrived in the Midwest without a dime to his name. At the time, deceitful men in the city took advantage of many new immigrants to run numbers for illegal gambling and for collecting bets on horse races. If these handlers got caught doing the dirty work of roughing people up for money, they could be replaced with new immigrants coming off the boats. It kept the crime bosses out of jail.

"Martin arrived in a strange country all alone, and he spoke little English. He was penniless and couldn't even muster up the price of a ticket to return to Europe. He was stuck, and he struggled with working in a dishonest business and committing the violence expected of him. While he was forced to accept this life, deep down, he was torn between his beliefs and the need to support himself. While he came to America in search of a better life, crime was the only road he found leading to it.

"But what began as survival, later became his own temptation."

Harriet could hear the empathy in her husband's voice as he described the predicament his father had fallen into.

"A couple years after my father first landed here, something unexpected happened. His boss died in a gun battle with cops who were trying to clean up illegal gambling. My father found himself the new leader of a minor syndicate. He assumed the role and set out to make his share."

The longer she listened to Warren speak, Harriet recognized her own growing sense of foreboding.

"Over the years, the business grew, and Martin created two separate organizations. One was for running gambling, and the other coerced merchants into carrying his line of expensive tobacco products. The second enterprise expanded to control supplies of meat, fish, and eggs."

Warren was deliberate in covering the details. He wanted her to know everything, the good and the bad. "It took time and a lot of bribes for both the local police and city officials, but Martin persevered. When he was quite established, he met a spunky impoverished woman with emerald green eyes. Her name was Julia. Shortly after she emigrated from England, Julia started working for my father, keeping his gambling and shipping records. He was fond of her from the first time they met and protected her from the hoodlums in her neighborhood. When they married, she became a great influence in his life and convinced him to keep clear of the deadliest sins. She was content and not weak to the endless gluttony of most criminal operations."

Harriet watched Warren speak with a sad look on her face.

Warren fixed his gaze on the old barn atop the hill. It was as if the faded paint held a story. "Once both my brother and I were born, life changed for my parents. Dad was determined to raise his boys in a good home and to return to an honest life. Mother left the business and set about the work of raising us children full time.

"Father tried pouring money into legitimate businesses but found he could never earn much unless he returned to the disease of tipping the scales in his favor somehow. Despite his dark occupations, Hudson and I attended school and had fairly normal childhoods."

Harriet sat quietly and focused on her husband. Warren decided to keep going while she was willing to listen. "Things were pretty good for my brother and me until the military draft sent Dad to fight in the bloody trenches in France. You know the Selective Draft picked on immigrants in those days. He never returned from the war."

Harriet gasped and covered her mouth. Her eyes welled with tears.

"A few years later, the Eighteenth Amendment passed making alcohol production illegal, and all hell broke loose. My dad was gone, and Hudson got pulled into the bootlegging business. Mother worried about us but couldn't keep me out of it either."

Harriet motioned for him to continue.

"My brother may have taught me the business, but I wouldn't do the things he did. I worked in the office and made many decisions." Warren looked down at the ground. "After Hudson died, my world fell apart.

"Before I knew it, an army of men came for me, too. I was shot and assumed dead. I had to escape somehow. I was banged up when I arrived in Minnesota. It took me a couple of years to fully recover. By the time I got back on my feet, it was too late to help Hudson's kids. His daughter was taken in by some nuns in St. Louis. His son was surviving on his own."

Her face turned pale. She was aghast at the senseless brutal attacks and murders. She'd read these sorts of headlines in the paper out of Minneapolis but had never known anyone who was involved.

Harriet sobbed and reached for Warren's hand.

"It changed me forever. I was determined to stay out of the business anyway I could."

Harriet stopped crying. She pulled her hands back. "You were one of them— Are you a murderer?"

Warren stared at Harriet. He would not answer.

"All this time you've kept this from me?" She covered her face. "Oh God, I'm married to a killer!" Her sobs turned into coughs and gasps.

Harriet went down on her knees and began to vomit on the ground. She took hold of the bench seat. When her retching ceased, she pulled herself up and staggered toward the lodge. Warren came around the table after her.

She stood straight with her arm extended. "Get away from me, you, killer! I don't want you near me or the kids!"

"Harriet, wait." Warren stepped between her and the lodge. "I was in the business, but it's not the way you think. There's more you need to know." He tried to wipe away partially digested food left smeared on her cheek.

She slapped his hand away and put her clenched fists on her hips. "What else, Warren? What other dirty secrets have you been keeping from me all these years?"

He could see the swarm of emotions racing through his wife. He sensed this announcement might light a match for her already explosive anger. "Hank is my nephew. He's Hudson's younger son."

She went into shock. Harriet covered her face. She shook her head as she backed away from the man she was starting to despise. "No, no, no! You can't do this to us! What happened to the Warren I married?"

She tore at her hair and made a tangled mess of herself. She cried out through the tears, "Why didn't I see this coming? Now I understand your weird behavior about protecting us around him."

Warren tried to defuse the tension with a calm voice. "Harriet, his family is all gone. We are the only relatives Hank has left."

"No, *you* are the only family he has left. He's not *my* nephew. I want nothing to do with either one of you."

Albert was standing on the porch now. He'd never seen his parents have a serious fight before. He yelled, "Mama, what's wrong?"

In an instant, her maternal instincts took over. "Go back inside, Albert, and get your sister. We are leaving right now!"

Albert wiped away his tears as he headed toward Kate's room.

Harriet turned to the man she once loved. "Did you think telling me Hank is your nephew was going to make things better? Now it's even more clear. You've been lying to me for years. This has become a bigger pile of lies. You are as bad as Hank. I don't know you at all! Stay away from me and the kids. We're leaving."

Warren was in tears. "Wait, I'll go. There's no need to uproot the kids from their home."

"No, you stay here. I'm not going to run this place alone. I'm taking the kids with me."

"Where in the world are you headed with them? "

"We can stay with my mother. Why do you care? You were looking for a wife to help hide from a heinous past. I can't imagine the unspeakable things you've done."

CHAPTER 29

The Reconciliation

It was a comfortable autumn day at Hubert Landing. Bright-colored leaves floated down from the maples when Harriet stopped the car to pick up Mildred Swenson.

As Mildred got into the car, Harriet reached over and took hold of her arm. "Thank you for doing this. This wouldn't be possible for me without you."

"That's fine, dear. It's my pleasure to help."

The two of them drove the wooded road to Clark Lake Lodge. Harriet parked the car at the top of the hill and crossed the lawn to the lodge's porch. She stopped at the screen door and began to knock.

Warren emerged from the lodge in clean clothes and a freshly shaven face. He gave a curious smile to Harriet. "You don't have to knock, Harriet. Please come right in."

Harriet paused and took a step backward. "No, Warren, I would prefer we talk outside."

He nodded and followed Harriet. "Let's take a table near the lake."

As Warren stepped off the porch, he noticed Mildred Swenson standing there in the shade of the pines waiting to join them. He stopped. "What's she doing here?"

"Oh yes, I forgot to tell you, Warren. I've asked Mildred to join us today. She's good at these sorts of things, you know. She can help."

Warren bristled. "Harriet, these are personal matters. We don't need to air our laundry in front of someone else."

"Hi, Warren. I'm glad the two of you are finally getting together like this. I mean you no harm." Mildred gave an awkward smile to match her position.

Harriet pointed at the first lakeside table arranged with four chairs. "Those will do."

Despite his preparations, Harriet was repulsed by the sight of Warren. He did not look well. His pale face made it look like he'd aged in the weeks since she'd last seen him. She began to take a seat but stopped. "I don't think I can do this!"

Mildred placed her hand on top of Harriet's shoulder. She gave her a reassuring squeeze. "Now Harriet, please sit down here across from Warren."

Mildred looked at each of them and nodded. "I want to let you both know I speak to many women and couples in our community who need encouragement. Our church refers me to those who may be more comfortable speaking to a neighbor they know well. There's no shame in talking about life's difficulties. Whatever you may share here today, stays confidential. We've known each other for many years. Please know you can trust me."

She waited for responses. Hearing none, she continued, "So, let's begin. Now Harriet, I assume Warren would like the chance to discuss things he feels are important to *the family*. I think it would be best to hear him out."

Harriet raised her gaze from the table to glare directly at Warren. The skin on her forehead was a map of wrinkled anger. "Family? These are *my* kids. He has no say in what happens to them."

The statement conveyed how great the divide was. Mildred recognized it would take real work to release these two from their battle-hardened positions.

Harriet couldn't wait her turn. "Tell me the truth, Warren, was this place bought with blood money?"

Her words pierced the tranquility of the place. Warren heard the tone and knew in an instant his response would need to be well chosen if he had any hope of salvaging his former life.

Mildred was shocked by the insinuation. To her, Warren had never been anything but a hard-working devoted father all of the years he lived in the area.

Warren looked at Mildred and knew he didn't have a choice but to answer with her sitting at the same table. "No, Harriet, we weren't assassins. We were bootleggers. We helped make regular people happy."

Harriet scoffed, "So, you're telling me you were a Chicago bootlegger who never killed anyone?"

He glanced at Mildred searching for approval but sensed from her blank expression he had to say more.

Warren exhaled. "Yes, I admit casualties were sometimes part of the business. But they were bad men, horrible men who were greedy and threatened good people. The world is a better place today without them. We certainly didn't get them all. No, some of the worst demons are still around today." He paused for a moment and let the message sink in.

Mildred's face turned pale and chalky.

Harriet closed her eyes. She had heard enough.

"Harriet, I need you to know I'm the same man you married and have loved all these years. You know me. What I did in the past doesn't change who I am. You and the kids mean everything to me."

She found some comfort in the thought but still shook her head. "No, you lied to me, and you lied to the kids."

It was plain to see her skepticism hadn't thawed. "You're right. I didn't tell you about my past, but you have to see how dangerous this sort of life was and how I never wanted any of it to follow me. It was a life I had planned to take with me to the grave. It's the reason I use my middle name Warren and adopted the last name Johnson."

Harriet slapped Warren. "What do I tell our children about their father—everything, or nothing at all?"

Warren covered his stinging cheek as he looked out across the waves like he was searching for something. He was tempted to answer the question, but he had heard Harriet say *our* children. It was the first sign maybe she could forgive him and think of him once again as a father and, someday, a husband. He faced her and turned his hands upward. "What will give them the best chance in life?"

Harriet knew this decision had to be hers.

Mildred was there to encourage her. She placed her hand on Harriet's shoulder. "Go ahead, dear. What do you want the children to know about their father?"

"I'm not sure what to do. I don't want them *acting* the rest of their lives or being suspicious of everyone they meet. I want them to have every opportunity." She shook her head. "I guess I think it would be safer for them if they didn't know about your past."

As the words floated in the afternoon air— she was satisfied with the statement. Harriet wasn't one to keep secrets from the children, but she thought it was best given their father's heinous past.

Warren pulled a handkerchief from his pocket. He turned away and coughed into it. Harriet and Mildred both watched him wheeze.

Harriet spoke first. "Are you all right?"

Warren crumpled the cloth up and stuffed it back in his pants pocket. "I don't know. I must have caught something. This will pass. I need some good rest."

Harriet continued, "Now what about your nephew? Is he a bootlegger, too?"

CHAPTER 30

Spies

"Warren, I'm scared. The newspapers say everything financial in this country is starting to collapse. People are panicking. I know families from our church who are leaving with a suitcase and the clothes on their backs. Is the bank going to foreclose on us, too? Are we going to lose the lodge?"

Hank looked at Warren and waited for him to respond.

Warren got up, walked around the table, and sat down next to his wife. Concern etched her features at the thought that they would be swept into the ranks of dust bowl families who'd lost everything. "No, dear. We will be fine. We've worked hard here and never relied on the bank to support us."

Harriet's features relaxed a little. "But I saw the bank manager speaking with you last week when we were in town. What did he want?"

"I've always kept some rainy-day money in a savings account there. It's safer than a cookie jar. Bill wanted me to know our local bank is in better shape than some big city operations you read about in the newspapers. He wanted me to help spread the word that there is no need for panic around here. All of their deposits are safe."

"I feel better hearing this, but what about our customers? What if people stop coming to the lake?"

Warren stroked the stubble emerging along his jawline. "Yes, things could get pretty tight. It might be awhile before most families feel good about spending money on vacations again. The few business travelers we get today won't bring us much, but we'll get along. We are pretty self-sufficient with your big garden and have plenty of firewood on the property for heat."

Harriet found comfort in his words and was tempted to apologize for her panic. Life would be hard enough without losing their home in the pines. She worried about the children and what the future might hold if things continued to get worse. But she knew they were blessed compared with many other families. "How do you think the big resort is doing over at Gull Lake? I bet they have a lot of bank loans to pay."

The statement surprised both men. Harriet had never spoken like a business owner.

Warren looked at Harriet and then at Hank. "You know, it's been a while since we made a spy visit. How do you feel about a car ride?"

Hank waited his turn.

"It's not spying if we are being friendly neighbors," Harriet said.

Warren wasn't buying it. "Oh, really. Since when have we shown them *any* friendship?"

Harriet fired back, "We've given them some business. Hank, didn't you stay there once?"

Hank looked sheepish. "Yes, I did when I needed to give your family some time."

"Did you enjoy the place?" Harriet asked.

"They seemed pleasant enough, but I wasn't there to use the lake or anything. I needed a spot to lay my head down for the night," Hank said.

Warren wasn't finished yet. "Harriet, maybe you should bring them a pie or a frosted cake."

She twisted in her chair and looked at Warren. "Why would we ever bake a pie for the people who are slowly stealing our customers? I'll do no such thing."

"Well, why not? You just said it's not spying to go over there—if we are being friendly neighbors."

Harriet stood up, untied her apron, and tossed it next to a pail filled with soapy water. "No, you're right. This is a spy trip. Warren Johnson, do you know you're nearly impossible? Let's go before I get busy with cleaning chores."

Hank offered to do the driving so Warren and Harriet could take in the sights. He pointed to a small unit on the hillside. "There is the cabin where I stayed." A business traveler was pulling a case from a car and unlocking the door.

Harriet was on high alert. "It's interesting to see they need to keep things locked up over here. We've never had any trouble in all the years we've been in business."

Warren shrugged his shoulders. "It's hard to say whether it's necessary because they are a larger resort with more people around, or if it's a sign of the hard times we find ourselves in. You never know where the next panic will come from."

Near the main lodge, Warren slid down as low as possible in the car seat as they passed a cleaning crew walking near the driveway.

"Warren, what's going on? Are you trying to hide yourself?" Harriet asked.

Warren put his hat on and nodded to the left. "Don't you think he looks like a manager for the place?"

"So, what?" she asked.

"Don't you think he might recognize us from the community and wonder why another resort owner is driving around their property? I'd rather not have to answer embarrassing questions," Warren said.

Harriet had never considered their appearances for the visit. "I guess so, but we're not breaking any laws. They are a business like ours, open to the public."

Hank laughed. "Maybe we should have brought a cake or pie along with us after all." He parked the car near a lakeside dining building and turned the motor off.

The three of them sat there taking in the view and the warmth of the sunlight. In the last hundred yards or so down to the water's edge, the well-manicured lawn was strewn with a curious new style of chair. Each one had a high-sloped back, low generous seat, and broad armrests. The adults seemed to really take to them, as the painted chairs appeared in high occupancy.

Harriet was puzzled and frustrated. "They still have quite a few families staying here. And will you look at those chairs? I've never seen anything like them."

"I've seen them in a magazine. They have a funny long name. I believe they first came from the upstate New York area," Warren said.

Near the edge of the lawn, a young mother and her family were packing up the last of their picnic items, preparing to leave.

"I'd like to sit in one."

The men were both surprised at Harriet's candor. She left the car, and Warren decided to join her. As they took a seat in the shade, Harriet marveled, "Say, these are very nice." Before long, the wonder soon faded. Harriet rose from the chair, crossed her arms, and returned to the car.

"Let's go home."

CHAPTER 31
The Fall

"Warren." Warren turned to look at Harriet. His skin was gray and pasty. His eyes seemed unfocused. She knew something was wrong. He clung there on the ladder with his paintbrush in hand and didn't respond. "Warren, what's wrong?"

Warren placed his right hand, still holding the brush, against his left shoulder.

"Warren, what is wrong? Why won't you answer me?" Her voice crackled with intensity.

Warren crumbled against the ladder. His knees buckled. The paint bucket and brush dropped from his hands and bounced on the ground. Red paint-spattered across the barn wall and the green grass.

"Oh, God!" Harriet rushed to the ladder and mounted the rungs. She took hold of Warren's limp body and pressed him against the ladder to keep him from falling. From deep in her chest came a blood-curdling scream. "Albert, come help me *right now*! It's your father. Something happened. Albert!"

From across the yard, Albert heard his mother's screams. He stood up from the lawnmower he was fueling and turned toward the barn.

She kept yelling, "Albert, I need you at once!"

Albert dropped the gas can on the ground and began to run. He could see his mother clinging to the ladder with her arms wrapped around his dad.

Warren's limbs were dangling straight down in a lifeless posture. His face was twisted unnaturally against the ladder.

"Mom, you'll have to let go of him for minute and come down so I can help." Harriet carefully released her grip on Warren and backed off the ladder. Albert took the ladder rungs two at a time. When he reached his father, he corralled him around the midsection. He exhaled. "Mom, I've got him now."

"Dad, can you hear me? Dad, wake up!" Albert shook his father continuously.

Harriet stepped to the side of the ladder with her arms still reaching in the air. "Don't let him fall!"

Albert was panicked. "Mom, what's wrong with Dad? He needs a doctor."

Tears streamed down Harriet's cheeks. Her arms shook. She covered her mouth with one hand as she wailed.

"Mom, Dad needs a doctor!"

In shock, Harriet stood frozen as her son gripped Warren's lifeless body.

"Mom, go to the lodge now and call Doctor Thomas. Hurry! I will get Dad down from up here."

Harriet began to nod with short violent head bobs. She began to stumble across the open field toward the lodge. She was almost to the cut lawn again when she stopped.

As Albert took hold of his father by the waist, he strained to lift the limp body from the ladder. As he twisted to pull Warren loose, the top of the ladder slid over a foot, catching on a thin strip of batten board. His dad's knees buckled once again, and Albert felt an unexpected shift.

Albert's heart raced.

Before he could rebalance the ladder, the left ladder stringer twisted away from the wall just enough to release from its catch on the trim board. The top end of the ladder started to slide across the wall toward the right with helpless acceleration. Albert took hold of his dad firmly as the two rode the ladder down to fall in a heap. The combined weight of their bodies snapped one side of ladder in two. Albert heard his own ribs crackle as his chest slammed down on the broken wood. When he regained his breath, he heard his father gasp and start to moan.

"Dad, you're alive!"

Warren moaned in a low audible tone once again.

"What's wrong, Dad? I can't understand you."

Harriet came running to their side. She helped Albert roll off his father. Warren gasped for air again.

Albert struggled to his knees. "Mom, did you call the doctor?"

"No, when I heard the ladder crash, I yelled at Kate to help us and I ran straight back up here."

"Dad's breathing a little. He's gonna need help."

She reached her hand out and took Albert by the arm. "Your sister is calling the doctor."

CHAPTER 32

The Confession

Hank waited in the car at Hubert Landing. He checked his pocket watch once again. It was 4:00 p.m. on the nose. He tapped the crystal and folded the watch cover shut. The ground shook as the black locomotive rounded the bend, pulling a line of rail cars. Steam poured from the base of the engine. The train's whistle made a long shrill announcement as the workhorse came to rest at the stop.

Hank approached the front passenger car. Through the steam, he saw a dark figure carrying a small case emerge. He approached the reverent man and reached out to shake his hand. "Father, thank you for coming on such short notice."

"Henry, I finally get to see where you've been hiding out." Father Whelan looked out across Clark Lake. "Oh, it's beautiful here. I wish we were here under different circumstances."

———— • ————

Warren was laying in the bed with his sleeping shirt unbuttoned at the chest while the doctor examined the sound of his heart. Kate was acting as a nurse while Albert tended to the resort affairs outside.

Harriet met the men at the entry. She held the screen door open and greeted Hank and his guest as they climbed the porch steps. "Welcome. Please come right inside. I hope you had a good train ride from Chicago."

Harriet's haggard appearance and forced smile were clues of how bad things were. Exhaustion was apparent in the dark circles beneath her eyes. It appeared she hadn't slept nor eaten since Warren fell ill.

Father Whelan arrived in his standard collar with a light overcoat.

"Hello, you must be Father Whelan. I'm glad to see you." Harriet gave the priest an uncharacteristic hug and turned to Hank. "Thank you for arranging his visit."

"Of course, Harriet."

"Father, welcome to the north woods. While you're here, please make yourself at home. We have a cabin ready for your stay. You can leave your bag here in the lodge for now. Albert will deliver it for you."

The priest removed his traveler's hat. "Thank you, Harriet. I appreciate your family's hospitality."

"Oh, it's no trouble at all. It's what we do around here," she said from habit.

The men stood and looked upstairs when Doctor Thomas pulled the bedroom door closed behind him. He took a moment to stow his stethoscope in a black leather bag as he prepared to leave.

"Would you like some coffee before you head up to see Warren? We also have water, or lemonade if you like." Harriet tried to sound cheerful, but the words came out strained.

Father Whelan replied, "Oh no, ma'am. I'm fine."

"It looks like the doctor is finishing with his daily check-in." Harriet walked to the foot of the stairs. She met the gray-haired physician as he came down. "Doctor, how is Warren doing?"

The solemn man looked up and scanned the visitors waiting at the landing with Harriet. He noticed Father Whelan's collar and felt at ease sharing the report. He took Harriet lightly by the arm. "Well, Harriet, while I'm certain Warren suffered a major heart attack the day he fell from the ladder, it's not clear how much permanent damage was done to his heart. For such a strong strapping man to be cut down like this, my assumption is the damage was quite severe. His heartbeat today remains very faint and somewhat irregular."

The statement confirmed her worst fears.

"I'm Father Whelan." The priest shook the doctor's outstretched hand. "I'm just now learning about Warren's condition. Do you mind explaining, what does an *irregular heartbeat* mean?"

The physician paused and took a breath. "Well, the sound of the heart is faint at best. At times, it skips a beat or two before it resumes. It may never return to a normal rhythm. I'm afraid at some point, he may even have another attack."

Harriet stepped closer. "What are you saying? Please, don't beat around the bush, doctor."

The physician stroked his bushy eyebrows. "To be honest, I don't know how long Warren has to live. His heart doesn't sound strong enough for a man his age." His sympathetic eyes focused on Harriet. "This is a difficult message, but I believe Warren should get his affairs in order."

Harriet stood silently as tears streaked down her face. She didn't try to wipe them away. Father Whelan stepped up beside her and put an arm around her shoulders. He retrieved a handkerchief from his pocket and offered it to her.

The doctor excused himself to visit another patient. Without a word, Harriet started up the stairs with slow deliberate steps followed by Hank and Father Whelan. She eased the door open to Warren's room. She took a moment to compose herself then moved close to the bed. "Warren dear, Hank brought a visitor to see you." She motioned to the men to join her at the bedside.

Hank and Father Whelan approached the foot of the bed and studied Warren. His pale face had deep creases in his forehead, which made him look aged far beyond his fifty-one years.

Warren stirred when Harriet massaged his hand. He looked at the two men at the foot of the bed and a slight smile came to his face. He addressed Hank with a raspy low voice. "This must be serious Hank if you've dragged a priest up here all the way from Chicago."

Hank had a difficult time hearing his uncle.

Harriet waived them closer to the bedside. "I'm going to let you men talk a while." She leaned down and gave Warren a kiss on the cheek before she left. "I'll see you later, dear." Harriet closed the door behind her.

Father Whelan made his way around the right side of the bed. Hank took the other side. Warren turned toward the priest. "Father, it's good to see you. What's it been, almost eight years?"

Father Whelan smiled. "Yes, Warren, it's been too long. I wish I were here for better reasons."

Warren turned his head toward the priest and waived him in closer. "Father, I'm ready now."

Father Whelan could see the hungry look in Warren's eyes. Hank stood up and started to pace near the door.

Warren continued, "Father, you and I went through a lot in the old days."

The priest nodded. "Yes, Warren, but your past is all forgiven now. God doesn't see those things anymore when he looks at you."

Warren shook his head. "No, Father. I'm still as guilty of those things today and even worse."

Father Whelan squinted, and his mouth drew to one side. He was surprised by the statement. He made the sign of the cross over himself, folded his hands, looked down, and became silent.

"Father, for all the years since I left Chicago, I've never cut my ties with the North Side Mob," Warren said.

Father Whelan sat upright and gasped. He stared into Warren's eyes.

The room became as silent as a winter night. When the floorboards outside the bedroom door creaked, Hank opened the door. Harriet stood there with a water pitcher in one hand, covering her mouth with the other. Tears dropped down to the insides of her forearms. When Hank moved closer, she shoved the pitcher at him and backed away shaking her head. She descended the stairs alone.

Hank delivered the water. "I should go now." He left Warren and Father Whelan alone, closing the door on his way out.

Warren resumed his confession. "When I left Chicago to save my hide, I had no intention of living a life of crime anymore. After the first couple of long winters here, my prospects were still thin. I needed more for survival but couldn't find a way to get it."

Warren began to wheeze and cough. The priest poured water and offered a glass. Warren sipped and coughed a little more to clear his throat.

"One day by chance in the village of Nisswa, I ran into a couple of Chicago thugs who were here trying to set up a small casino in an abandoned building. Though they were friends from the past, I told them to knock off the local gambling. They might blow my cover if the Feds came around."

Warren paused to rest a moment. "The next thing I knew, a week later, they closed up shop and the whole thing disappeared. Before they left town, one of the goons reached out to see what else they should be doing. We talked a lot about the liquor business and bringing booze in through Detroit."

Father Whelan nodded and listened with his eyes closed.

"A couple of weeks after that, I got a call from Tom at the general store across the lake to let me know I had a visitor interested in lodging. In the early days, I didn't have a lot, so this was a big deal for me. I took the boat over there, and a familiar man stood on the dock in a suit looking straight out of Chicago. It was Dean O'Banion."

The priest looked down at Warren.

"One of the goons told him where I was hiding, and he came to see what I wanted to do with my share of the business.

"To be honest, I thought I had walked away from it all when I left Chicago.

"We spent the next four days in the original farmhouse here working out the North Side's plans for how to run our side of Chicago. I agreed to oversee entertainment for the clubs, find quality liquor supplies, and distribute the goods. Dean took care of the speakeasy owners, gambling, protection, and directing the guys on the street.

"We also made plans for how I could remain anonymous—do my part from behind the scenes. We planned for a few of my head guys to see me from time to time by coming here. Most posed as ministers or salesmen when they came north on the train.

"Hank was one exception who just stumbled in here while trying to get away from the killers on his tail."

Father Whelan studied the grave-looking man unable to leave his bed. "Warren, did you decide who would be killed in Chicago?"

Warren took a few deep breaths. "Father, I've committed about every sin there is. I used people and endangered lives while stealing liquor. The men killed people for me who posed a threat to us or the business. We were guilty of cheating in gambling. We regularly took the Lord's name in vain. We celebrated gluttony, malice, and drunkenness, and we hoarded lots of liquor. It's been so long since I've attended Mass regularly, I can't even recall when. We broke the law on almost all of these things, and, when we were caught, we lied to the cops and even judges and juries while under oath. I'm sure I've missed many sins on this list and for those unknown, I confess as well." His tone was one of deep regret.

Father Whelan sat still and stared down at the floor for several minutes as he considered the confession. "Are you sorry for the sins you've committed and resolve not to commit them again?"

Warren focused his thoughts on the question. "Yes, I am, Father."

Father Whelan gave Warren a prayer penance and offered forgiveness.

Warren faded back on the bed as if all his energy was gone from purging the darkness from his soul.

Father Whelan caught Henry out on the landing. "You can come back in now."

Hank took his place in a chair alongside the bed. He reached in and squeezed Warren's shoulder. The muscles seemed weak and loose on his bones.

Warren's eyes closed on the edge of sleep, but he stirred once more. "Out there."

Hank was nearest to Warren. He leaned down and gave his shoulder a gentle shake. "Warren, what did you say?"

Warren's eyes flickered open for a moment. "Out there."

Father Whelan glanced at Henry and turned back to Warren. "Warren, *what's* out there?"

Warren's right arm wavered as he raised it off the bed a couple of inches and pointed. His arm collapsed back down on the blankets.

Hank guessed, "There is an old barn here on the property. I understand it was part of the farm Warren bought many years ago."

Warren mumbled inaudibly with his eyes shut. His breathing faded to puffs of exhales as he slept.

The priest looked at Henry. "What would a *barn* have to do with anything?"

Hank shrugged his shoulders. "I have no idea. It's where he fell off the ladder when he had his heart attack."

"What was he doing when it happened?"

"Harriet said he was painting the faded red siding on the barn."

There was a pause in the conversation. "Warren isn't a spring chicken anymore. Why wouldn't he have his son Albert do that type of work?"

Hank rubbed his face. "I couldn't say."

—— • ——

Father Whelan settled into his cabin before walking over to rap on Henry's door. "You got a minute?"

"Sure, Father. Come on inside and have a seat."

The priest stayed standing. "There's something I need to tell you."

Hank remained in his chair. "OK, we're alone here."

"They won't be looking for you anymore. You're safe now."

"Who won't be?"

The priest came in and sat down. "Neither the Murder Twins nor Capone will be looking for you."

CHAPTER 33

Erased

"Henry, it happened when you got burned in the fire. You know, after we got you all bandaged up at the church, I drove back to the old warehouse alone."

"Yes, Father."

"Well, I ran into the same young Irish policeman who came to the church the night you were shot. He said, 'As long as you are here, Father, I have a request for you.'

"I was curious. 'Oh, how can I help?'

"He made his grim request. 'Well, you know so many local people on both sides of the law. I was wondering if you would also be willing to help confirm the identities of the dead victims?' He tried to warn me that it might be gruesome.

"I can still feel the anxiety of being surrounded by those charred corpses. After all my years as a priest, I'd never thought I'd come face-to-face with hell."

Hank's mind was stuck on the fact that this occurred while he was making his escape by train.

"I kept a firm grip on my Bible. I told him, 'If I can stomach it, then yes, I will try to help you. Of course, there is no guarantee I will know any of these hoodlums unless they attended a funeral Mass at my church or something. Most of them generally don't come to Mass.'

"He nodded in agreement and said, 'All right, let's start by the door and work our way through the building.'

"Step by step, we walked the wreckage and looked over the remains. I asked questions like: 'What are all these large metal rings? Was this a bicycle factory?'

"He was patient with me. 'No, I'm afraid those are the barrel rings from stored whiskey, which remained after the fire.' A corpse of a short man lay among the ashes and metal. I pulled back some smoldering wood slats and studied the gold dentistry work in the front teeth of the victim's mouth. Officer Mulaney peered over my shoulder. 'Do you know this one?'

"I was pretty sure. 'Yes, based on the teeth, I think this is Tony M, as they called him. He had been a fighter in his younger days. He is a part of Capone's Outfit.'

"While Officer Mulaney made notes in a small book, I continued the search crawling over the twisted building beams and smoldering wood debris next to the remains of a large freight truck. Down through the charred lumber, I saw a distinct patch of human skin. I pulled some loose timbers back. I let him know. 'I think I may have found something under here.'

"The policeman looked up from his notes. 'Wait for me, I'll be right there.'

"So, I pulled back a piece of roofing tin. It was hard to look because the face of the victim was burned beyond recognition. 'No rush, I won't be able to give this one last rights.'

"It hit me just then. I still had your dad's jewelry in my coat pocket. At the church office, we were marveling at how his initials were the same as yours."

Hank's eyes widened.

"Lying on my stomach, I stretched my arm down through an opening in the heap and tugged the man's left arm into view. I retrieved the gold band from my coat and worked it on the deceased man's ring finger. I smeared some ashes on the ring and replaced the cuff link on the man's sleeve. I tucked the arm back into place under the pile. Before I could finish, Officer Mulaney came out of nowhere.

"He startled me. 'What do you see in there?'

"I lurched back and turned to him. I'm sure my face was flushed. It took me a moment to regain composure. 'This one sure appears dead.'

"Mulaney had to notice how he surprised me like I was doing something wrong. But he brushed off my reaction by saying, 'Even as a cop, I've never gotten used to dead bodies.'

"He wasn't fazed. 'Let's pull back this mess and see what we've got.'

"I was nervous having him help because I still had one cuff link squeezed tight in my hand. When I got the chance, I slipped it back into my coat pocket.

"We took turns pulling the collapsed tin pieces and charred lumber back. When we created access to the victim, I could see the coat and shirt sleeves on the man's right arm were melted to ashes."

"The officer asked, 'I don't suppose you can help identify this one?'

"I stepped closer into the newly liberated space. I took a knee next to the victim. As I bent down close to study the remains, I told Mulaney, 'It won't be easy with his face and hair burned like this.' I noticed a silver cuff link poking up through the ash around the right arm. This didn't match the gold one I had attached to the left sleeve.

"So, I reached in my coat and took the gold cuff link in my hand. With a tight grip on the jewelry, I reached down and pinched the silver cuff link from the body. I rubbed them together and picked the gold version out for the officer. 'Here's something. Could this help?'

"The policeman rubbed the ashes off the gold. 'Hey, there are initials engraved on this. It looks like HLM. Do you have any idea who this could be?'

"I had to be coy, so I took my time. I spoke in a confident deliberate tone. 'Yes, I do. I can't believe Hank Macklan finally met his match. He and his father both had long histories of working for the Northsiders. I believe they were beer runners.'"

Hank found it odd to hear a story of his death.

"The officer stood upright and said, 'This one was important to the North Side. I've been told he was a right hand for George Moran.'"

"I also shared, 'Years ago, the family attended my church. I knew Hudson, Hank's father, too. He worked for Dean O'Banion sometimes. There's been so much death in this family. Rumor is Hank's mother even died from being poisoned by a rival mob. His dad could never prove it. Either way, this was a tragedy.'

"He then asked, 'Father, I'm curious. Will you conduct a funeral for this type of known mobster? I've heard some priests refuse to give Catholic burials to those who wouldn't change their ways.' The man had raised a good point."

Hank took notice of this question.

"I said, 'Well, I don't know for sure. You are right. We can deny a Mass of Christian Burial for any person who has deliberately chosen to live in opposition to our faith and refused to repent. We also consider the impact of holding such a service on the rest of the truly faithful who may consider it a dishonor to the beliefs they hold fast to.

"I pointed out the inclusion of other church leaders. 'I must reach out to the church diocese for their final say. Hank has a sister who lives out of state somewhere. If she's in good standing with the church, we'd consider her faith in the decision, too.'

"A few days after you made your escape to the north woods, I held your funeral Mass."

Henry pondered the strange deception. "Oh?"

"Yes, and by the way, the church was pretty full for a guy who works behind the scenes." The priest gave a faint smile. "When your sister Gloria stood near the casket in the back of the church, I consoled her while she wept. She said, 'I'm surprised to see so many people here today. My brother was not a good man, and he kept to himself mostly.'

"I shared my sentiments with her. 'I want you to know, Henry, has been coming to see me the last couple of years. Deep down, despite his business, your brother was a type of good man.'

"So, you see, Henry. In Chicago, no one is looking for you anymore. Your slate was *erased,* just like your Uncle Warren's, or should I call him *Edward.*"

Hank was moved by the thought of his funeral being attended by many people who thought he was dead. "It's hard for me to believe. You have covered my tracks and made it possible for me to start a new life."

"I'm sorry I had to include your sister at your funeral. But Gloria had to *believe* you were dead to keep everyone safe. You'll need to speak to her right away. At first, she might be frightened by the sound of your voice, but she'll rejoice when she hears the truth and why this happened. Be sure to tell her *you* didn't even know about the funeral."

———— • ————

Kate had prepared a light meal. Father Whelan sat with Hank. The priest had only planned to sit for a few minutes before returning to the bedroom, but Harriet approached the table. Father Whelan pulled a chair out and said, "Harriet, please join us."

Harriet took a seat on the edge of the chair. Father Whelan motioned to Kate, but Harriet held her hand up, "No, I don't want anything to eat."

The priest looked at her with compassion. "You should eat something, Harriet. You're withering away."

Hank changed the subject. "Harriet, Warren mentioned the barn when we spoke to him. Do you know what he might want us know?"

Harriet struggled to look at Hank. "I can't imagine why. I have a notion to burn the old barn down tonight. Warren spent too much time out there. The work might have killed him."

The statement hung there with an air of condemnation.

Hank looked at the practical side of the decision. "If you do want to torch it, we should pull Albert's old car out of there first. There may be a few other tools out there to collect as well."

———— • ————

Father Whelan spoke to both men. "I assume the local priest would be happy to come out to take your confession and deliver the sacraments. But Warren, I know the life of secrecy you've been living. It delights my soul to be able to help you today. But I have to tell you something. When I asked to join Hank on this trip, I was thinking mostly of myself."

Hank looked at Warren and then at Father Whelan with a furrowed brow. "What are you trying to say, Father?"

The priest wiped his already dry lips and exhaled with the weight of his shame. "I didn't exactly come all this way to take your confession, Warren. I came here to speak to both of you and to give you *mine.*"

Hank raised his hands in the air He had a dazed look on his face. He stood and walked around to lean on the footrail of the bed. "Father, what is it *you* could have done?"

The tone implied a priest, of all people, would never sin.

Father Whelan held his hands up in front of him. "Now take it easy, Henry. I want a chance to explain things to you both."

The priest took a deep breath and sighed. "It all started in the early days when St. Mary's Church opened over in Cicero. At the time, Chicago was growing fast, really fast. The new church saw members pour in every day.

"I was a bit jealous since things weren't happening at the same pace in my part of town. But they were short priests to take care of their growing flock. It's when I got the call to help them take confessions during the week. This seemed like a reasonable request and the least I could do."

Hank interrupted, "But what does this have to do with *your* confession? So far, you sound more like a saint than a sinner."

Father Whelan looked at each of them and returned to baring his soul. "At St. Mary's, we had many young families coming to confession as I had expected. At times, I had a few local mobsters come through as well. Now, while I won't break the sacred seal of confession, let's say this last group often carried a heavy burden and was hungry for absolution."

Hank looked over at Warren and shared a nod.

"Now, I'm a priest, so these things shouldn't affect me. But at the same time, I was taking confessions back at my parish from people like your father, who was working for the other side. I'm human, so I couldn't help but compare these conversations as if listening to the different sides of the same story.

"For the most part, I've found gangsters are pretty skittish about giving traditional confessions." Father Whelan looked at Hank. "I think it's the issue about knowing right from wrong but choosing to ignore those beliefs to do the Devil's work.

"The ones I got to know the most preferred to talk to me from time to time but only outside the confessional.

"This is where things get tricky. A confession is unloading the list of sinful acts that happened in the past. Over time, I noticed these informal talks were usually discussions about things they planned to do in the future."

Hank leaned in. "Wait a minute! So you're telling me you *knew* about Torrio and Capone's plans even before they took place?"

Father Whelan looked out the bedroom window. He stared at the pine boughs waving in the breeze. "Yes, Henry, sometimes I did. It was the same as when I heard about the Northsiders plans from your father and *you.*"

Hank rubbed his face with both hands. "But hold on. This was outside the confessional, so you could flap your gums about these things with others anytime you wanted?"

Father Whelan gave a slow nod. "That's true, Henry."

"So, Father, whose side are you on anyway?" Hank stepped closer to the priest. "Did you have something to do with the deaths in my family? My mother?"

In the bed, Warren leaned toward the holy man with raised eyebrows.

"No, no, Henry. You have this all wrong!" Father Whelan ran two fingers underneath the shirt collar cutting into the back of his neck. "No, it wasn't a matter of which gang I favored. I was always on *God's* side. I wanted all the sin, violence, and killing to stop!"

Hank's cranberry-red face steamed with anger. "What have you done? What have *you* done?"

There was no turning back now. "Well, I didn't mean for anyone to get hurt. I thought if liquor loads were slowed from coming in, the source of all the evil would be cut off for a while." After a moment, the priest's confession continued. "So, on occasion, yes, I did share delivery plans for booze shipments I knew were coming in."

"So, after all this time, *you* are the leak I've been searching for?" Hank thumped the top of the dresser with his closed fist. "The guy who helped Capone in whacking our loads?"

The priest hung his head.

The longer Hank listened, the more the discontent grew within. "Father, I trusted you for who you were. How could you of all people do this to us? This is the reason Allen and Remi got shot up!"

Father Whelan squirmed like he was twisted in a trap. "I know, I know. I felt terrible about those two. I admit there was always risk. The information wasn't perfect. I never knew who was going to be there. The few details I got were usually about what loads were planned and maybe when they would move."

Father Whelan cowered near the bedside. "I thought if the speakeasies closed up shop early sometimes, drunk husbands might not beat their wives for one night, and we'd have a few less men in prison or in the coffins rolling down the center aisle of the church."

Warren closed his eyes, and Hank shook his head in disbelief.

"Henry, I want you to remember I helped you, too."

Hank took a step back. "What do you mean?"

"The river route. You know where Capone was sneaking his loads in. You hijacked two of his liquor loads, didn't you?"

Hanks mouth fell open for a moment. He gasped. "I didn't know you got information directly from one of Capone's thugs. I thought you stumbled across a rumor somewhere along the line," Hank stammered, as he paced around the bed. "This is why you showed up at the warehouse fire the day you found me near the river! Because you told them we were hiding liquor there?"

Father Whelan looked down and made a couple of slow nods. He stared at the foot of the bedpost. "I was horrified by so many dead bodies. They didn't try to steal the booze, they tried to have *you* killed! That's the day I stopped trying to meddle in everyone's affairs."

Hank was in shock. He had heard enough. He raised his hands in the air. Father Whelan had betrayed the trust given him by the family. "Father, you need to give me some space on this. It might be best if we call it a night."

CHAPTER 34

Search for Answers

Three days after Warren's death, the twilight air chilled to fifty degrees with barely any wind. Next to a can of kerosene, Harriet stood, holding a lit lantern at the foot of the barn. She turned with tears in her eyes toward Hank and Father Whelan who stood beside her. "It has to go. Warren worked himself to death out here, and I want those memories gone."

Hank nodded. "Let's do a walk through one last time before you start the fire, Harriet." Father Whelan and Hank lit a couple of lanterns.

Remembering Warren's last words, Father Whelan stepped forward. "There has to be something here. Henry, are you positive he never mentioned anything specific about the barn?"

Hank shook his head. "No, nothing particular comes to mind. I was out here plenty of times with Warren while he worked on equipment for the lodge. I never saw anything unusual."

Hank swung open the large doors. In the gray light, the sounds of their voices echoed inside the nearly empty barn. Gone were the cars, ladders, and tools. Father Whelan stepped inside, raised his lantern, and looked around. Faint light filtered down through gaps of missing floorboards above.

Harriet noticed his curiosity. "Oh Father, Warren warned the kids and I to stay out of the old hayloft." She pointed to the end wall of the barn. "He even cut off the wooden ladder nailed to the wall over there so Albert wouldn't be tempted and wind up getting hurt."

Hank walked along the perimeter and made his way back to the storage room at the far end. "This should be the last corner to check out."

He pulled the door open and stared at some crates and a stack of firewood.

One by one, Hank handed Father Whelan a crate, and the priest arranged them in the open space for Harriet to look through. When the firewood remained, Hank called out to Harriet. "Should we save this pile of wood, or do you want to let it burn up in the fire?"

She poked her head inside the storeroom. She didn't want to be a bother but thought about the long cold months ahead. "It might be nice to have the extra wood this winter."

Father Whelan didn't hesitate. "OK. I've got this. I'll fetch the trolley." He headed outside to retrieve the wheelbarrow.

Hank began to pull wood away from the back wall and carried the pieces to the storeroom doorway where the wheelbarrow stood ready. As he worked his way down the pile, he noticed an out of place looking handle fastened to the lower wall about a foot above the floor. He pointed. "Would you look at this?"

Father Whelan had returned with the emptied wheelbarrow. "What is it, Henry?"

"Step in here a minute with your lantern I need more light. What do you make of this?"

The two men cleared away the last of the split wood, and Hank stepped to the wall. He tugged on the handle, but it held fast. He lifted his lantern and examined the wall up close.

The priest noticed a metal latch fastened to the last piece of barn wood. Father Whelan reached over, rotated the latch handle vertical in its channel, and drew back the slide. He found a similar latch down next to the lower shelf. He loosened it as well.

Hank pulled on the wooden handle in the middle of the wall once more. It seemed to give a little. This time, dust escaped from the seam of the wood boards near the two metal latches. The whole clad section swung out from the wall structure a few inches on blind hinges buried beneath the panel.

Harriet heard the commotion and joined the men at the most opportune time. "What on earth have you found back here?"

━ ● ━

Hank dragged some timber bunk materials on the floor out of the way. He swung the six-foot section of barn wood open and raised his lantern. Harriet gasped. "What is this?"

The three of them stood there staring at a narrow set of stairs cleverly hidden behind the secret panel. The stairs led up toward the hayloft.

Harriet was dumbfounded. "But Warren said it was too dangerous to go up there."

At the top of the stairs, a wooden hatch door covered an opening to the loft. Hank braced for the climb.

The precarious stairs were a narrow steep incline and lacked a handrail. In the dark shadows of the lantern light, Hank took one step at a time, keeping his left hand along the outer wall for balance while his right gripped the lantern's wire handle. At the hatch, he hung the lantern from a nail protruding from a rough sawn floor joist, appearing placed for such a purpose. He used both hands to push the thick hatch door open into the hayloft. A light swirl of dust descended from above.

After three additional steps, Hank paused, waist deep in the loft, to reach down and retrieve the lantern. He raised the light through the hatch and stood there on the stairs in silence. His upper body rotated back and forth with the lantern.

Harriet looked up at Hank's legs as he stood on the stairs and turned to Father Whelan. "What do you think is up there?"

Father Whelan stepped to the stairs and raised his voice. "Henry, what do you see?"

Hank didn't move.

Harriet could wait no more. "Hank, have you found anything?"

Hank stirred. Backing down the stairs one step at a time, he reached the base once more and turned toward Harriet.

"What is it, Hank? What did you see?"

Hank looked at each of them and rubbed his bearded chin. "We can't burn the barn."

Father Whelan placed a hand on Harriet's shoulder.

Her brow furrowed as she spoke. "Why not, Hank? What's up there?"

Hank looked up at the stairs. "I don't know exactly yet, but it looks like an office. Warren was keeping a lot of records up there."

Harriet moaned, "This is more of the lies and the secrets he kept from me! I'm going to burn this place right now."

Hank stepped in close. "No, Harriet, you can't."

Her face was flushed. "Give me one good reason why not."

Father Whelan nodded, and Hank turned to face her directly. "Because it looks like Warren was keeping things up there you may need now."

"What do you mean?"

"Well, I don't know exactly. There is information about the lake lodge and ledger books of some sort."

"Show me." Her words echoed in the darkness of the barn.

Hank put his hand up in front of her. "We could, but as you can see its tricky getting up there. We would be better off waiting until tomorrow in the daylight before climbing around in the old hayloft. As you showed us, some floorboards look pretty weak."

Harriet could still see the image of Warren falling from the ladder on the day of his heart attack. "OK, fine. We'll wait until morning, but I still plan to burn this place. It's evil!"

— ● —

Harriet stood in the dining room, holding a quart jar of cold coffee mixed with cream and sugar. She set it down on the serving counter for a moment while she liberated three porcelain coffee cups from a stack. She could wait no more.

Moving to the table, she said, "Father, if you're finished with your breakfast, I'd like to head back to the barn. I'm not sure why Henry is such a slowpoke this morning, but we don't need to wait for him. He knows where we're headed."

At the barn, Harriet scowled when she saw the large door left partially open. "That's odd. I thought we closed everything up last night."

Father Whelan looked at her and shrugged. "I don't remember closing it, but maybe Henry did."

In the back storage room, the pair stared up at the open floor hatch. This too matched the state of the barn door. Its red paint was mostly gone, leaving the wood covered in a layer of dust.

The morning light streamed from a pair of small windows located in the loft above. The priest held on to Harriet's basket of coffee and mugs as she began to climb the stairs. Through the hatch, Harriet heard a distinct scuff of a crate being moved. With care, she made her way up, pushed the hatch open, and emerged into the loft.

Hank froze with a wooden crate in his hands.

"Hank, what are you doing up here so early? We missed you at break—" Harriet stopped mid-speech as the presence of the place hit her.

The office, cloaked in a haze of morning light filtering through the dust-laden air, was orderly, carefully constructed, and had a solid reinforced floor built atop the original barn planks. Ceiling beams had been constructed above the windows on the back wall, allowing natural daylight to filter in.

A desk, much too large to have been brought up the narrow stairs, stood ready. Side drawers flanked both sides, and an armchair on rolling wheels sat ready for use. The wood-paneled walls of the office were plastered with maps, drawings, and yellowed newspaper clippings. A lantern, perched atop a vertical open-sided bookcase, posted as a remaining sentry over the former nighttime operations. The desk was topped with a typewriter, a clock frozen in time, receipts, stacks of ledgers, an empty glass, and a tall bottle with a portion of amber liquid still in wait, all organized with purpose.

On a side table, a step lower than the desk, rested three open crates like the one Hank held in his hands.

"How is this possible? When did Warren do all this?" Harriet's eyes drew to a curious phone mounted on the wall. "What is this?"

Hank remained still. "It looks like a telephone."

"I know. But how long has it been here?"

Hank stammered, "I'm not sure. I've never seen any of this before."

"We went years without a phone in the lodge. Warren said we couldn't get a phone line here in the woods."

Father Whelan emerged from the floor hatch and, hearing the question, stepped to the phone. "But what sort of phone has no ringer?"

Harriet looked a second time and made a closer inspection. She examined a pair of empty brass pegs protruding from the front of the phone box above the mouthpiece and void of the standard ringer bells. She picked up the cone-shaped earpiece from its rest and listened to the crackle on the line.

A switchboard operator barked a greeting, "How may I connect you?"

Harriet spoke into the mouthpiece, "Oh, I'm sorry. I'm not making a call. I was testing the phone to see if it still works." She hung up the earpiece immediately. "This is a working phone! *Why* would Warren need this out here?"

—■●■—

Father Whelan moved to a busy wall covered in clutter. Newspaper clippings of gangland news were tacked in place in layers. Prominent among them were the reports of Al Capone's war with the Chicago Northsiders over the illegal liquor business and black-and-white pictures showing bodies lying on the street, littering sidewalks, or slumped in cars after being gunned down. Warren's handwriting on the clippings recorded the names of unidentified victims and dates of the attacks. It almost looked like he was keeping some sort of score.

Harriet looked over the priest's shoulder. Her hands covered her mouth and tears formed at the corners of her eyes. Reading the headlines, she wondered aloud, "Why would he still track all this hatred? He was out of the crime business."

When she moved to the next wall, a large map of Canada was placed right above one for the United States with Warren's handwritten label—*Northern Supply Routes*. Tacks were pressed into Windsor, Ontario, Regina, Toronto, Winnipeg, as well as a curious one in Central Minnesota. Strings were tied to each tack, then strung around various tacks in Minneapolis, Detroit, and Milwaukee. Each continued to three tacks placed in an overlaid detail map of Chicago.

The third wall contained long lists of musical groups, singers, dancers, and other entertainment, along with their city locations, phone numbers, and notes. There were clippings from newspapers, magazines, and fliers about the musical and entertainment performers. A racy photo of some dancing girls caught Harriet's discerning eye. *What sorts of sinful businesses was Warren tangled up in?*

Harriet grew angry. She took hold of Hank by the collar, and he set the crate he was holding on the table next to the others. She pulled him to the wall of maps. "What was he doing? Tell me right now. What was Warren up to?"

Hank remained silent and looked at the desk. He didn't see a reason to ruin Harriet's memories of her husband.

She raised her voice. "After all this time, Hank, *what the hell did Warren have to do with the bootlegging business?*"

Father Whelan stepped in and pulled Harriet's hand away from Henry's shirt. "Harriet, remember Henry isn't the one responsible. I don't think he knew about this office until now. Henry, am I right?"

Hank turned around. "I had no idea Warren kept this place." He stopped short of saying more.

Father Whelan sensed it. "Henry, what aren't you telling Harriet about Warren. He's gone now. She deserves to know everything."

Hank paced the room. "I'd rather not say."

Harriet was crying. "Why not? Why can't anyone tell me what Warren was really up to?"

Hank couldn't stand it. His mind flooded with the pain of losing his family and the personal misery about not knowing what happened to his mother. He looked at Father Whelan.

The priest raised his hands. "Henry, I don't know this part of Warren's life."

Hank sighed. "Harriet, you better sit down for this."

Harriet perched on the edge of the desk. She refused to touch the chair Warren used.

"My uncle told you he worked in the Chicago breweries many years ago. The truth is the breweries were only how he got *started* in the crime business."

Harriet paled. "Are you telling me he was still a mobster when we were married?"

Hank wanted her to know the whole story. "My uncle wanted out of the crime business, but the business wouldn't leave him alone up here."

Harriet tested a loose string on her skirt. She stared at the wall covered in local maps and property plots including Clark Lake Lodge.

"Warren came here to get away from crime. That was the truth," Hank said.

"Yes, he told me that much."

"There is more to that truth." Hank stopped to rub his sleep-deprived eyes. "The truth is Chicago crime wouldn't leave him alone. At first, he was an advisor to Dean O'Banion for finding booze and entertainment, like bands and dancing girls. Before long, Dean was killed, and Warren's role grew."

Harriet began sobbing, but she waved her hands for Hank to continue.

"As more North Side leaders died, he eventually ran the whole show. I mean he made the decisions but kept his name and face out of Chicago."

Harriet decided to take Warren's chair after all. She plopped down and uncorked the bottle on the desk. She smelled the contents before pouring herself a glass.

Father Whelan stepped in and took the booze away. "Now, now, Harriet, this is difficult news. I'm here to listen if you want to talk about things. This liquor won't help the situation."

She pointed at the wall. "Why did he have a phone without a ringer up here? Was he using it to conduct his horrid business affairs?"

Hank nodded. "Warren likely used the phone for arranging booze shipments and entertainment. If one of the guys wanted to talk with Warren, they had to speak to him in person."

Harriet stood up in shock. "What exactly are you saying?"

Hank danced around the answer. "Warren's men in charge met with him from time to time."

Harriet closed her eyes for a moment before she spoke. "I don't remember Warren leaving or taking trips to Chicago." Then it slapped her in the face. "You mean these strangers came here to the lodge?"

"Yes, Harriet. It is time you know." Hank cleared his throat and moved in close and took the spot on the edge of the desk. "Those gangsters weren't coming here to cool off and hide out from rival gunmen. They were coming here to speak to Warren, the patriarch himself."

Harriet twisted uncomfortably in the chair.

"They came here to talk about threats to the booze and gambling business and ask the boss about what their next strategy should be."

A chill ran the length of Harriet's spine. Nausea stabbed into her midsection. She wrapped her arms around her stomach and slumped forward. Her eyes had the steely look of a caged animal. "Hank, how can you ever live with yourself? You knew this about Warren all along! Why would you keep this from me all these times you came up here?"

Hank looked away from Harriet. "Because, I was not only Warren's nephew, I became one of *them*."

Harriet turned toward Father Whelan. "This place must burn before Albert see's any of this. He doesn't need to know about the horrible monster his father was."

She made her way to the floor hatch and descended without saying more. Father Whelan kept an eye on her as she left.

Hank looked down at the trail of dark spatters on the floorboards where Harriet's teardrops had fallen. He shook his head.

"Father, we need to sort out Warren's business affairs now. But I don't think we'll have much time."

Hank walked to the table where Harriet had left the coffee jar along with some mugs. He untwisted the jar's cap and poured two mugs of creamed coffee. He added the amber liquor Harriet had poured from the bottle to each. Handing one to Father Whelan, Hank asked, "So, where do you want to dig in?"

———— • ————

Late the next day, the desk was piled with ledgers. "Father, these are records of gambling debts. This pile over here is records of liquor shipments. These are records of balances speakeasies owed, and the green books have lists of entertainers hired. Warren kept lists of policemen, attorneys, and elected officials partial to the cause," Hank said.

Father Whelan looked at a green book in disgust. "Henry, over here on the table, I collected the records Warren kept on Capone's crew, contract hires, friends, allies in government and the courts, Capone's distilleries, and other known suppliers. Warren was meticulous. He did this with the Genna family and other gangs, too."

Hank was exhausted.

"Henry, what is wrong?"

Hank raised his arms in the air and turned in a half-circle. "In all of this, I can't see where Warren kept any of his own money."

Father Whelan walked among the piles and scratched his head.

As Hank watched the priest wander around the room, he began to focus on the outer walls once again.

"You know something odd about this room, Father?"

The priest stopped moving. "No, what is it, Henry?"

"It's the wall with maps of the lakes area. Why would Warren keep this stuff up here? He could have pinned this information up in the lodge rather than in his secret mobster office where he was cramped for space."

"Do you suppose he took the same approach to this lodge business? I mean keeping close tabs on his competition and their employees?"

Hank studied the wall. "Wait a minute. On these plots of land around Gull Lake, there are several handwritten notes. See here, there are also outlines for some cabins along the lake, a golf course, a pier for boats, and more. How was Warren getting this information about them in advance? Did he have someone on their payroll? That's how we do things in Chicago."

———— • ————

Harriet fumed. "I don't *ever* want to go back up to the office again. When I go back over there, I'm bringing my box of matches and some kindling wood." She took a step back from Hank.

"Wait, Harriet. We need to show you Warren's records before you destroy everything," Hank pressed.

Dark rings showed beneath her swollen eyes. "No, you won't."

Father Whelan sighed. He understood the sick feeling Harriet must have had with this discovery. He stepped in. "Harriet, please listen to me. There was more to Warren than you knew about, and it must feel incredibly deceitful. To close this chapter for you and the children, we need to show you the records we found before you erase them with fire."

Harriet stood motionless, looking down. "The whole thing makes me so sick. I trusted him with my life, and I was in danger the whole time. He lied to me!" Her legs began to quiver. "I'll give you ten minutes up there and no more. I can't stomach the thought of the place."

She dreaded the very sight of the barn now. While once she thought of it as a happy place where the children learned to ride their bicycles, now the red barn paint reminded her of the bloodshed Warren had on his hands. The hurt was deeper than his crimes. The whole foundation of their marriage was a swamp of deceit. It was apparent he didn't care for her or the kids. Warren was another bloodthirsty gangster who came here to start the family he needed to cover his tracks.

Harriet stood with her arms crossed at the foot of the desk. She was repulsed by the piles of crime records.

Father Whelan and Hank brought her various items to look at.

Hank brought one particular plain-looking brown leather document pouch to Harriet. "It took us a while to find this. It was tucked in the bottom drawer on the right side of the desk." He unzipped the pouch and withdrew a blue ledger book.

"There is an entry in this one I want to show you." He turned the pages to a paper marker poking out of the top of the ledger. He ran his finger down the page halfway and tapped the book. "Here it is." He turned the book, so she could read the entry titled, *Legal fees for LLOC Holding Company*.

Harriet was unphased by this detail. "So, what does this mean?"

"It didn't mean anything to either of us. It looked like another of Warren's endless business dealings. I thought maybe this was a front for making silent donations to political campaigns or other such activities," Father Whelan said.

"You mean making *bribes*? Is this what you wanted to show me?" Harriet's voice rose with each word.

Hank broke in before she could get too worked up. "We assumed the same thing at first. I read this entry and kept on moving along because there is a lot to look at in these books. Later in the day, Father and I were studying the property plot maps on the wall over there, and I noticed something familiar."

"Yes, and what did you see?" Harriet was anxious to get this over with.

Hank pointed to the drawing of the Clark Lodge property. "Here in the corner of this property plot, see how the title shows *LLOC Holdings*?"

Harriet's face turned a deep shade of red. "So now the mob owns our lodge and the property? Was Warren still working for them because he owed money for the land we live on?"

Hank wanted to stop her from spiraling out of control. "Whoa, Harriet— You have this all wrong." He needed to reset her thinking. "Harriet, LLOC is a personal *family* business that the mob has nothing to do with. With Warren gone, you've become the owner."

"What? No, I'm not! I don't know anything about this."

"We didn't think you did. No one did. It looks like Warren created a couple of these holding companies. He was investing rainy-day money for Hank, too. It's in a separate one," Father Whelan said.

Harriet's face had a look of disbelief.

Hank wanted her to understand. "We found the Minneapolis attorney who set these companies up and called him. Yes, we confirmed this is real. I wrote down his phone number for you. He wants you to call him when you're ready."

Harriet was quiet. She stepped to the plot map of Clark Lodge and ran her finger back and forth over the words for LLOC Holdings. After a few minutes, she took a step back and looked over the rest of the wall.

Hank and Father Whelan gave her all the time she needed.

"What does this mean?" she finally asked.

"Harriet, what are you asking?" Father Whelan asked.

"What does LLOC mean?"

Hank chimed in, "I asked the attorney. It was pretty simple—Lake Lodge On Clark, or LLOC for short."

It hit her. "What is this?" Harriet spun around to face Hank and Father Whelan. She turned part of the way back toward the wall to point at a large property plot surrounding Gull Lake. "What is this?"

She swooped in close to the wall and tapped her fingers on a *LLOG Holdings* symbol. "What is this right here? Are you telling me *LLOG* has something to do with us, too?"

Hank nodded twice at Harriet, who turned to look at Father Whelan. The priest was impressed with how quickly she had connected the dots.

Hank confirmed her assumption. "Warren didn't owe the mob any money, Harriet. We found out Warren was investing money into the property over on Gull Lake. You know that big modern resort you feared might run you out of business someday? Well, guess what?

"*You* own it!"

Harriet was biting her fingernails.

Hank repeated the statement. "Yes, *you* own the majority of it, and I own the rest."

Harriet couldn't comprehend the notion.

"We are debt free, I might add," Hank said.

Harriet sat in a chair. She covered her face with her hands. She was caught in a swirl of emotions. Was Warren the kindest man she'd ever known or a monster who killed people for money? In her mind, he couldn't be both.

Hank added more confusion. "The attorney stated, if we prefer, no one has to know we are the owners. We could pay the manager to keep making the daily decisions for the business. The other detail the attorney mentioned is that Warren set up a trust account in my sister's name."

Harriet was overcome with emotion. Warren had planned for her and the kids after all. The images in the newspaper clippings plastered on the walls showing bodies cut down by prohibition violence only added to the confusion of the situation.

She turned the chair around to face Hank. "So LLOG is a holding company for the property on Gull Lake."

Hank nodded as she turned to leave. "Yes, that's right, Harriet."

Afterward, in the nighttime quiet of her bedroom, Harriet turned out the lights and began to mull things over. On one hand, like it or not, she was the owner of the vacation property on Gull Lake. But on the other, she couldn't see how she could ever get past the thought that people had died along the way to buy it. When she closed her eyes, she could still see the images from the black-and-white newspaper clippings.

How would she ever explain their sudden wealth to Albert and Kate? They were old enough to ask a lot of questions, and they deserved honest answers.

It was a tough dilemma. She now owned a business bought with blood money. Even if she were to part with it, she assumed it would fetch a life-changing price. Could she live with the idea of buyout money if she didn't have to be a part of the business for the rest of her life? Was it fair to Albert and Kate not to benefit from the estate their father left because *she* disapproved of how he paid for it? Harriet turned the lamp back on and opened her Bible.

When the morning finally came, a sleepless Harriet quelled the debate raging in her conscience with a kitchen diversion. She made an oversized breakfast of coffee, pancakes, and sausages for everyone. She even baked bread for the lunch meal.

Hank was in a haze of his own when he arrived at the lodge. Harriet poured coffee for him and offered Father Whelan a cup, too.

As the men sipped on the piping hot coffee, Harriet made her suggestion. "I suppose we should go see the other property."

Hank was curious. " Harriet, won't things look pretty much the same as our other visit when Warren was with us?"

"But that was before. Now everything has changed. Before, I was looking for reasons to *hate* the place. I was trying to understand how they were stealing our business. Now, I have decisions to make. Things will look different to me today."

Hank marveled at the truth of her statements. "Sure, why not? After breakfast, I will bring the car around to the front. Father, would you like to join us before you head back to Chicago this afternoon?"

Father Whelan was curious about Warren's secret. "Why yes, I would find it quite interesting. And assuming you take over the reins there, it would be good to know where you've landed."

Hank drove with Harriet riding in the front seat and Father Whelan in the back.

When they arrived at the lakeside, Harriet stared at the dock lined with fishing boats. She remembered the day she and Warren watched the same sights. "Oh, this explains it."

"What does it explain, Harriet?" Father Whelan asked.

"The last time Warren and I came over here, he was mesmerized by the new Evinrude outboard boat motors. Now I understand. It wasn't because he'd never seen one before. It was because he bought them and wanted to see how they were running for the guests."

Some of the cleaning staff members were coming out of an empty cabin. "Oh, there's another thing. When we were here last, Warren acted all goofy around the staff. He even slumped down in the car's seat when we passed them on the road. I thought he didn't want our rivals to spot him on the premises. Now, I realize the help could have recognized the owner. He was hiding, so I wouldn't find out he owned the place."

"I understand some things, too. Harriet, when you and I weren't getting along, Warren offered to find me a room nearby. He told me when you weren't around, 'Don't tell Harriet, but the new resort is pretty nice.' He advised me to stay over here if I needed. It makes sense if he owned the place," Hank said.

Father Whelan was taking it all in. "This looks very modern. You say they also have a large golf course?"

Hank said, "Sure, let me drive you around the other side of the resort."

CHAPTER 35

Gull Lake

There was much to be done at White Pine Cove on Gull Lake. After a late lunch, Hank returned to working on a troublesome lawnmower in front of the maintenance garage near the main driveway. When he pulled the starter cord, the motor gave a frightful belch of blue smoke and puttered for a few seconds before it quit.

As he pulled the cover off the motor's air filter, he heard the powerful hum of an automobile approaching on the drive. He looked up to see a black Ford V8 sedan push past on its way toward the lodge. In an instant, the sun's light reflected directly off the car windows, leaving Hank with a glimpse of the dark hats of two men.

He dropped his screwdriver on the ground and bolted toward the lodge. He cut through the trees to cross the lawn, while the car made the long loop around the property. Hank found Harriet digging in a flower box near the front door, his face was flushed. "Harriet, there are men on the property coming this way in a black car. They might be here after me. Let's get you inside right now."

Harriet glanced over her shoulder and dropped her work gloves. Hank followed her inside and then visited the back office before he ran back outside again. Harriet kept her eyes on the road coming up through the woods. Ten minutes later, a young woman from the cleaning staff came walking up the drive with a cartload of bedding to be laundered. She parked the cart outside and walked into the lodge. Harriet was still staring out the window.

"Mrs. Johnson?" The cleaning lady waited a minute, before asking, "Mrs. Johnson, are you all right?"

Harriet broke from her hypnotic stare. "Oh, yes. I'm fine, dear."

"Mrs. Johnson, there were two men in suits here."

Harriet spun around with wide eyes. "What did they want with you? Are you OK?"

The young woman was surprised by the concern. "Of course, I'm all right. The men told me they were from the state Department of Commerce. They wanted to request a copy of your business license. The older gentleman left his calling card." The woman handed the card to Harriet. "He said he will be contacting you soon."

Harriet sighed in relief.

"Are we going to be all right, Mrs. Johnson?"

Harriet regained her composure. "Yes, dear, of course."

———— ● ————

A pair of workers dressed in light coveralls raised the restaurant sign in unison as they ascended a pair of wooden ladders spaced ten feet apart. They looped the brackets of the new sign over a pair of wall-mounted supports and snugged down the first clasp with a metal wrench.

When the work on the right end was complete, the wrench was tossed across to the workman on the left side. After completing a one-handed catch of the wrench, saving a trip back to the ground, the workman smiled. "Nice throw, Bill. Did you happen to play baseball before you got in the sign business?"

Bill smiled.

The workman on the left secured the clasp on his end and began to feed short strands of electrical wire through the wall as an electrician pulled the lengths into a junction box. Through an open window, a voice came from the darkened room inside. "You guys hang out on the ladder a minute would you, at least until we turn the power back on? Then we'll know if everything is working all right."

Bill turned on his ladder rung and drew a cigarette box from his coveralls. He peeled a stick match across the back of the box and struck a flame. He exhaled the first smoke and watched three kids in the distance playing catch with a ball. He felt like a bird in a tree looking down on a green summer park. While he had no experience raising children, he could see the contentment and joy of the parents sprawled about taking in the children's games from the sidelines.

Harriet led Hank to the road in front of the restaurant. The two of them stood with their backs toward the building while they studied the dock in the lake. Harriet commented on the need for more boats. From the corner of her eye, she noted the men on the ladders unwrapping the protective canvas draped around the sign. The men released the tarp. It fell to the ground with a muffled thump. The sound captured Hank's attention, and he turned to see the source of his curiosity. The electrician set the fuse in place and the neon sign crackled to life.

Hank smiled. "Wow, Harriet! What have you done here?"

Even in the light of day, the white neon color beamed the new restaurant's name, *Henry's*. Beneath it, the smaller words, *Fine Dining,* were illuminated in light yellow. "What do you think?"

Hank couldn't contain his beaming smile. "We've come so far. I have to say, this sign spells high class! I wish Warren was here to see the place."

Hank walked over to the entrance and turned to Harriet. "I can't believe you put my name on the building. Even the rich dark brown brick sets it apart from any other place I've seen in the north woods."

Harriet cleared her throat. She knew this was the perfect time to have the conversation. "Well, I think the name makes a statement, and people who are on vacation want to splurge on themselves."

Harriet didn't want to spoil the moment, but she felt unsettled after the events of the past few months. Harriet spoke to Hank with a caring tone, delivering a message long overdue. "I'm sorry. I was wrong about you, Hank.

"When you first arrived at our dock, I assumed you were a greedy blood-thirsty killer who only cared about himself. While I'll never approve of the bootlegging business, I've since learned you are actually kind and quite considerate. You've surprised me.

"Warren invested your money in this place, too, so the restaurant is your business to run. You don't work for me. We are partners in this property. Our guests don't need to know the details of who owns what. They just come here to have a good time. I'll help you, and I ask you to help me."

Hank extended his hand to Harriet. "Let's get something straight. If this restaurant is going to draw people in, I need to play a different role. Starting today, you'd best call me, Henry."

Harriet shook his hand. The agreement was complete. "I am so excited for you to see the new tables, chairs, and linens. We have a few set up inside. Let's take a look."

The place was immaculate. Henry was impressed with the look of the flooring, trim, and lighting. It reminded him of the feel of posh restaurants in Chicago.

Harriet laughed as she walked through the arrangement of tables. She ran her fingers across the new linen tablecloths and felt the smooth fabric. "OK, I'll stop spending your money now. I have an account you can take over when you're ready. Besides, I know you have a great taste when it comes to food, so you decide the menu."

Henry took a seat at a corner table. He pulled his hat off and turned it around between his hands. "But wait a minute. To do this right, I'll need some help. If we get busy, I can't be both the cook and chief bottle washer, too."

Harriet let Henry mire in his concern. In a low tone, she whispered, "Are you afraid of an honest day's work?"

He didn't like the insinuation. "No, I'm not. I'm worried about this place filling up and a hungry crowd staring at me while I work alone."

Harriet knew he'd had enough. "Of course, we won't let it happen. I have an oversized cleaning staff right now because I planned a few extras for the restaurant opening. One of our employees, Cynthia, knows her way around food. I mean she's into matching flavors, textures, colors, and more. She's a stray from the big city somewhere, moved here a couple years ago. She's on her own, and she'd like more of a career. Cynthia oversees the cleaning crew today and is good with people."

Henry felt some relief. "Would you give her up?"

"You aren't looking for a wife are you?"

Henry smirked. "Why? Is she pretty?"

"I can't be the judge for you." Harriet shook her head. "I've heard one of the other women comment she was surprised Cynthia was still single. You need to know, she's a hard worker. I never worry about the crew. She keeps them on their toes. At the same time, you'd take notice if she slipped on a fancy gown, put on some dress shoes, and let her hair down. She doesn't live like that today, but she looks like she should."

Henry was speechless. He stared open-mouthed at Harriet.

She could see the confusion in his gaze. "What is it? What's going on in your mind?"

Henry broke out of the trance he was in. "To be honest, I haven't thought about a beautiful woman for a long time. If she's half as attractive as you've described, *you* better be the one to hire her for the restaurant manager. I don't think I would have a clear mind to do the interview."

Harriet laughed. "Yes, I can speak to Cynthia about it. I know she's anxious to do something bigger around here. But you must keep your eyeballs in their sockets if you work with her. No romance on the job. Business comes first."

Henry turned his palms up. "When did you become such a bear cat?"

"It comes from tough living. We had to scrape for everything at Clark Lake the past few years. The twenties brought in some customers, but business wasn't *roaring* like you heard city folks talk about. I was in complete shock when I learned about Warren's war chest of investments."

Harriet pointed toward the front door. "About this place: Are you planning to be open for day visitors coming in for the restaurant or will this be reserved for the resort guests who stay with us? I think people might come by boat from all around the lake to dine here."

"It's a good question. To start with, we should open the door to anyone who wants to eat here and see how things go. If it gets hectic when the cabins are full, we can limit the list at some point."

—— • ——

The following afternoon, Henry worked on setting up the new kitchen. Harriet poked her head through the double swinging doors. "Henry, can you come to the dining room, please? I'd like you to meet one of our employees."

Henry washed his hands and wiped them dry with a towel as he made his way toward the window-side table. Harriet was seated next to a woman with a work scarf wrapped over her head. As he approached, the woman untied her scarf and pulled it free, revealing long auburn hair carefully drawn up to keep it off her shoulders.

Henry circled the table to face the pair. He drew a chair back and took a seat. Harriet began, "Henry, I'd like to introduce you to Cynthia, your new chef and restaurant manager."

Henry removed his hat and ran his hand back through his thick head of brown hair. He blinked a couple of times before he thrust his hand out. "I'm pleased to meet you, Cynthia."

"It's a pleasure to meet you, Henry. I appreciate the chance to work with you."

Henry took her hand. Even though he knew better, he wanted to start a personal conversation. "I'm curious, Cynthia, where are you from originally?"

Cynthia was stirred by the appearance of her new boss. His smile was warm, and his handshake conveyed a reassuring feeling of strength. "You can call me, Cindy. I am from the Minneapolis area. I moved up here when things got tough in the city."

Henry smiled. "I moved here for similar reasons."

Harriet looked back and forth between the two of them. She sensed a good connection.

Cynthia leaned on the table. "Oh? What line of work were you in?"

There was a pause as Henry wanted to start off right with his new restaurant manager.

Harriet noticed the hesitation and interceded. "Henry is my late husband's nephew. He was in the Chicago entertainment business."

Cindy nodded her head. "That sounds interesting. I'd like to hear more about that sometime." She was feeling a little forward. "So, Henry, do you have a wife hiding around here in the woods somewhere?"

Henry smiled, got up, and turned toward the window. Cynthia possessed natural charm and seemed to have a great sense of humor.

Harriet leaned over and whispered near Cynthia's ear, "No, he's never been married."

CHAPTER 36

Demise of Demons

Unknown to Henry, his lingering fears of being hunted by the Murder Twins were unfounded. Two years earlier, on a lonely road near Hammond, Indiana, their disfigured bodies were discovered at dawn. Following lives marred by lawlessness, violence, and murder, the rage of John Scalise and Alberto Anselmi was finally extinguished. The Murder Twins died the same way they waged war on the Chicago streets, together, in gunfire.

Throughout their time in the United States, the men were driven by greed to conduct whatever dirty work was asked of them without lasting loyalties.

In the end, they underestimated the powerful reach of the Al Capone connections when they conspired with rivals against him. Capone insured the physical beatings of the double crossers were severe enough, that in the end, they longed for the execution by gunfire.

CHAPTER 37

Winds of Change

Mornings at White Pine Cove began quietly except for a few fishermen eager to get out and wet a line.

"Henry, I need to speak to you," Harriet said.

Henry poured Harriet a cup of coffee.

"You, of all people, know how hard I've tried to make this place my own. I thought this might be a good home for Albert and Kate."

Henry nodded. "Harriet, I think you have done well."

She took a sip and set the cup aside. "Thank you, but after all these months, I still can't get the idea out of my mind how we can live as if nothing ever happened. I can't explain it all to the kids either. I want a better life for them *outside* the lingering shadows of their father."

Henry left his cup on the table and stood to look out the window. "Harriet, I think I understand, but you have to level with me before you go further. Is it *me* you take issue with? The fact I was a mobster and now work beside you as a partner?"

Harriet was silent.

Henry filled the void. "Because, while this feels like home to me now, I can still leave this place if I need to. I want Albert and Kate to have the best chance."

A tear streamed down Harriet's cheek. She wiped it away. "I appreciate it, Henry, but no, I don't want you to leave. To be honest, I am still shaken by how naive I must have been to live with Warren all those years while he was directing his Chicago business. Being here on this property now feels like I am still living the same way. I need to make a change in my life and get away from here with the kids."

Henry's face turned solemn. He hadn't seen this coming.

Harriet crossed her arms and stepped back. "Now, I have been thinking about this for a long time. My mind is already made up. I have been approached to sell the Clark Lake Lodge property. Even during these tough times, the acreage has grown fairly valuable to the right people. I feel it was paid for with good honest hard work. I have a clear conscience."

Henry didn't know what to make of this.

"Furthermore, I don't want or need any part of the money from this place." Harriet swept her arm in a wide arc, encompassing the estate beyond the windows. "I'm signing my share over to you."

Henry became concerned for her. "Wait a minute, Harriet. You can't walk away from all of this."

"Yes, Henry, I can and must walk away. Please think of it as your inheritance from Warren. Part of it you earned, and part of it you now inherit. I must do this now and won't feel bad about it in the least. You will be giving me my life back. Please help me to make this happen for my family."

Henry rubbed his face and sighed.

"I am going to sell Clark Lake Lodge and move with the kids to California to be near my mother. She needs my help, and there are good schools and more opportunities for Albert to find a job in the future. I've spoken to the attorney. He will have papers for us to sign in the next few days."

It all seemed so sudden. "Harriet, are you sure about all this? I don't quite know what to say."

"Don't say anything. Help me get my life and sanity back."

CHAPTER 38

Dark Skies

Late in the day, children played along the beach despite the unbearably sticky summer air. The sky across the lake grew dark, and low rumbling thunder challenged the stillness of the afternoon. The change in weather caused the parents to corral their children and head toward the lodge.

Standing on the dock, Henry scanned the watery horizon for a final fishing boat still unaccounted for. When the craft rounded the point with white wakes rolling off the sides of the hull, he breathed a sigh of relief.

Henry directed them to bypass the dock, which was being pounded by the growing waves to land the boat directly on the beach. He tried to yell over the howling wind. "There's a rainstorm coming. We'll need to pull this up for the night!"

When the bow of the boat pushed safely into the sandy shoreline, the fisherman helped his wife collect her things and get out of the vessel. He pointed toward the sky across the lake. "We came in because the clouds beyond the point are a strange dark greenish color. We saw streaks of lightning coming down over there. This storm seemed to come out of nowhere."

With the boat secured, Henry rushed to the lodge.

In the back office, the radio tubes warmed to a crackling, popping haze interlaced with the sound of an emergency weather broadcast. Henry, straining to hear the announcement, caught the words *imminent storm* and *threat of danger* before steady static poured out from the speaker as the transmission cut off. With his breath rising in his chest, he searched the radio dial in vain for another broadcast.

Henry was on the move now. From the lodge, he sprinted to the cabins along the lake, pounding on each door, and telling guests, time was of the essence to take shelter in the lodge.

He helped a young family out of the last unit by carrying one of the children. With his arms wrapped around the child, he turned to look back at a mountain of dark thunderous clouds bearing down on them. When a wild wind gust rattled the cabin windows across the property, fear of danger swept through him. Henry made quick steps on the path to the lodge.

As he ushered the family into the building, lightning surged from the sky and split a pine tree with a mighty crack. The blinding flash and subsequent thunder sent Henry diving to the ground with flashbacks of being shot at. The top of the tree broke off and crashed on the very cabin the young family had vacated. Henry got to his feet and rushed into the lodge, pulling the door closed behind him.

Flickering electric power blinked the lights off and on. Henry gathered two old oil lamps and lit them for the guests huddled in the windowless basement rooms. He stood guard at the top of the stairs with a view through a first-floor window. He took a step closer when he noticed a curious wall of white chop racing in from across the lake. An instant later, small hail pellets began to bounce off the lawn chairs and tables. When the frozen scourge grew to the size of small potatoes, it littered the lawn with pine boughs and branches while it pounded the guest's cars parked along the drive. The rain was so heavy, the lake and sky appeared to be one.

Wind, coming in blasts from across the water, tore through the resort and uprooted trees. A large white pine crashed on a car in its path. Sheets of rain waved down in angles, pooling on the lawn. The explosions of lightning and thunder waged war in all directions.

After several minutes, the wind in the trees ceased as abruptly as it began. Free-falling rain dropped straight to the earth. In the distance, an alarming roar was growing closer. The sky became as dark as night with an eerie greenish hue. Henry watched in awe as the waves on the lake went slack before the water appeared to retreat from the shoreline pulling back fifty feet or more. The air pressure inside the lodge was nearly unbearable.

He bolted straight down the stairs taking two steps at a time. A father rushed over to meet him. "Henry, what is it?"

Henry's face was pale, and he stammered. "Everyone, get on the floor now and cover your children. There's a tornado coming!"

The sound, like a steam locomotive roaring into the lodge, silenced the last of his words. The building shook violently. With a horrendous screech, the roof and all the beams on the top floors above were torn off the structure. In a flash, the basement room became light, then completely dark as the remaining walls crashed down sending broken glass skittering down the stairs into the basement. One of the oil lanterns survived the collapse leaving a yellow glow over the wreckage.

Rainwater spilled in through the gaps in the ruins above.

Henry was cut on his right arm and one hand. He got to the lamp and crawled over a pile of debris toward the sounds of children crying in the first storage room. He held the lamp high and watched the faces emerging from the corner behind an iron boiler.

"How many are hurt?" Henry's voice shook.

A young father turned from his wife and children to give the report. "The kids are scared, but we only have a few cuts and bruises. My wife lost her eyeglasses back here somewhere. Otherwise, we are fine."

Another man stood up from behind a large freezer located across the room. "All of us taking shelter on this side are OK, too. There are no serious injuries."

Henry still felt the weight on his chest. He carried the lantern back into three more rooms. It was a miracle. All the basement sanctuaries remained intact, and the guests survived unscathed.

Henry stood in the open space between the rooms. "OK, everyone, can I have your attention? There's a lot of broken glass and lumber with sharp nails sticking up all over, so I would keep the kids in place for a while. I'm going to need a few strong men to help me clear a path up through the stairwell. Right now, it's blocked, but I think we can make our way out of this mess.

"I need some volunteers. Who can help me get us out of here?"

CHAPTER 39

Visions

Ms. Evelyn Smith walked the property, toting a pair of sturdy suitcases. Clothed in a splendid blue dress and smart tan leather shoes, she stopped to fuss with a curl of her already perfect hair. After curious exploration, she found him there, perched on a wooden bench, sitting alone in the quiet of the outdoors. As she approached, she was startled by the breathtaking view of the sparkling lake.

Hank Macklan, a man who'd lost everything, sat forlornly with his head in his hands, across the property from the storm-ravaged ruins of his once-great lodge.

For an instant, she paused there, just behind him, looking down at a good-natured man with both the capacity to be charmingly human and also, when pressed, to be as fierce as a wild bear.

She was his eternal flame, naturally beautiful, gifted with smiling eyes, and she was about to come to his rescue. At thirty-four years old, a vibrant woman with an infectious spirit was about to collide with, and forever change, the trajectory of the life of Hank Macklan.

Her thought was, the very sight of her, after all this time, might draw a profound reaction, though of what sort she was uncertain. She reached down and placed her hand on his shoulder and gave him a gentle squeeze.

Buried in a transitory state of mind, with senses immune to the physical world around him, the troubled man gave no response.

Evelyn persisted. She grasped his shoulder again, but this time, shook it with a bit more vigor. "Henry?"

Upon this second intrusion into his private thoughts, he lifted his head, regained focus on his surroundings, and searched for the source of the angelic voice he assumed to be imaginary. There, in the periphery of his view, he caught the image of her.

With his head upright, he turned toward the bold blue figure standing quite near to him. Given his peculiar state of mind, he failed to recognize Ms. Smith.

Considering the surprise she had given him, she stepped to the front of the bench and leaned down to look directly into his eyes. She touched his hand. "Henry?"

Henry was unable to speak, his mouth opened, his breath came in shudders, and his heart pounded. His long-lost love stood right in front of him. "Evie, is it really you?"

A pleasant smile spread across her face. "Yes, Henry. It's me."

"My God, Evelyn, I can't believe you're here!" Tears formed at the corners of his eyes. "But there was a funeral for me. How did you know I was still alive?"

"Oh, I spoke to Father Whelan more than once after your funeral. Eventually, when he realized I was no threat, he told me your funeral was held for your protection."

"You are an angel answering my prayers." Henry stood up and took the woman of his dreams in an embrace.

When he released her, Henry turned with his arm extended and pointed across the property. "I've lost everything now. The storm destroyed the lodge, most of the cabins, and even the restaurant."

"Henry, I wasn't sure I'd find you today. On the second train, I read the newspaper headlines and learned about the terrible storm that came through here. I worried whether you were all right."

"We were so lucky. No one was hurt. The guests, the staff, all of them were unharmed beyond minor scrapes and bruises." Henry picked up a fallen tree branch and tossed it out of the way. "I found out this morning even the insurance is gone. The company I used went bankrupt in the big financial collapse last year. My attorney tells me they don't even exist anymore. I have no way to pursue it."

"How awful, Henry. I'm sorry to hear about it."

He took Evelyn's hand and started a slow walk around the property. He told her about the former lodge and all the families who vacationed there. There was much history to share.

A couple of hours later, when they returned, Henry looked at the matching luggage standing tall along the end of the bench.

"I'm sorry, Evie. I don't even have a place left for you to stay here tonight."

Noticing the reference to the luggage, she released Henry's hand and pointed. "Henry, just so you know, those aren't mine."

The statement was puzzling to the man who'd spent the morning on a bench in a depressed state. Henry looked at Evelyn and again at the suitcases before shrugging his shoulders. The tornado had done some curious things, but someone had left these bags here.

Evelyn took hold of his hand again and squeezed. She couldn't hide the smirk on her face. "Oh, I brought these bags here all right, sweetheart, but you need to understand, they are not mine. Those suitcases both belong to *you*."

Henry stared at them once more. They were unfamiliar. He had no memory of such luggage.

Henry took hold of the first case and placed it down flat on top of the bench seat. He popped open the two brass buckles and lifted the cover.

There, nestled securely in the padded bag, was a tarnished saxophone.

Henry beamed. "Hey, is this what I think it is?"

"Yes, Henry. It's the very same one. It might need a good cleaning, but you can bring the magic back."

Henry pulled the horn loose from its rest. The feel of the instrument in his hands brought a flood of memories. "It's how we first met."

Evelyn nodded. "I know."

Henry's smile faded. "I could use a good session about now."

He placed the brass instrument back in its case and closed the lid. Henry took hold of the other case and placed it down on the bench next to the saxophone.

He tried to release the brass buckles on the lid but found them locked tight.

"Oh yes, I forgot!" Evelyn reached around the base of her neck and retrieved a thin gold chain. She slipped it over her head and released the clasp. When she raised one end of the chain high, a small brass key dropped down into her waiting hand, and she presented it to Henry.

His eyebrows raised as he first looked at Evelyn and then studied the key. With care, he unlocked the buckles and snapped each one open. He looked at Evelyn again. "Let's solve this mystery."

He lifted the lid, rested it against the back support of the bench, and looked inside with a gasp. The case was filled with tightly packed canvas money bags. He pulled a bag loose from the case and tugged to loosen the cord tie on the end. He reached inside and ran his thumb over the stack of bills. Each was a crisp one-hundred-dollar silver note. He looked up at Evelyn.

She smiled. "You do remember our arrangement?"

Hank looked back at the money, then turned to her. "Yes, I gave you *some* money to stash for me long ago. But, not nearly this much. How is this possible?"

"Luck, I guess?" Evelyn blushed. "Henry, you never really told me what to do with the cash, but said you trusted me to take care of it like it was my own. In my life, I'd never actually had much of it, but I heard about people making money by investing. I've always been pretty careful with these sorts of things, so I invested some of it. At least for a while."

Henry looked at the bags. "You certainly didn't earn this betting at the dog track!"

"No, I wasn't investing in fun." She tucked a stray curl behind her ear. "In the early days, I put most of it in the stock market and used some to buy land. After several years, I got nervous about how high the stocks had grown, so I sold everything off in early 1929, well *before* the crash. When I couldn't get my hands on gold, I used the cash to buy silver instead and held on to it. It turns out silver was a good way to keep the value you had earned."

"You mean *we* had earned," Henry corrected.

"But, Henry, there's more."

He nodded. "Go on, tell me the rest of what happened."

"No, Henry, there's more *money*. A *lot* more! I just brought one suitcase of cash with me on this trip in case you needed some right now."

CHAPTER 40

The Boat Ride

"Evelyn, we'd better get going now. It could be a half-hour boat ride down there."

Evelyn grabbed her sunglasses and a light jacket. "Yes, dear, I'm all set. Tell me again why we aren't taking the car? Wouldn't it save some time?"

Henry paused before speaking. "I don't think the car would save much considering the roads aren't very direct. It's better this way and sort of tradition. You'll understand once we get there. It's the closest bus stop to the lake. It's all preplanned."

"Well, it does sound like an adventure."

"Will Sarah be joining us? She loves the powerboat."

"I know, but since she's a teenager now, friends have become pretty important. When I think back to her childhood, I'm amazed at her recovery after being so frightened during that attack on our Chicago home. She's no longer afraid to go out." She leaned against Henry. "Tonight, she has plans to attend a birthday party. So, it will be you and I for the boat."

Henry smiled. "Glad your daughter is starting to have a social life. It may take some time, but we'll get used to the idea she's growing up."

The lakeside boathouse was built of dark-stained timbers, gray wood shakes, and a foundation of impressive fieldstone. Henry's greatest treasure waited silently in the dark water. The custom-built Larson powerboat, tethered to the rails by braided ropes, stood ready to demonstrate its exhilarating speed.

Stepping through the door to the boathouse, Henry helped Evelyn traverse the interior platform and settle into the highly varnished cedar strip boat. Near the steering wheel, she found a place on the red vinyl bench seat.

With the boat untethered, Henry dropped in next to Evelyn, twisted the starting key, and turned the big motor over. The throaty six-cylinder roared to life with a deep pitch sputtering up through the water at the boat's stern. With the engine warmed, he eased the craft out of the boathouse, navigated the rock barriers, and broke out onto the open lake.

He put his arm around Evelyn and gave her shoulder a squeeze. "Here we go, baby."

She took his left hand, and he poured on the power. The boat erupted to a horizontal plane and reached cruising speed in seconds. It was a beautiful day with the sunlight sparkling on the water. The heavy forest created towering shadows along the shoreline in sharp contrast to the endless blue skies above. Running the shoreline and lake narrows southward, the couple headed toward Steam Boat Bay.

— • —

In the busy resort community on the south end of the lake, a lone man stood at the shoreline overlooking the water. He was conspicuous in his professional dress clothes on the warm summer's day. The sun worshipers on the beach paid no attention to the man they assumed to be an accountant or possibly the manager from the resort office.

Passing the point of the bay, Hank scanned the developed shoreline for locations where a bus might park. He didn't see his guest until they were nearly right in front of him. He pointed him out for Evelyn's benefit. "There he is." Henry waived to the man.

Henry cut the power, and the boat slowed until it nudged up against the cushioned piers of a resort dock. With a leather briefcase in one hand, the man trod the length of the dock and efficiently secured the boat with a length of rope.

Henry kept his voice low. "Welcome. It's been a long time."

The man took a knee on the dock, reached down, and shook Henry's hand. "Yes, it has. And who do you have with you in this beautiful boat?"

"Oh, sorry, this is Evelyn. Evelyn, I want you to meet Mr. Johnson."

"Hello, it's nice to meet you."

"Please, Evelyn, call me Al."

She nodded. "Say Al, what a smart-looking briefcase you have there. What line of work are you in?"

Al paused and looked out across the lake. He turned toward Evelyn and said simply, "I'm in the insurance and investments business."

Evelyn smiled.

"I'm one of the big-city business agents who comes to see Henry from time to time to talk strategy and how to handle business risk." Al smirked. "Despite his looks, Henry is quite brilliant."

Evelyn looked over at Henry and thumped the side of his leg. "Is that so?"

Henry didn't like the attention and glanced around the shoreline. "We should get underway. There's room in the second seat. Do you have any other baggage?"

Al smiled at the notion of hauling bags in a boat.

"Well, it's a long story, but no, I don't have any bags, but I did bring a package for you, Henry." Al opened the briefcase, pulled out a brown paper bag, and passed it to Evelyn, who set it on the boat seat.

Al remained on the dock while he scanned the inside of the craft with a curious look on his face.

Evelyn smiled at him. "Al, would you prefer to ride in the front seat?"

He smiled. "Oh no, ma'am. I was looking around to see where Henry has the set of oars he plans to use to row us to the cabin today."

Evelyn got a twinkle in her eyes. "There must be some history with you two and boats. Is this why Henry insisted we pick you up by water?"

Al stepped aboard and settled in the second seat. "Oh, there is history all right. In the past, I might have preferred to leave Henry on the dock rather than get into the same boat with him. Maybe we can tell you more of that story a bit later."

Henry powered the boat's engine back to life, pushed off the dock, and began to motor out across the bay. He slid his hand down inside the paper bag Al had brought along. He recognized the hard feel of the shape and drew out a glass bottle. It was filled with single-barrel bourbon whiskey. He raised it high in the air, glanced back at Albert, and shook it. Henry laughed as he had never laughed before.

Being fully aware of the truth of things, Henry felt blessed to be alive.